Hands That Break...

Hands That Heal

Gary Kaschak

Xulon Press
www.XulonPress.com

Xulon Press books are available in bookstores everywhere,
and on the Web at www.XulonPress.com.

Dedication

This book is dedicated to all the Becky Chapman's, Paul Strong's and Joshua Gibson's of our country. They can be found somewhere in every town in America, and truly are the real heroes in our lives. It is also dedicated to my loving daughters Kara and Emily, and especially to my wife and good friend, Maureen, who gave up so much of her time to "run our lives" during the writing of this novel.

Acknowledgements

I'd like to thank the following people who gave up several hours of their time to read, edit, evaluate and comment on my book. The positive comments served me well, as I was further encouraged by the wonderful remarks, and humbled to realize how much this novel impacted their lives...

Thank you to Linda Thompson, my assistant volleyball coach at Our Lady of Mt. Carmel; to Eucharistic Minister John Rich; and to Sister Agnes Heffernan. Thanks to Coach Terri Maser, Jim and Shirley Nugent, Carol Gillard, and Elyse Emmerling. Thanks to my daughters, Kara and Emily, for persevering amidst a busy lifestyle, and for supplying me with endless ideas for characters and personalities. Special thanks to Janet Ciel, my first reader, who diligently read and edited the original manuscript, and to my good friend Dr. Virginia Reed, who was right there from the beginning, cheering me on and offering great advice. Special thanks to Judy Comer, a total stranger in my life, whose inspiring words lift me each time I read them. To my Godmother, Margaret Lipka, who's enthusiastic comments and truly positive nature infected me with the desire to continue. To my mother, Irene, for her candid observations and words of kindness. To my brother-in-law Paul Gillard , the *real* Paul Strong. I thank you for all your support and for supplying me with the foundation of a truly remarkable character.

Finally, to my editor, coach and friend, Anton (Tony) Marco. Right from the beginning you made me feel like I had a message, the talent and "the right stuff". You have been patient and supportive. Your advice has been invaluable, and your teaching skills are second to none. I look forward to working with you on future projects.

Author's Notes

The characters and events in this novel are fictitious. Although many of the situations and events are similar to actual events, they are nothing more than an extension of this writer's imagination. Two characters in particular, Becky Chapman and Paul Strong, contain traits of real people encountered along life's journey.

Becky Chapman is a combination of the strongest traits of several girls I'd coached from Our Lady of Mt. Carmel (Berlin, New Jersey) girl's volleyball team from 1999 to the present. Her character is pure and perfect, willing and cooperative, spiritual and determined. She is a combination of the faultless parts of real people, and although she is a conjured character, there is no doubt there are real Becky Chapman's in the world, and a character many girls' can identify with and find a part of within themselves.

The character closest to a real person is Paul Strong's. He is full of life and energy, a devoted family man who always wants to do the right thing, and is willing to make sacrifices to improve the conditions and the quality of life of those fortunate enough to be involved in his life, yet expects nothing in return. He is a man of wisdom and high-standards, who truly cares about the important things in life. Yes, I've coached volleyball and worked in the newspaper world, so the natural thing for those close to me was to assume Paul

Strong was my character, but that is far from the truth, for I fall far short of many of his qualities and attributes. That honor goes to my Brother-in-law Paul Gillard, who is everything and more than the memorable character of Paul Strong. He is a real person.

Several events in the novel were gathered from real-life situations worked into the story line, with a real-life "coincidence" discovered months after the novel was completed. It was this discovery that truly validated a major theme in the novel, that coincidence doesn't exist, things happen for a reason, and we all can "read the signs" given to us every day by simply opening ourselves up to interpreting them. This final "sign" involved two of the most respected people in the lives of my family, and was discovered unintentionally.

The prevailing theme in the novel is the Hands and the things they do for the good. I learned the I love you sign for the hearing impaired from a legendary softball coach from Southern New Jersey, Mr. Bob Carp, who learned the sign from his daughter, Tricia, via a Special-education class she was taking in college. I soon discovered the magical qualities of the simple gesture with the hand given at just the right time. Extended index finger, pinkie and thumb creates a universal symbol with the unequaled ability to send a powerful message of caring, along with the therapeutic message of feeling better about yourself, right now. It is more than just I love you, for it is a message placing things into a proper perspective, allowing the receiver to understand instantly that "You're O.K., I'm O.K." and not to worry. Bob Carp recently told me he uses the signal only at certain times, when sensing a young girl requires a lift from the burden of the moment. "It's my way of telling them to take it easy, that everything is fine, and not to be so hard on yourself," Carp said. "It's much more than I love you... It's, I understand what's happening, and that I care. It's a reminder to them that life isn't perfect, that I'm here for you, and we'll get through it together."

Images of my Father-in-law, John (Jack) Gillard are spread throughout the novel. He is part Joshua Gibson, part Jack Chapman. The real-life Jack Gillard had a similarly unique way of communicating with his football-playing sons, Patrick and Paul. Pacing the sidelines of both high-school and college gridirons, he'd occasionally let out a loud, shrill whistle during particularly stressful parts of games, reaching the ears of his tuned-in sons. It was their way as well, a reminder that "You're O.K., I'm O.K." and "not to worry." His passing six years ago created a big void in the lives of his family and friends.

Knowing these real-life "signs" given by the two most-respected men we'd known made it rather simple to include and expand upon them as part of the story-line. But the real kicker was recently discovered dealing "coincidently" with the lives of these two great men, tying in neatly with a later chapter in the book when Paul Strong and Joshua Gibson exchange opinions on "coincidence," and "Divine-intervention." For how can it be, that two men so respected and admired, two men who'd impacted our lives and shared loving signs on gridirons and softball fields, could also share March 22nd, as their birthday?

Coincidence? Divine-intervention? You decide which one after reading this novel.

—Gary Kaschak

CHAPTER

1

"Get my bag," snapped the nurse, the harsh and commanding tone immediately recognized and deciphered by her twin 13-year old daughters, Colleen and Maggie Shea. Without hesitation, as if they'd practiced or learned it, the girls bolted for the family car as if their lives depended upon it, for this was not a practice or a drill, it was the real thing.

Their mother, Annie Shea, knelt beside the injured player, 13-year old Becky Chapman, who had the 200-pound base of the volleyball pole completely enveloping her right hand, the wide base temporarily shielding the severity of the blow.

Quickly jerking forward, my 180 pounds easily shifted the weight off Becky's hand, rolling the pole and base free of her shattered limb, and out of harm's way. But the horrible damage had been done, that was clear enough…

Immediately after the accident, my time had literally stood still. Surveying the scene before me, I determined that this accident was serious indeed, we'd need an ambulance, that was for certain. I also thought, *seasons over for this girl before it even started,* a most unfortunate beginning for both new player and new coach.

I felt a jostle, and the nurse's black bag shifted into Annie Shea's experienced hands seconds later. *How lucky,* I thought, *to have a nurse for an assistant coach on our volleyball team.*

Annie was reaching inside the black bag, fumbling for bandages and antiseptic. She went right to work on the limb, now swollen and puffy, purple, black, and pulsing unevenly.

I held Becky Chapman's left hand, and several of her players stroked her long blond hair, giving her as much comfort as we could, waiting for the ambulance to arrive.

Then, as I looked down at Becky, lying there on the cold gray floor of our old gym, broken hand and all, I saw something astonishing: this young lady was smiling-*smiling*. A few tears rolled down her cheeks, but she didn't cry or yell or scream; instead, an uncanny, peaceful glow seemed to surround her, while her teammates wept without restraint.

This was only our second volleyball practice of the season, yet this young girl, still a stranger to me, seemed more intent on easing *our* pain at her anguish, then bothering herself with her own injury.

I saw her make eye contact with each of the girls, her deep blue eyes magnificent, riveting. She said calmly, "Don't worry, it's only a hand, and it'll heal." A sudden warmth overcame me, as if I were being blanketed by a veil of inner security. *Why*, I wondered, *do I feel actually relieved under circumstances like these?*

Minutes later, an ambulance arrived, and two volunteers rushed in towards us. Becky slipped her left hand from mine, and raised it high, her index-finger, pinkie, and thumb extended outward, then waved a wide arc, slowly, as if to cover all 12 of her teammates and coaches within her gesture.

As the ambulance volunteers prepared Becky for transport, gingerly hoisting her up onto the portable bed, she continued to lift her left hand, stretching the three digits of her hand as far as she could. The volunteers cautiously rolled her from the gym, all of us trailing behind, caught up in

Becky's plight—and bewildered at her mysterious hand signal.

The volunteers opened the back door of the ambulance, and carefully slid the bed and Becky inside. Annie Shea climbed in too, and Becky simply said in a voice gentle as an angel's, "Coach Paul, will you please call my mom, and ask her to meet us at the hospital?

CHAPTER
2

County Hospital was conveniently located near St. Luke's, no more than two miles on a straight line from our small gym and school. County was one of four hospitals located within a 30-mile radius of our community of 60,000 plus, and I was more than relieved, knowing Becky would be treated quickly. Hopefully, she wouldn't be in severe pain for long.

During the five-minute ride to the hospital, and for a full hour following the accident, my mind kept replaying the scene that had led up to its awful climax. I carefully visualized the event, pictured the girls who'd been involved, and wondered what I could have done to prevent this freak accident. I knew full well I was playing Monday morning Quarterback, and that hindsight is 20/20, and that I could only do my best to prevent a repeat in the future.

In those five minutes just before the accident, coach Shea had selected Becky as one of four girls who would set up the volleyball net to begin practice- usual procedure at St. Luke's for long before my tenure as head coach ever began. Two girls would grab the portable net at one end, and two would stabilize its opposite end, a simple task once the front pair began walking the net onto the court. The trick was to retrieve the large object from "the hole," the space in which all the gym equipment was stored after practices and games.

So far as I knew, the girls had never had a problem performing this task for the team. The technique had been carefully demonstrated during day-one practice, and I was confident the girls understood it well, and that no harm would follow: Once the front end was angled to begin the net's customary roll across the court, the back end would follow "automatically," just like any other learned routine, one the girls actually looked forward to doing.

Today, Sharon Lee and Joanne Cross, two of our three seventh graders on this 13 girl team, had been chosen to handle the front end of the net, while Janet Moore and Becky were to hold the rear. Usually, a coach would "spot" the girls, but this time, caught up in the distractions of practice, neither of us stepped over to assist the girls- and we soon paid for our oversight.

Everything went smoothly at first: Sharon and Joanne bent the front pole down at just the right angle, and began to move slowly out of the hole towards mid-court. But they forgot to check whether the back-end team was ready yet, before their short walk.

So when the two front-end girls began to roll their net-standard forward, the back end team of Janet and Becky wasn't quite ready. Janet was standing upright, holding the pole in its upright position, and Becky was still kneeling at the base of the pole. Before she could get up, a small portion of the netting wound itself around one of the canisters. Becky pulled hard in a vain attempt to free the fabric from the wheel, but with insufficient leverage, she stood no chance- the net was trapped like an insect in a spider's web, and could only be set free by raising the back pole.

But Becky couldn't see this; it was her first time on the pole, and her inexperience proved disastrous.

As the pole inched its way forward, Sharon and Joanne peered back and noticed Becky on the ground, and at the same time they felt the tension from the stationary base, and moved the base just far enough to allow the flat back end to raise up, perhaps six inches on one side.

It was then that Becky seized her opportunity to free the netting from the back wheel. She slid her right hand underneath the base, and pulled the netting free. But as she pulled, Sharon and Joanne relaxed their end of the pole, and the back base came crashing down onto Becky's vulnerable hand.

I remembered all too clearly: At first, a total silence had fallen across the gym, like a forest going quiet with the arrival of a predator. But seconds later, Sharon and Joanne both let out blood-curdling screams, loud as twin sirens blaring in the night.

Instantly, I sprinted towards Becky, and lifted the pole off her shattered right hand and witnessed the legend of Becky Chapman being born.

CHAPTER

3

Now I quickly found a parking spot in the hospital parking lot for my 10-year old Ford, less than a stone's throw away from the hospital entrance.

County Hospital was an important place in my life: Both my wife, Emily, and I were born there 36 years ago, and our daughters, Karen and Megan, now 13 and 12 (and key members of our volleyball team) came into the world in the same rooms Emily and I were born in. This incredible coincidence had not gone unnoticed by the local media, and the story became public. I was a reporter for the local newspaper, and my face was known throughout the county, which only served to strengthen the story. As a matter of fact, the story changed my career's direction, for within weeks of my sudden stardom, I was promoted to political columnist. My profile ran alongside my by-line on a daily basis, so around town, our family was very well-known, and treated kind of like celebrities.

The entrance to the hospital's short, narrow runway opened to a sprawling waiting room. Behind the desk there, the story that popularized my family was framed and mounted for the whole world to see and cherish. Millie Parker, now plump and gray, had discovered the story years ago, and she still remained behind that great desk like a permanent fixture, checking people in, and calling the shots with the precision of the very experienced receptionist she was.

"Paul!" she rasped as she spied my six foot frame, "Paul Strong- where have you been hiding? Come over here and give old Millie a big hug."

And I knew a big hug was exactly what was coming. Millie pulled her 300-pound frame from behind her desk, and wobbled over to meet me half-way, her body bouncing and shaking as she held her stubby arms out to me. I reached down to hug her, but was too late already. She held me a not-so-gentle bear hug, easily lifting my 180 pounds into the air, and shaking me like a rag-doll.

"All-right-already!" I cried. "It's good to see you, too, Millie."

"What's goin' on Paul? I haven't seen or heard from you in over a year. What's wrong, don't you love old Millie no more?"

"Of course, I do," I laughed. The old black woman eyed me, one hand on her hip in a defiant and playful pose, the other hand in front of her face, her index finger waving back and forth.

"Oh, you call that love?" she bellowed teasingly. "Remember Paul, it was old Millie who got you where you are today."

With that, she grabbed me by the arm, and literally dragged me to her desk, pointing to the story and photos she'd assembled 11 years ago.

"This is Paul Strong," Millie announced to anyone within earshot, "and this story from 1968 is about him. This here is *Paul Strong*, folks!"

Millie's raucous voice stunned the room full of a dozen or so people for a moment, but most of them quickly turned away to their own personal problems. I turned to Millie, who wobbled back behind her desk.

"Millie, I'm here to see an accident victim, probably came in about an hour ago."

"What's her name?"

"Becky Chapman," I replied, "She's on my volleyball team, and I think she broke her…"

Millie's overpowering voice cut me short: "Oh, I know the one you mean!" She rose from her chair, and her cheerful face grew softer, her eyes kinder, and her body language seemed to dwindle from dominating to submissive.

"Yes, Becky' is here," Millie said almost reverently. "She's in room 309."

The look in her eye, her whole demeanor puzzled me.

"Millie, is everything O.K. with Becky?" I asked.

"She's just fine," she said. "Her hand is set in a cast, and her prognosis is good. Broken hands heal, Paul."

"Yes," I said, still amazed at her awe-struck look. I've known Millie all my life, and if she has something to say, she says it without hesitation. On the other hand, whenever I tried to pump her for information, she wouldn't give.

She was a living paradox.

"Paul, before you go in to see her, I want to tell you something about Becky," she said solemnly.

Millie whisked me into the open conference room located behind her desk. She closed the door, and we both sat down.

Millie said, "Becky Chapman was born in this hospital, too Paul. I remember the exact date, July 29, 1966." Her photographic mind and in-depth knowledge were no surprise to me.

Millie paused for a moment, then held her hand out to me, and I took it in mine.

"That girl has a gift," she went on. "She is special."

I was confused, I'd never seen Millie like this before. Sure, I knew she was a very emotional, and spiritual woman, but this wonder of hers over Becky piqued my curiosity to no end.

Millie squeezed my hand tightly; her hand felt clammy to

mine. ***Odd***, I thought.

She went on. "Back after that girl was born, I saw her leave the hospital," said Millie. "And there was this shining, a greenish-blue aura all about her little frame, and that's when I knew." She paused.

"Knew what?" I asked.

"I just ***knew***," said Millie.

Hey, this is bordering on the bizarre, I thought. I knew very little about what some people have called the "human aura." I'd heard that certain people had an unusual ability to "read" the "outline" of the human soul. I'd never given stuff like this much thought till now. But I had a lot of respect for Millie and decided to listen to her with an open mind. She went on.

"Paul, you can consider yourself blessed to have Becky Chapman on your team. I guarantee she's gonna change your life."

"Huh? She's going to change my life?"

Millie grinned, like she was some kind of keeper of the future who knew time would prove her right.

"Paul, have I ever steered you wrong? Have I ever given you bad information? Have I ever in your life misled you?"

It was true: Millie had been an important source in the past, helping me with story leads and key information. She was being forthright now, for sure, and with an eerie assurance.

"O.K," I said. "Exactly how is this Becky going to change my life? She has a broken hand, she'll probably quit the team, and that's the last I'll have to do with her."

"I'm not really sure how she's gonna do it," said Millie, "but just let it happen."

Millie smiled and said no more. I rose from my chair and gave her another hug, and we exited the office together. As we did, she took my arm once more, and I let her walk me to the side of her desk.

"Paul, I've seen that girl three times now," she said, "all three times in this hospital. And that aura I told you about, the greenish-blue aura, it's the strongest aura there is," Millie said, "and Becky has it, and it's stronger and purer today, 13 years after her birth. I know, cause I saw it again when she came in a while ago."

"Now understand," she said mysteriously, "an aura doesn't always grow. On the contrary, aura's often shrink or disappear altogether as children get older and learn about the world, is influenced by their surroundings. I've seen that happen many times, but I've never seen an aura grow like this."

Millie spread her arms, as if to demonstrate the size and scope of Becky's aura. Tears of joy filled her eyes, and she smiled broadly, and turned several times in circles.

She stopped, and seeing my astonishment she said gaily, "Paul, I know you don't really understand what I'm saying, but you know old Millie don't tell nobody wrong."

She gave my arm a last squeeze and bid me a peaceful "Goodbye!" that seemed to enter my body along with the thoughts she'd just shared with me. She was about to walk away, but I said, "Oh, Millie, you said Becky had been to this hospital three times. What was she here the other time for?"

This time her face flooded with sadness, and she said, "Becky's father, Jack, died in this hospital three years ago, and Becky was here when he died."

"I had no idea," I said.

"Now, I've got to get back to hospital business, so I don't have time today to fill you in on everything that happened," said Millie, "but I do believe in due time you'll learn the truth of that glorious day."

"Glorious?" Now I was really confused. "I thought you said Becky's father *died.*"

"I did say that," said Millie quickly. "Oh, there's most

often lots of grief when a loved one passes on, but I saw a true miracle on *that day*, you can bet your bottom dollar, a true miracle from God himself, say Amen!"

"Well, I hope you tell me some time soon," I grinned. "If you don't tell me, who will?"

"So far, I can see this whole thing pretty clear," said Millie. "I don't know how or why we're put into the circumstances life gives us, but all you got to do, Paul, is *follow the signs.*"

And with those startling words, she turned to face a summoning co-worker, and leaving me standing confused, curious, energized, puzzled, and at the same time, eager to learn the truth of what she'd shared about this Becky girl.

CHAPTER

4

The plaster cast on Becky Chapman's right hand wasn't pretty; it exposed only her thumb and the very tips of her fingers. The 200 pound steel base's fall had shattered numerous bones just above the wrist. Becky was told she'd need to wear her protective cast for up to 10 weeks—coinciding exactly with the end of the volleyball season. "It's bad luck for her, but broken bones heal," said Millie Parker, "and once they do, Becky's life'll go on with just some inconvenience and a little discomfort."

Let me say right now: We were one cautious group of coaches following Becky's accident—and for good reason. Back in 1979, accidents like Becky's were treated without blame, or finger pointing, but had that accident occurred in the 90's, we would surely have found ourselves under a microscope, facing possible dismissal, and maybe even a lawsuit, instigated by today's always-lurking lawyers out for an easy buck.

But these weren't the 90's, and although we felt responsible, the public didn't hold us accountable for Becky's unfortunate accident.

We changed some of the rules following the accident. Coaches only were in charge of setting up the net, which the girls appropriately named "Breaker." (That wise decision has stuck for these many years), and amazingly, "Breaker" has stood also the test of time, and remains like a silent guard in our humble gym. A few tattered holes have been mended in the webbing of "Breaker's" netting. But the same wheels responsible for Becky's accident still turn. And despite the pain "Breaker" caused 20 years ago, I still pause now and then to think back to that day, and in a strange way I'm delighted that "Breaker" is still with us, to remind me most of Becky Chapman.

But back then, we assumed that Becky's short stint with the team had ended. Becky was right-handed, and even if she could learn to serve with her left hand, there was no way she could play volleyball with that heavy plaster cast. She was finished, and we thought we'd certainly never be able to accurately rate her talent as a volleyball player.

But we soon began learning about one of Becky's foremost attributes: resiliency. For just when most young people would have called it "quits," Becky called "a beginning." Would a little thing like a broken hand keep her down? Not this girl, no, not Becky Chapman.

But who was she really? She had only been a student at St. Luke's for one year, and although my daughters knew her, I knew very little of her, her family, or anything else about her background. But now more than ever, my writer's instincts drove me forward to find out more.

Becky had looked just like any other new player on that first day of practice; but that was then, and this was now. We were holding a new practice in just a few hours, and I fully expected Becky Chapman to be absent.

As we drove to practice that afternoon, my daughters, Karen and Megan, seemed unusually quiet for the 20 minutes it took us to get to St. Luke's gym. I asked them the usual questions about school, but both girls, even the usually chatter-mouthed Megan, answered in very few words. And not only were they curt, they seemed a bit depressed.

What could account for this sudden change of attitude in

my two ordinarily highly energetic, fun-loving young girls? Had something happened at school? Was either of them in trouble? What was the problem here?

We pulled into the school parking lot, our short drive having felt like it had taken 40 minutes, and I breathed a sigh of relief as I parked the car, turned off the ignition, and shifted into "Park."

We were always the first to arrive at the gym, a habit I formed early in that first coaching year. I needed the few minutes before the others arrived to mentally prepare myself. I was also concerned with the players parents' perception of me if I wasn't the first there. I'd impress them, I thought, by showing that kind of consistency and sense of responsibility, and that I truly cared. I personally didn't appreciate lateness, though I did recognize that these young players were seldom at fault for being late, since they were all several years shy of completing the Driver's Education curriculum.

It was Megan's job to retrieve the key to the gym, which was kept next door, some 75 feet away, where the Irish Order of Nun's lived together. (That arrangement still exists 20 years later; the nuns just don't leave the keys to the school and gym lying around, *period*!).

Not that the old gals didn't trust me. No, it wasn't that at all. "It's for your own protection Mr. Strong," Sister Fran Drake had told me in her strong brogue. "This way, you'll never come under any suspicion. So just come over here any time you need the key."

I watched Megan walk slowly to the brick convent, head down, sullenly. Again, I was puzzled—before, she'd always bolted to the door of the convent, eagerly rung the bell to the right of the door, and enthusiastically hailed the lucky Sister who answered the door. Her demeanor this time was so different, I decided to trail behind her.

Just as she reached the door and pushed the white button,

Sister Fran Drake herself, the "Mother-Superior" of the school, opened the door and peered down at the young girl. "Meg," she said with her usual warmth, "are you here for the key, young lady?"

"Yes," Megan said glumly. She did force a smile for Sister Fran's benefit. "We have volleyball practice."

Sister Fran Drake retreated inside for a moment, but quickly returned with what looked like at least a 40-key ring. She fumbled for the gym key, but I knew Megan could tell just which one it was—the only silver key on the ring. Still, Megan waited politely for Sister to go through all her careful motions. Sister Fran then repeated her set speech about the responsibilities that came with Megan's acceptance of this ring of metal. Megan had heard it each and every day we'd practiced, from whichever Nun happened to answer the door.

"Am I clear Meg?" said Sister loudly. "Will you bring the keys back promptly?"

"Yes," said Megan meekly, amazing her father with her sincere patience. "I'll bring them back in just a minute."

As Megan turned to make her way to the gym, she and Sister Fran both noticed me standing near the side of the door. I said my hello to the Sister, and motioned Megan towards the gym door. "I'll be right over, hon," I said. "I just want to have a few words with Sister."

Megan turned and again walked slowly towards the gym, keys in hand, and I turned my attention to Sister Fran. "And how are you tonight Sister?" I said. "Beautiful night isn't it?"

Now, Sister Fran wasn't one for small talk; she customarily cut right to the chase, and so she did this moment. "In case you're wondering why your daughter's so glum, the girls are all upset about the Chapman girl," said Sister. "They all love her so. But Megan will get over it, just give her some time."

Her abruptness startled me a bit; in one brief sentence she had probed my unspoken question about the girls' attitudes.

"Well, I guess the girls would be upset about the accident," I said. "But Sister, can you tell me what's so special about this girl? I've never seen the team so concerned over something?"

Sister Fran's look into my eyes seemed almost hypnotic. Her thin lips curled slyly, as an in-the-know detective's might. When she was quite sure she had my undivided attention, she said, "It's hard to explain just why, but Becky Chapman is a very special young woman. She's got a peculiar hold on you—you'll see when you come to know her better."

"Think about this: Becky has a broken hand, but both your girls—all the girls—they have broken *hearts*. And I suggest your practice tonight be a light one, you know. The girls have Becky on the mind right now, not volleyball, and you're not going to change that right away."

I pondered what she was saying; she seemed to be echoing Millie Parker's feelings about Becky. Before I could speak again, Sister Fran Drake said, "Goodnight," and retreated into the Convent's mysterious confines. I stood there for a few moments, wondering exactly what I should do.

The parking lot was beginning to fill with cars, as parents dropped off their daughters for practice. I gathered myself, as parents waved to me, and kids entered the gym. *I'll wing it lightly*, I thought, *but the team really can use practice. I'll say a few consoling words to the girls, and we'll just move on, period.*

Megan had already unlocked the gym as I strode towards the school parking lot adjacent to it. I figured several girls had gone in ahead of me and snapped on the overhead lights, which took a good 20 minutes to reach their full brightness. I unlocked the trunk to my car, flung the net filled with a dozen balls over my shoulder and slammed the trunk shut and went into the gym. Half the team had gathered inside; they were talking quietly among themselves.

Lynn Modell, Sharon and Joanne, a trio of great friends, formed one group; they paused in their conversation as they looked up and noticed my presence. Mandy Morrison, Katrina Glover, and Karen also formed a small circle; none of them met my eyes as I passed them. Only Megan, the one girl looking a bit interested, stood isolated; she methodically bounced a stray volleyball off the far wall, looking deep in private thought.

Within minutes all the players and coaching staff had arrived at the gym—all, of course, but Becky Chapman. I blew my whistle to take roll call, and the girls' mood as they sat in a tight circle at mid-court remained eerily silent. You might have thought a family pet had just died, and the whole bunch was grieving together. This made me even more curious to understand how a 13-year-old like Becky Chapman could have affected them so deeply—especially since this was just her first year on the team, and we'd had only two practices. I hadn't thought Becky was our best player, nor necessarily even a key player, at least in terms of sheer athletic ability.

But I glanced at my clipboard and began taking attendance. As I called out the names, I was met with dispirited responses. When I'd finished, I thought it might be best to ask coach Shea to give us a complete report on Becky's condition.

Afterwards, I would review the new rules regarding the thing that had injured her and get practice going.

At my right, coach Shea had barely begun to speak, when several of the girls turned toward the sound of a car engine outside, but rumbling throughout the gym. A moment later the far door to the gym opened slowly, revealing the silhouette of a girl.

Instantly the grimaces of the girls near me turned to smiles. Before I could say anything, the entire team rushed by me towards the girl in the doorway; standing alone, her broken hand raised high, a smiling Becky Chapman.

CHAPTER
5

The rush of jubilation suddenly filling the gym reminded me of Christmas day for a gaggle of six-year-olds, with Becky the biggest gift. Becky raised her sparkling cast high for all eyes to behold, as if she was proud it, flashing the hardened plaster like a trophy. So quiet moments earlier the gym, now rocked with shrill, happy laughter.

I approached the pack Becky was in the middle of, and her eyes met mine as I greeted her with a smile. She smiled back; as a matter of fact, she'd always seemed to be smiling when I'd seen her.

"Hi, coach Paul!" she chirped gaily. "I'm sorry I'm late for practice."

"Sorry? I'm happy to see you here at all," I said, for want of something "righter" to say. "How are you feeling?"

She again held up her broken hand for me to see. Then she raised her opposite hand and said softly, "*This* one still works."

Like a burst of thunder the girls clapped and cheered louder than I thought any group that size possibly could. I confess that I got caught up in that joyous moment, too. Dropping my "coachly cool," I joined in the general glee and whacked my hands together till they hurt.

When at last I felt the cheers ebbing, I shouted, "All *right* then—let's *get* to work."

The applause picked up again as the girls escorted Becky triumphantly to the opposite end of the court. As usual, Maggie led the way; this time her left arm enveloped Becky tight as a vice. Katrina and Janet flanked Becky's right, and happy teammates trailed behind, skipping and dashing like small children.

I stood in place for the few seconds it took the girls to reach their destination, bemused at this remarkable attitude change. I thought I'd fathomed something of the complicated minds of 13-year-olds, but what just happened took even me by surprise. I mean, who ever dreamed Becky would show up for volleyball practice in her condition?

"Come on, we're ready for practice now, coach Paul!" yelled Janet. "Should we go get 'Breaker'?"

I spent the next few minutes discussing the new rules about handling our friend "Breaker"—which had been a breaker indeed under the old ones. After I'd done that, coach Shea and I retreated into the "hole" where "Breaker" was stationed. We pulled that infamous gear out into the open, as the girls watched us, quietly and intently.

"Remember, ONLY us coaches will be responsible for the 'old Breaker' from now on, "I said, as we dropped the wheels into place along center court. "Now—let's get going!"

I rolled the balls out from the carrier, and coach Shea took half the team to begin our serving drills. The remaining players, including Becky, stayed with me.

I caught her eye and said to her, "Could we talk a moment?" I blew my whistle and directed the other girls toward coach Shea. Then I walked with Becky a few feet into the hallway leading to the school's classrooms.

"Becky," I said, looking down at the cast on her hand. "I know you want to play, and I appreciate your desire. But how can you play with that cast? Not to mention you're right-handed..." My voice trailed off; I was struggling to find a way to complete my thought. "Look," I said, "even if you could learn to serve left-handed, the league won't let you play with a cast on. I'm sorry, Becky, that's the league rule."

Becky looked up at me, her eyes smiling like clear blue glass as they always did. Her head nodded, seemingly in agreement with what I'd said. "Sure, coach Paul, I know I won't be able to play right now. But I'm part of this team— I'm an *Eagle*—and I want to do whatever I can, any *way* I can to help, even if it's just cheering the team on or keeping score. I'm an Eagle, and we Eagles are fighters, aren't we, coach Paul!"

I couldn't help but smile. *Why isn't the world made up of Becky Chapman's?* I thought. I felt so proud of her, I wanted to reach out and give her a big bear hug. Of course, I thought better of that; a male coach has to keep an appropriate distance from a girl he's talking to in private. So I simply smiled back at her.

"Becky," I said, "you've got me—I can't help but love your attitude. Now, what do you say we join the others? I'll find something for you to do."

"Yes!!!" she cried. She reached over and gave me a big, quick hug that felt almost like an electric shock. She let me go, shot me another beaming smile, and sprinted back into the gym.

Somehow, just then I felt rejuvenated, as though a jolt of perfect peace coursed within me, sort of vibrant, I thought. Maybe I was just pleased that Becky was back, and with the way things had shifted so suddenly since she entered the gym only minutes earlier.

Whatever it was, I was beginning to sense what Millie Parker and Sister Fran had told me about Becky. One thing was certain, positive: Becky Chapman was going to make a difference to this team, even if she never played in a single game for the St. Luke's Eagles.

CHAPTER

6

That practice went incredibly well. I never felt such cohesiveness on any team I'd ever been involved with, as a player or a coach.

The players felt it, too. They sang and cheered, listened to us coaches and helped each other out at every opportunity. They were simply alive with enthusiasm, and my focus was so direct, I lost track of the time completely, till the moment the girls' parents returned to the gym to pick up their daughters.

During the two hour practice, I'd put Becky in charge of retrieving loose balls during serving drills. It was a boring, but useful ritual. And despite my suspicions that she'd tire of it quickly, she seemed to enjoy it. Still, I figured I should think of something else for her at our next practice, maybe something more important.

My wife, Emily, kept charge of the scorebook; she also served as an assistant coach, helping with certain drills. Scorekeeping was no option for Becky, though. Becky had only practiced once and didn't know volleyball very well yet, so I couldn't have her help coach the girls; in fact, she herself needed help in all phases of the game. I racked my brain for an answer, but I came up empty. If she wanted to "practice" with the Eagles, Becky would have to retrieve balls, or just sit and watch. ***That'll be her choice, period***, I thought.

I blew my whistle to signal the end of practice. I knew none of us wanted it to end, but tomorrow was another day, and tomorrow we'd hold another practice. We needed plenty of practice to get ready for our first game of the year, which was scheduled for only two weeks away.

The girls gathered and formed a seated circle near mid-court, in the shadow of "Breaker" and waited for me to wrap things up, as their parents stood impatiently by. "Girls," I said, "let's do it again tomorrow!"

Another peal of high-pitched thunder pierced the gym as the girls in unison let their feelings fly. *This team is really something special!* I thought, as they sprang to their feet as one.

We coaches excused the players and collected the equipment. Across the gym, every team member collected her own gear and huddled once again around Becky, and her Mother, Maureen.

I had met Becky's mom at the hospital, but only for a few minutes. Family only had been allowed in her room at the beginning of her trauma, and we weren't then in any frame of mind to be especially social to each other. Now she looked over at me as I began to position "Breaker" for his short ride to the "hole."

"Wait!" she cried. "Wait just a moment, coach."

I halted abruptly, and she approached me, wide-eyed and smiling. *So this is where Becky gets it,* I thought.

"Coach Paul," she said, the girls want to have their picture taken with Becky, and they want it taken standing next to...Breaker!"

"Really?" I said.

"Yes, really, coach Paul" said Becky. "The accident was my fault—I wasn't paying attention when it happened. I want "Breaker" to know that he's still our friend. And—will you be in the picture too, coach Paul?"

I thought, *She actually acts as though this metallic*

webbed piece of equipment has feelings! Or is she just kidding me the way teenagers do? No, I thought, *she's for real, and she's gotten the entire team to buy in to the idea. And what was the harm?*

"Sure," I said, "where would you like me to stand?"

Becky took gentle control, directing each girl to her proper place for the photo. Her mom, Maureen, stood by waiting, camera in hand, for Becky to give a "thumbs-up." Becky took just a few more moments to position the team just right. Then at last she sat down—on the very base that had shattered her hand—and her volleyball season.

"Perfect!" said Becky when she'd surveyed the scene. "We're ready now, Mom."

Broad smiles filled the room as Maureen's mouth formed the familiar "cheese." As a flash, then another one followed, nervous laughter echoed throughout the gym.

Maureen placed the camera back into her purse, and the gym soon emptied itself of all the players and parents except Maureen, who remained with my wife, Emily, Karen, Megan, and Becky.

"Coach Paul," Maureen said sweetly, with a smile almost as dazzling as Becky's, "may I please have a word with you?"

"Sure," I said. "I've been meaning to talk to you, too."

I had tons of questions to ask her—about Becky, their life, and especially about Becky's terrific attitude. I also wanted to know what "the hand" gesture was—did it mean anything significant?

But I put my personal agenda on hold for the moment and let her keep talking. "Coach Paul," she said. "I just want to assure you that in no way do I hold you responsible for the accident. And she's probably already told you this, but Becky wants you to know that she'll be happy to do anything, ***anything,*** that might help you and the team at practice."

"Yes I know, Becky did tell me that," I said. "And I had her run down loose ball tonight, but…"

Maureen shook her head several times to silence me. She apparently knew where I was headed, and she stopped me in my tracks.

"That's just fine" she said assuringly. "Becky will be pleased to run down balls for you, if that's what you need."

I smiled and knew she was telling the plain truth. Boring as I might have judged this kind of menial task for a girl Becky's age, Becky and her mother convinced me the assessment was wrong.

And they both made me feel comfortable with this, so my mind began concocting additional tasks for Becky to help with. *Even if she's willing just to chase balls for 10 weeks,* I thought, *this girl deserves something more.*

"Well, all right then," I grinned, "I'll have her chase balls for now."

Becky's mom thanked me and left. Then Emily and I gathered "Breaker's" two ends and rolled him into the "hole" for the night. We shut off the lights to the gym, locked the two doors, and headed for our car with the bag of balls, a few clipboards, and other volleyball items.

Outside I was surprised to see all the girls on the team, gathered around the Chapman car. Several of the girls' parents had also joined the conversation that was going on; I quickly counted, at least 10 adults and 13 girls.

Emily and I, surprised still once more, tossed the equipment into the car, and walked the 20 paces to where the others were standing. It was a beautiful evening, maybe 30 minutes before the sun would disappear behind the horizon and darkness settle into the valley.

"What's going on?" I said glibly. "Having a team meeting without the coach?"

"Coach Paul," said Jane Modell, Lynn's mother, "we'd like you and Emily to listen to an idea we've been talking about-is that all right?"

Emily and I walked over to Jane, who was standing near Becky and some of the girls. I looked at them, all smiling, all obviously very eager to share something they considered important with us.

"O.K." I said. "What's the deal?"

Before I could get a response from anyone, I instead got 13 hand gestures—just like the one Becky had thrust into the air at the height of her injury—from all the team members. They took me by surprise, to say the least.

My wife and I watched them for a moment, then looked at each other in wonder. Then we looked back at the girls, who kept gesturing, as if they were waving tiny flags. We smiled, dumbfounded in that parking lot at this remarkable display of camaraderie.

"O.K., enough suspense!" I said at last. "Would you girls please tell me what that hand-sign means?"

All hands came down in unison and Becky came forward. She looked ready to begin speaking, but before she could, Maureen stepped forward, and Becky paused and gazed with obvious respect and admiration at her mother.

"Coach Paul," Maureen said, several years ago when Becky was in the fourth grade, her father, Jack, was involved in a terrible automobile accident, that left him in a deep coma." Her eyes glistened with tears, she swallowed and after pausing a moment continued to speak, with all eyes on her.

"For several weeks, the outlook for his survival was grim."

I looked around at the group; everyone was eagerly waiting for her next words.

"It became apparent to us early on that if Jack did ever come out of his coma… he would never walk, nor probably ever speak again."

All of our eyes were teary now, as Maureen continued.

"Our emotions were all over the place for those two weeks. Jack was my life, our life, and we couldn't imagine living without him. He was the best man God ever created, and he was slipping away, and we couldn't even say good-bye."

Maureen paused to collect herself, and I now heard louder sniffles around me. She went on.

"I went to the Doctor in charge. He had told me I should prepare myself and Becky for Jack's death, that there was simply nothing more that could be done for him. At first I'd been both resentful and angry. How could they have given up hope so quickly?"

Emily reached over, placed her hand in mine, squeezing tightly. Maureen said, "So I decided to keep Jack on life-support, against the medical staff's wishes, and I kept believing God would do something for Jack, maybe even a miracle. I spent hours at the hospital chapel each day."

"Then one evening, Father Benedict, a Priest who made rounds at the hospital, came into the chapel as I sat there, sobbing and praying at the same time. He was an older man, very wise. He just placed his strong arm around me and I wept for what must have been at least an hour, yet never moved from my side or even said a word. When I had finished crying, I felt all my energy spent, yet somehow, I was left at peace with myself, and with the whole situation."

She smiled then went on.

"Father Benedict spoke comfortingly to me for a while-his voice, his touch were so spiritually powerful. Then as he led me out of the chapel, he told me what I should do. So I went to talk to the Doctor's."

I was so tuned into her words till this point, I hadn't noticed my clammy palms or my perspiration-soaked brow. I wiped my forehead and my hands with the cuff of my shirt.

Maureen said, "I told Dr. Johnson what I had to do- he was in charge of Jack's case. I said "We'll all come together at Jack's bedside tomorrow, the entire family, and we'll pray for him, talk to him, until he either comes back to us, or until it's time for him to leave with God."

As Maureen paused for a few seconds I tried to imagine what it must have been like for her back there in that hospital. *How could anyone have been so strong in that situation? How would I have reacted?* I thought. *How would my family have survived without me?*

Tears trickling down her cheeks now, Maureen said, "I went home that night and organized a family meeting. We were fortunate that most everyone lived in the general area; those that didn't had sensed the end was near for Jack, and they'd already flown in. That night we all gathered at my house, and I shared with each person—it took hours for us all to come to peace with Jack's going."

I suddenly noticed that Sister Fran Drake seemed to have appeared near me, almost out of thin air. *She must have noticed us gathered in the parking lot*, I thought. I don't know how long she'd been there, but she was listening intently, with a knowing smile. She apparently had known these details the rest of us were just now learning.

Maureen glanced at Sister; Sister nodded, and Maureen went on:

"During our few hours together, I convinced everyone that we should never play God with Jack's life, or ever with anyone's life. If it was God's will for Jack to live in this vegetated state, then I'd care for him. And if God wanted him to come home to heaven, then that was acceptable to me as well."

At least 15 minutes had passed since Maureen had begun sharing with us, yet we were all still transfixed at her every word.

"The next day we arrived at the hospital," she said, "maybe 30 of us in all. Becky, nine at the time, was still numb with grief and unsure of herself. She needed me to be strong, so with God's help, I was."

"The hospital rules were very strict; Jack could have only three visitors at a time in his room, for only fifteen minutes each set of visitors. Of course, as Jack's wife, I was allowed free access at any time, and I took full advantage of that privilege. I was there night and day, talking to Jack, holding his hand, combing his hair, even shaving his face when he needed it." She smiled tenderly at this memory.

"That day, though, rules or not, I wanted the entire family, all 30 of us, to be at Jack's bedside; even if we could be there together for only a few minutes, it had to be—and that very day, I sensed."

"The head nurse objected to my request rather sternly, but I was determined not to take her 'no' for an answer. Perhaps I was disrespectful to do so, but I simply told her, "It has to be this way," and motioned the whole family into Jack's room. I knew she wasn't going to call hospital security to kick me out!" Maureen grinned.

We listeners expelled relieved little laughs, and Maureen said, "I now have to add something new to this story. "You see, I come from a family of singers. While I grew up, whenever family—aunts, uncles, cousins- got together at our house, we all sang. And not just any songs, *Irish* songs, and barbershop harmony! My maiden name is Walsh, and singing was what us Walsh's did best," she said with no small touch of family pride.

"My Uncle Tom and his bother, Patrick, always were the first to begin singing, and long after all of us younger ones went to bed, we'd hear them still singing, always right on key."

We laughed again, and Maureen said, "Is it O.K. if I go on?" We broke the night with a resounding "Yes!" and she took a sip of water from Becky's sports cup and told us more:

"So there we were, 30 of us packed around Jack's bed,

like sardines. There were a few tears as Jack's parents, John and Dorothy, stroked his hands and arms."

"At that moment, Uncle Tom's sweet, angelic Irish tenor lifted quietly in song, as it had at so many family functions in the past, bringing tears to our eyes at weddings, funerals, and special occasions. Ah, he had a voice to die for!"

"Uncle Tom knew what Jack's favorite song was—"Ol Man River,"—and that's what Uncle Tom sang into that hospital room and gently echoed down the halls."

Most of the girls squinted, unfamiliar with that old song; Maureen saw this, and she took the next few minutes to sing a few key verses of the song. Then she tried to explain to us why it had been Jack's favorite:

"Ol' Man River is a song about a black man in the South, who worked on the Mississippi River, during our country's slavery days. The Mississippi was that "Ol' Man River.""

"Now, the man singing the song is a hard worker who simply dreams of freedom, wishing he could cross the Mississippi and into another world far from his slave life." "It's a song about the basic freedoms in life that aren't always available to us just because we want them to be. It's about hard work, and people who have much, and people who have little. And it's about growing weary of life sometimes, and wishing we could just give up."

Katrina's voice broke through then: "Mrs. Chapman, I'm not sure I understand—why would your husband so much enjoy a song about *giving up?* From what you said, he sounds like a very strong person."

"That's a great question," Maureen said, but before she answered it she sang the entire song, in a voice worthy of her forebears that rang across the parking lot. She finished, "I get weary, an' sick of tryin', I'm tired of livin', an' scared of dyin', but Ol' Man River, he just keeps rollin' along." Then she caught her breath and said, "The last verse is about giving up, you said? "I've sung it to you the way it was written—now, I'll sing it for you the way *Jack* used to sing it:"

"I may get weary, but NOT sick of tryin', NOT tired of livin', NOT scared of dyin', but Ol' Man River, he just keeps rollin' along!"

The group applauded Maureen, and she bowed her head graciously. Then she lifted her chin and with fire in her eyes said, "*Now* do you understand? Our Jack WOULD *NEVER* GIVE UP!"

Darkness had begun to settle in, and street lamps were flickering on all over the parking lot, but none of us wanted to leave and miss Maureen's triumphant conclusion:

"So Uncle Tom sang that song, Jack's way, and before he was done, we all had joined him. I don't think in all of our lives we'd been so lifted up," she said.

"None of us wasn't in tears when that song ended. We reached out to hug each other and hugged and kissed, all 30 of us. One by one, each family member squeezed Jack's lifeless left hand. He may not have squeezed back, but I'm sure he knew we were with him," Maureen said. "He had to have known."

"At last the room emptied of family, but for myself and Becky inside. Becky wanted to stay with me. She took my hand and put her head on my shoulder. She looked down at her Dad and, placed her free hand inside his. She looked me calmly in the eye, and I knew at that moment, as she did, that it was time."

Maureen's eyes, shining with the parking lot lights, looked past us all, as if she could see beyond time. Then she said, "But before I finish my story I must tell you one more thing." She paused, gathered her thoughts, and finished her story.

"Jack had been the Director of Operations for VOICE— the national group for the disabled. Its name stands for "Volunteer, Organize, Inform, Create, Evolve." Jack's specialty with VOICE was helping hearing impaired children, and he knew sign language as well as you and I know English."

"Jack had this thing with Becky. Prior to dance recitals, Becky would always be nervous. She'd peer out into the auditorium, and when she spotted Jack, he'd simply lift his left hand with these three fingers—as you all did earlier- and Becky's fears would disappear. You see, that signal means, "I love you" in sign language for the deaf- but for Jack and Becky, it even meant much more. For them it meant, "I'm O.K., you're O.K., and of course, I love you." It always helped Becky get through her stage fright."

" Now I can end the story of that night properly. Jack did go to heaven that night," Maureen said, "and I felt a truly amazing unreal peace as I felt him leave- and I really did, I *felt* him leave. He was gone from the life we knew, but I know he is still with us, girls, I just know it."

"But before Jack left us," she said then, "he left us one final message."

We huddled closer together now and waited, total darkness having enveloped us outside the parking lot lamps that hummed above us.

"Becky," said Maureen, "I think you should finish."

Becky came forward and stood next to her mother for a moment, and they exchanged a hug. Maureen walked over and lowered herself into the spot where her daughter had sat.

"I was sitting next to my father when God took him home," Becky said. "I could feel it happen, too; it was incredible, simply incredible."

"We cried, mom and I, as Dad left us. We cried for a moment and, held each other tightly. We stayed there for a few minutes, not letting go. But then, we wiped away our tears and, got up to tell the others. The nurses burst back into the room then to check Dad's monitor, but they were too late."

"They worked on his body like crazy people, but it was over. Dad was gone."

We looked at the ground and then at each other standing in that parking lot, and searched for some "right thing" to say. But Becky hadn't finished.

"Just one more thing," she said. "When I'd come to his bed to give Dad one last hug, I'd noticed something strange. His left hand was open, in the signal we always had for each other. His fingers were stiff and unbending, yet somehow, they had formed our signal. I began to cry, and my Mother came over. I showed her Daddy's hand."

"She looked down at it, then opened her mouth in disbelief and asked me. "Did you do that? Becky, I can't believe you'd do that as a joke, 'cause it wouldn't be very funny."

"I said, "No Mom, it was just like this when I came over!""

"Mom and I held each other, cried, and then said a prayer for my Dad. He was gone, but he'd left us so at peace. And he'd left us a message, a sign from God, Dad's last message to us, I'm sure of it," said Becky. "he was letting me know that everything was O.K.""

CHAPTER
7

The sound of the telephone's ringing startled me as I gazed out the kitchen window at the apple orchards that spread for miles beyond my back-yard. I'm not sure how many rings I missed before I finally picked up the phone.

"Coach Paul," came Jane Modell's familiar voice. "It's Jane, have I caught you at a bad time?"

"Not at all," I replied. "What can I do for you today?"

I recalled then that Jane had asked last night to talk to me about an idea she'd had. But of course, we were in no mood to discuss the matter after Becky and Maureen had told their moving story.

"First, how did you feel about the Chapman's' story last night?" she asked with an almost childlike awe. "I tell you what, that girl and her mother really touched me- well, they touched us all, don't you agree?"

Of course I did. My Family had been equally touched by Becky's story; we had stayed up late that night, talking on our deck about it till well after midnight. The quiet, serene way Becky had spoken, her calm movements, her sense of assurance had moved us all to tears. How grateful we were already that she had come into our lives!

"Yes," I said, "that was quite a story. What a strong family—especially Becky, for such a young girl."

Jane agreed with me, and I had never till then heard her

sound so upbeat. Then she paused a moment and said, "Coach Paul, as I told you, the other day I had an idea I wanted to talk to you about. And especially after last night, I just *know* now that my idea would be absolutely the right thing to do."

"Go on," I said.

"I've designed a patch that will fit perfectly on the volleyball team's jerseys," she said. "It shows' the hand signal for the deaf that Becky taught us, the one that says everything is o.k., the "I love you." I'd like to get your approval, to make these for all the girls, so they can wear it out of respect for Becky, her father, her family- and our team and the school!"

I paused for a moment. It sounded like a great idea, but even if I bought into the idea, I'd need Sister Fran's permission. She, not I, controlled the school's athletic program. It might not be easy to persuade her; she and the other Sisters were sticklers for "tradition."

"I like your idea," I said. "But will the nuns?"

I could sense Jane Modell smiling knowingly on the other end, and I realized she'd already anticipated this difficulty. She paid attention, and knew how to work the school system. She had three daughters enrolled there, plus a husband who contributed much of his spare time from his plumbers job to keep the old building from totally collapsing. And neither he nor Jane, was ashamed to remind those in charge of all his free service.

"I've already talked to them," she said. "They'd be delighted with these patches—Sister Fran Drake told me so herself."

I paused again for a moment, then said, "All right, bring the patch over to my house; I'd like to see it."

"Be there in five minutes!" she chortled.

CHAPTER
8

The patch was perfect: A left hand, gold-stitched onto a background of green, our school colors. There they were—index finger, pinkie, and thumb, all raised, just like Becky had first displayed to us the night of her accident. It was inspiring and looked very professional. I liked it, and I wanted it.

"This is a work of art!" I told Jane, who'd been standing by my side, eager to hear my comments.

"I'm glad you like it," she said, giddily as a school-girl. "It won't take me long to finish- in fact,... I've completed six already!"

I wasn't surprised that she'd more than anticipated my answer, that she'd known long before she asked me what my opinion would be:, that I would absolutely embrace her idea. Still, she had respected me enough to ask me about it, and for that, I certainly thought well of her.

What a nice touch this'll add to my first year, I thought, *a spiritual symbol for a Godly school. We'd be foolish not to take advantage of Jane's generosity.*

"How long do you think it'll take you to finish making the rest?" I asked, and I saw Jane's eyes brighten with joy.

"I think I can have them ready by the end of practice tomorrow," she said. "Wouldn't it be nice to have them by then to show the girls?"

"You bet!" I replied. "Why don't you come by after practice, and I'll give you a few minutes to reveal your handiwork to the girls. How's that sound?"

"I love you, Coach Paul!" she squealed. Her arms flailed, then wrapped around my defenseless torso. "I'll work on them tonight, and I'll have them ready tomorrow—*ooh*...I can't wait to see the expressions on the girls' faces."

I couldn't either; I felt like jumping up and down myself. But I would make sure to display the calm a coach ought to at such times and leave the revelry to Jane and the girls, and simply go about my business as coach. Well, I would show *some* excitement, but part of a coach's leadership is to separate himself at least slightly from the reaction. I would stay "in charge," and remain cool as a coach should—and, leave the rest to the girls and their moms.

As I walked Jane to the door, I said, "I'll let you get to work then. Come to practice tomorrow the minute you finish the final patch."

Jane sprinted with the smallest, quickest steps imaginable to her car and pulled out of the driveway and into the road in an instant. She did take a second to wave frantically at me, standing in the driveway, and she honked her horn gaily as she drove from sight.

I returned to the house; Emily and my daughters had gone to the mall earlier, leaving me alone with my thoughts. Now, as I waited for them to return from their excursion, I smiled, imagined the girls reaction when they learned about the patches. Karen would be satisfied, but not go "ballistic"; but Megan would be unable to contain herself. Like night and day, these two were, but I would keep silent, leaving what was to come completely to Jane. She could announce in any way she saw fit the addition of the patch to the green and gold uniforms. This was Jane's baby, and I would "humbly" remain in the shadows.

An hour later, the family car pulled into the driveway,

Emily inched her way into the garage in her usual precise spot, and turned off the car. The girls stormed into the house, remarkably free of shopping bags, having apparently returned relatively unencumbered from this particular shopping venture.

Megan was the first to burst into the house. She could spin a tale from the events of a mere five-minute walk in the park. She exuded energy, enthusiasm, and passion while taking the most inconsequential moment and painting intricately detailed epic word-pictures from the moment she returned home from school, till the moment her tired eyes closed for the night.

Karen tended to keep her emotions all in, maybe thwarted by Megan's dominance in this area. But I doubted that was why. Instead, I figured that her personality, so unlike Megan's, simply enjoyed accurately recounting events, when she decided to share them with us. So I could count on Karen to take Megan's rushed words, decipher them, eliminate "opinion," and deliver the clean truth, free of warts, free of charge. That's why I was so astounded that night to hear Karen dominate the conversation. But she evidently felt like talking, so we'd allow her all the time she needed.

It was a splendid night, as there on the deck, the four of us sipped cold drinks and gazed up at the thousands of stars sparkling so clearly above our country home.

What a perfect setting for Karen to open up in, I thought, and she proceeded to take center stage.

Karen began her impromptu conversation with fanfare, sharing about a number of issues, including items she needed for her bedroom, albums she was interested in purchasing, and what we were doing for summer vacation next year (-a full 10 months away). She rattled on for 20 minutes—occasionally Megan interjected something, but this was Karen's soap-box, and she held the floor.

But soon she switched her topics from the mundane to things not physically "touchable," but real just the same. It turned out she was curious about and wanted some real answers to some tough spiritual issues. "What is heaven *really* like?" she asked. "Why did Becky's Dad die at such a young age?" "Why did Becky break her hand, the one part of her body she needed the most to play volleyball?"

On and on went her questions, and I felt feeble indeed, giving what I thought were such weak answers. Yet, thinking back on those responses to her queries, I believe even far more thorough preparation for those life-questions would have given me adequate answers. After all, some of these issues seem destined to be reserved for the after-life, and scholars and clergy around the world have argued about them for years.

And that's what I told Karen. She went on to ask about "fairness" and "sadness" and "teamwork," and I reviewed her face to see if my all-too-humble words were getting through. And, I must say, I was very proud that this 13-year-old girl was starting to "get" such important issues at such a young age.

We finished sipping our drinks around 9:30. Karen leaned down to where I sat, on the lounge chair of the deck, and placed a warm, pleasant kiss on my right cheek. She said goodnight, thanked me for taking time to share with her, then did the same to both Megan and Emily. Megan jumped up from her chair and gave her usual hugs and kisses, and she, too, went inside.

Emily and I looked at each other and shook our heads. "That was intense," Emily said. "I can't believe that was Karen asking those questions. Where do you think they came from?"

"I don't know," I shrugged. But maybe I really did know, and so did Emily. I thought, *It's Becky Chapman who's turned the wheels in Karen's head, no doubt about it.* In a very short time Becky had brought a team together, she'd inspired Jane Modell to create a unique patch for the team uniforms, and now she'd prompted Karen's curiosity about life's deeper issues.

"I'm really looking forward to tomorrow," I told Emily after a short pause. She lifted an eyebrow questioningly, and just then I remembered that I hadn't yet shared with her Jane Modell's patch idea.

"Why, what's going on tomorrow?" she asked.

Then I heard her ask again, "What's happening tomorrow?" I had obviously been too deep in thought for a few moments to respond to her. This time I acknowledged her.

"Sorry," I said. "What exactly did you say, honey?"

"I said, 'WHAT'S GOING ON TOMORROW?'"

"I'm sorry, hon," I said, and took the next few minutes to let Emily in on the patch idea. She loved it as much as I did. Now we both looked forward to see the girls' reaction at tomorrow's practice.

CHAPTER

9

As usual, when the alarm clock thundered on the night stand next to my bed, I tried and failed to grab another five minutes' sleep. Giving up the attempt, I fumbled for the proper button to turn the thing off, found it, and clicked it. Mercifully, my action eliminated the clock's annoying racket.

I reached over to hug Emily, but her spot was vacant. I fumbled for my glasses near the foot of the bed, but with my increasing myopia, I couldn't spot the exact location where I'd dropped them the night before. My hand finally found their target; I placed the glasses on my face, took a quick look around the room, stretched out, and yawned. Then I popped out of bed and entered the kitchen. I looked there for Emily for a few minutes; then out of the corner of my eye caught sight of her standing on the deck, a cup of coffee in hand. She turned and spotted me and smiled. I went out the door to the deck, and she greeted me with a tight, almost painful hug.

"How long have you been up?" I asked. I peered through the kitchen window, and spied 7:29 on the kitchen clock.

"Oh, quite awhile. I just couldn't sleep last night," she said.

We went back inside together, woke the kids, had our usual "breakfast of champions" and went our separate ways.

Of course, the girls caught the bus to school, just in time as usual, waving to us from the yellow vehicle as it cruised away from our house. Emily kissed me goodbye moments later, as she left for work as a part-time receptionist for Dr. York, the local veterinarian.

Emily wanted to be home for the kids after school, and she managed to be, always. She would work until 2:00, arrive home by 2:15, and have a snack ready for the girls by 3:15, the minute they walked through the door.

I had the distinction of being the lone political columnist for our local daily paper, "The Valley News." I had worked my way up the ranks over the years, toiling long hours for little pay to start, as a cub reporter. During my seven years at the paper, I had become the youngest political columnist in the state, and by this time my work schedule was pretty much mine to call.

Today I needed to drive three hours north, where I'd be meeting Joshua Gibson, the crusty 95-year-old, former mayor of our township. He'd agreed to let me interview him for a piece I was working on, comparing the politics of 1929, when Gibson ran the show, to the situation in our time, under our current mayor, Madeleine "Sunny" Light.

People said Gibson's thinking faculties were still very much intact, but that he'd become a recluse, pretty much holed up in his lakeside cabin for 50 years. He lived with a niece, Rosemary, in what someone had told me was "an old cabin," at the end of a long dirt road on the southern tip of "Rye Lake."

I had never met Gibson, or been to Rye Lake, but I was curious to do both as I pulled away from my house at 8:30. I figured I'd arrive by 11:30, tape our conversation (which I expected to last about an hour, 90 minutes tops), and head back home for today's volleyball practice, which I'd pushed back to 5:00, to allow for any travel problems I might possibly encounter.

This story's 50-year comparison between the two political eras was my idea. What sparked it was an issue that had suddenly become the source of a thorny debate in our town of over 60,000 people. A 200-acre tract of township land that had always been thought to be off limits for development since the township was incorporated 200 years ago, was now on the verge of disappearing, as the township wrestled with where to place the ever-growing population of our ever-spreading community.

What some people called "The Purists," folks mostly 60 and above, held the belief that to disturb this pristine natural beauty would be tantamount to committing the worst of sins. At recent town meetings, they had passed out flyers urging the citizens to stop the would-be developer, "A.J. Craft."

Craft was the current "duplex king" of our state. He'd been developing acres of untouched nature by the hundreds for years; now he had come south like a Napoleon, and our region was next on the list of this "conqueror."

Our present Mayor, Light, seemed to be torn between the needs of the growing town she had lived in her entire 48 years, and the feelings of the older residents, many of whom had shaped the town and whose ancestors had settled and died here.

But she could see tax advantages to Craft's proposal, ones not only enticing but necessary ones to address. Over 200 homes could be built on the contested land, Craft pointed out, and that would be a boon for the whole community. New homes would attract new business, and new business meant new tax money, new tax money meant more growth, and more growth meant even more tax money.

So Mayor Light was torn, as she'd admitted to me off the record during an interview three months earlier. The future was looking her straight in the eye, but she felt she had to remain on the fence. I understood her dilemma; there were still tricky politics to be played here: 1980 was an election year, and the land, were it developed now, wouldn't be open for development until well after the election one year way, so to stand against Craft would involve risking her re-election over this one heated topic. Plus, she didn't want to end up being shunned, ostracized in the town she'd always called home. During that interview, the mayor had told me, "You can't please all the people all the time," *That's a useful cliché for both politicians and volleyball coaches*, I'd thought as we shared the moment with a chuckle.

What had complicated the initial struggle for the land was the search for the deed to it. Long-time residents claimed that the land had always been zoned for what it now was—nature. So there was no way it could be developed, and that had been taken for granted all these years.

But the shrewd Craft had other plans. Somehow, in an exhaustive search for the old deed, the vital paperwork had been misplaced, and when that had been discovered, the lawyers had rushed in like roaches when lights go out. The Craft camp, a dozen or more of the most brazen "suits" in legal history, weren't to be taken lightly, and the township's legal team couldn't match them. But they had taken their case up the political ladder, and the courts had decided to allow six months more for a deed search. If by such time, if the deed couldn't be found, the mayor and her eight committee members would be free to decide the fate of the land—and possibly their own political fates as well. So the stakes here were high.

Now, the elders of the town believed that Joshua Gibson knew the whereabouts of the deed, and he was their last hope. Craft's noose had started it's deadly squeeze, they knew, and there was one rung left before the top of the scaffold, and that was old Mayor Gibson.

I hashed all this over in my mind as the three-hour drive went without a hitch. The directions I'd received from the old man were perfect, much to my pleasant surprise. *Yes,*

Mayor Gibson may be old, but his mind's still sharp, just like I've been told, I thought. I looked forward eagerly to meeting him moments from now.

The long dirt road leading up to the Gibson camp was bumpy, narrow, but worn. I slowed to five miles per hour, and took in the surrounding beauty of the lake and forest. The first few miles coming into the Rye Lake area were filled with summer homes, but they curiously lacked many signs of life. A few boats dotted the lake, old men fishing from them in silence broken only by my 10-year-old Ford. Along the way I spotted four deer, three squirrels, three chipmunks, and scores of rabbit. *There are more animals here than people*, I thought on that drive towards Mayor Gibson's place.

The mail-box at the entrance to the Gibson camp was shaped like a duck. It had the words "J.P. Gibson and Company" etched on both sides. The box wasn't numbered, just named. Well, no surprise there; this was the first sign of any residence in over three miles. *The old man' was sure living out his latter years in the middle of nowhere,* I thought, *but it's so beautiful, who can blame him?"*

The road eventually split after about a half mile, challenging me with my first and only decision regarding directions. But this was different than most problems one encounters on the road; there was nothing for miles—no gas station, no telephones, no people.

I opened the door and stood outside the car, hands on hips. I looked down both forks in the road and saw nothing. I looked at the directions Gibson had given me, he hadn't indicated this fork in the road. I stood there shaking my head, wondering what to do next.

I decided to just leave it to chance- I'd simply flip a coin, and heads would take me to the right, tails to the left. *A simple decision*, I thought, as I reached into my pocket, feeling for the quarters I'd accumulated from the toll-booth at my final exit.

The quarter I pulled from my pocket was old and worn from years of handling.

The year "1929" was inscribed just under the Father of our Country's profile. *That was the last year of Gibson's second term as mayor, and the last known recording of the deed*, I thought. *Coincidence?* I thought as I flipped the coin high into the air.

I held my hand out for the quarter's return and closed my eyes for only a moment, wishing for "heads." But the coin never hit my palm. I looked toward the ground, fumbling for the coin in the dirt road, but I couldn't find it. I glanced up, into the late morning sun. Nothing.

Just as I began to mouth the words, "what the," a voice broke in sharply, sending my surprised body into a sudden spasm.

"Shouldn't throw your money around like that, son!" The voice had an old man's vinegar in it. "When you throw around your money, you're likely to lose it."

I looked over and caught a wink at the end of this crisp advice. Mayor Gibson, whom I supposed this lively codger to be, opened his hand and placed the quarter into mine, then took my other hand in his and shook it firmly.

"Joshua P. Gibson at your service," he said, "and you are Paul Strong."

I wanted to ask him how he'd been able to sneak up on me, and clutch that quarter from the air without making a sound. But he was extremely quick, for his or any age, and before I could get my mouth open, he said, "let's go," and he placed his old body with surprising agility into the passenger side of my car.

This old man has to be in supreme shape for a man five years shy of 100, I thought.

Five foot ten, perhaps 160 pounds, a full head of gray hair, he wore rimless Ben Franklin-style glasses, with high magnification, I guessed. He sported a baseball cap, suspendered overalls and dusty old work boots. He had a magnificent tan, and his handshake had been with the powerful grip of a man half his age.

I didn't know what to say, but I blurted out, "I wasn't sure which fork to take in the road," as I followed him into the car. "You didn't make any mention of this fork in the road in your directions."

The old man said nothing, only pointed to the right as I started the car.

I knew it, I thought. *I knew it would be the right fork in the road.*

I drove about a half mile filled with twists and turns and wondered if I'd have continued on if Gibson himself hadn't come along. The road soon trailed west, but was then joined a few yards further up by the road that had gone east only awhile back. Now I understood: both forks in the road met again at this spot, to form the single road Gibson had diligently informed of in his directions.

Gibson must have sensed that I was about to speak, but he beat me to it. He said, "Sometimes when the choices aren't very clear, we must rely on what we've learned. "Sometimes what we *see* is not what we *really see*. You have to train yourself to look *beyond* that what you see." *He's a man of wisdom, this one*, I thought. I only hoped that after this day at the lake, my words to the girls on the volleyball team would be as powerful as his words were to me at that moment.

I nodded, soaking in his observation. I was repeating it in my mind when up ahead the shape of a huge log cabin hit my eyes. Old Gibson was right again, that, "We must rely on what we've *learned*"-was true." I'd thought there was only one road leading to his camp, yet I'd seen two. I'd also thought, from what I'd been told, that the old mayor lived in a ramshackle little cabin. Now I was learning the truth was different. *Got a feeling this is going to be one interesting afternoon*, I thought as Gibson signaled me to stop and park the car.

From the left of this giant structure, a cool breeze with a pine smell caught me. I was taking it all in, the structure and the odor, while Gibson signaled me up the cabin's four very wide stairs and onto the deck, which was massive as well, and appeared to circle the cabin entirely. Six-foot beams connected the deck to the roof, which looked more like a wood awning, angled in such a way as to keep the sun away wherever it's position might be in the sky.

At least 15 old, wooden rocking chairs were neatly spaced along the front of the deck. I estimated at least three feet of room was between each rocker; all were at least two-and-a-half feet wide. Wooden buckets, I counted eight, possibly just for decoration, were spaced across the deck and in the front corners. I estimated the cabin was somewhere between 100-120 feet wide. Adding in the width of the deck, which looked a good six feet, the house had to be over 130 feet wide, and with its towering, seemingly endless roof, this cabin was an awesome sight.

The unusual doorway leading into the cabin was wide and high as well. I started to enter, Gibson already ahead of me, inside. As I walked through the massive door, I guessed it was at least nine feet high and, perhaps five feet wide. One small window was cut at about eye level; the word "Welcome" was carved just above the glass, a good three feet from the top. All this, made the door seem even larger than it was.

Gibson waved me inside.

"This cabin has been here for over 100 years," he said. "Bet you've never seen such a wide opening to a house, have you?"

I certainly hadn't. It was the biggest house door I'd ever seen- and then I dropped my jaw as I stepped into the most awesome room imaginable.

"Have a seat over here by the fireplace," Gibson motioned. "I'll find Rosemary and ask her to get us something cold to drink."

Gibson stepped out of sight for a few moments to look for his niece. I took this opportunity to have a look around, *Magnificently built*, I thought, *rustic, and furnished with all the amenities you'd expect if it were built circa 1850.*

But before all, the fireplace stood out in the giant front room- immensely wide, like everything in the place, and incredibly high. The hearth itself was as deep as it was wide, at least six feet in both directions. The mantle was adorned with dozens of old black and white photos, mostly of the lake and, curiously, several of our town.

The photos of the town itself were very old. In over half of the photos, the main road into the center of the bustling business sector was unpaved. Also decorating things were drawings of the lake, the cabin, and nature scenes, and a photo from 1904 with a young Gibson dressed in a navy uniform, a pretty woman seated to his left. I noticed that the overwhelming majority of these were framed in cherry wood, setting off a dazzling display of color in the afternoon sun. A magnificent, tall Grandfather clock, stood silently in the far corner, the hands fixed at "7:29." *"Strange,"* I thought, as just then a new, female voice broke the silence.

"Hello Mr. Strong, I'm Rosemary. Welcome to our humble home in the woods."

I held out my hand to a blue-haired woman. Her grip was strong for her size, five-feet-two, perhaps 110 pounds, 70-75 years old. She held my hand for several seconds while she made small talk, and then released her grip.

"You have a strong aura," she said, smiling. "Have a seat right here, I've prepared some home-made lemonade for you."

"Aura, did you say?"

"Yes, I said you have a strong aura, it's very clear to me," she said, winking at me with her left eye.

"That's odd that you should say something about my aura," I said. "I recently ran into an old friend who also made some comments about auras."

Then old Mayor Gibson said, "Rosemary has always been able to size up a person, just like that." He snapped his fingers, and the sound echoed through the giant room. "Don't know how she does it, don't care to know either. But her gift does come in handy when we first meet someone new."

Rosemary rose from her chair, poured the lemonade from a frosty-looking silver container, then returned to her seat.

"I suppose it's God-given," she said. "Now, I don't do anything else, like read palms or any of that mumbo-jumbo. But I do see the shapes of people's characters, and I can analyze those pretty good, too."

"Now, I can see that you're a man of integrity- that's first and foremost on my list. Also, kindness and generosity, and they're next in line."

I was humbled by her words, and when she finished speaking , I simply said, "Thank you." Even if her talent wasn't authentic, she'd left me feeling alive and appreciative.

"Now, don't get all full of yourself over that," Gibson growled gently. "In fact, why don't you begin the interview now? At least I feel I'm at ease to talk now, but just don't mess up my quotes."

I nodded and turned on the tape recorder. I began with the usual opening interview questions: "What was the most difficult decision you ever had to make?" "Tell me about some of your adversaries?" "How did you raise money for your campaigns?" and so forth, and Gibson answered briskly, as if it had all just happened. It didn't take long to confirm my impression that Mayor Gibson was no ordinary man.

After what seemed like a few minutes, I glanced at my

watch. A full two hours had passed, much to my surprise.

"Would you like to take a break?" I said, though I wasn't really eager for one; I was finding this the most interesting interview of my journalistic career, and I wanted to go forward.

"I don't need a break," said Gibson. "Fire away."

I asked more questions, and another 45 minutes whizzed by. It was now 2:30, and I'd forgotten all about the volleyball practice I had scheduled for 5:00. It was Gibson who reminded me.

"Didn't you say something about leaving by 2:00 for some practice?"

My shoulders slumped and I slammed my forehead with the palm of my right hand.

"I can't believe I forgot," I groaned. "Can I use your telephone?"

Gibson directed me to the kitchen, where the ancient-looking telephone was kept. I promptly phoned Emily, who'd just arrived home from work, told her what had happened, and asked her to call the team and, move practice up to 6:00.

"Call the Modell's first," I said. "Jane's no doubt feverishly finishing those patches, and this'll give her more time."

I hung up and returned to the huge room, gathered my belongings, and made my thanks to my hosts. Before I said goodbye, I asked Mayor Gibson if I could call if I needed anything else for my column.

"Of course," he replied. "It would be my pleasure."

Rosemary and Gibson walked me to my car. I slid inside and, closed the door. As I was about to back out, I remembered that I'd promised the senior citizens back home that I'd do them the favor of asking old Mayor Gibson about the contested property deed. Gibson looked surprised at my question. He squatted on his haunches, his eyes now level with mine where I sat in the car.

"That land can't be touched," he said. "It's set aside, all 200 acres, just as it is."

I reworded my sentence, to be sure I made it clear that the deed was either missing or lost, no one knew which.

"Oh, I understood you the first time," he quipped. Looking perturbed, he said, "You sure they searched everywhere?"

I briefly reviewed everything I knew about the situation: about the developer, A.J. Craft and his team of lawyers, and the six-month deadline that had now reached it's third month. I told him about Mayor Light's dilemma. His eyes misted over at the news.

"Young man, that deed *must* be found," Gibson said with startling firmness, "it's *imperative* that it be found." Then he turned abruptly, fists clenched, and headed for the cabin.

Close by, Rosemary smiled, her kind eyes instantly at mine. In a gentle voice that matched a gentle spirit, she said, "Paul, the mayor was the last person to know the whereabouts of that deed. "He's talked about it on occasion. He knew this day would come eventually. But amazing as it seems, he just simply doesn't remember where it is."

I shook my head in disappointment, said goodbye to Rosemary, and headed down the long dirt road, leaving a trail of dust behind me. A minute later, the cabin was out of sight as I looked through my rear-view mirror.

I plugged my recorder into the car's lighter socket, and for the next three hours listened intently to the interview with Gibson, analyzing his wisdom, reflecting on the kind words of Rosemary, and thinking about that great cabin and the beauty surrounding.

But all together, I felt well up in me one strong urge that went beyond mere "journalism." *Somehow I had to find that old deed.* Mayor Light needed me to, I told myself. "Yes, I *must* find that deed."

It was now 5:45, and I was driving the last few miles to

the gym. I turned my thoughts to volleyball, remembering the notes I'd made about tonight's practice.

I pulled into the school parking lot, 10 minutes early. I jogged to the convent, got the key from Sister Fran, ran to the school, opened the doors, and quickly snapped on the overhead lights. The sound of cars and car doors opening and closing outside led me to the gym door, where I welcomed the girls, who all seemed to appear at once, and together we went inside. Moments later, Coach Shea, Emily, and all 13 players were present and accounted for.

And just like that I shifted from being columnist Paul Strong, to being "Coach Paul."—and got practice going.

CHAPTER
10

One true measure of a capable volunteer coach is the ability to separate work from play. You don't earn any money volunteer coaching; yet it's not uncommon for your work day to stretch well beyond the normal eight hours, creating an "overlap" on occasion.

And I still had my mind on my time with Gibson as the girls took the court for that third practice. I was ready to write, on the spot. But right now, I was distracted, and I needed to pull myself together to do volleyball for at least the next two hours.

I closed my eyes and imagined a giant volleyball. I would be the focal point of these 13 girls for the next two hours, and I wanted desperately to give them what they deserved. So, like a dieter resisting the urge to plunge into a giant slice of pie, I pushed the Gibson article away. Will-power somehow, won. I kept focused on that giant, imaginary ball, then I opened my eyes, and blew my whistle. Now I was ready; the story would wait until later.

We broke into two groups to begin serving drills. Serving is the single most important aspect of volleyball at this level. Simply put, the team of girls these ages that serves better almost always gains the victory. I had studied the score-books of the previous 10 years of volleyball at St. Luke's. Not only had the team never made the playoffs, they'd never yet had a winning season, 29 wins, 91 losses was the school's dreadful, cumulative record. Three of those years, including two of the last three, had produced no victories. In other words, St. Luke's was the doormat of the league. Teams salivated when we were their scheduled opponents. I had put my journalistic instincts to work as I combed those books, and had diligently logged any bit of information I felt would further our cause.

And it had all come down to serving. Our best opponents had successfully served with greater than 80 percent accuracy; yet we showed a poor 50 percent, and that barely. Our average loss was by a 15-5 margin, and we had *never* defeated a team with a winning record. Still, it was clear to me that if we could improve our serving skills, we could at least be competitive.

So tonight, as we had been, we spent a good deal of our practice time honing our serving. Two teams of six each competed against each other, each girl serving 20 times at the start of practice, and they'd serve another 10 each at the end. The thirteenth girl, Becky Chapman, was in charge of tallying each girl's success at serving. We had 10 practices set before the first game. That meant, each girl would get to serve 300 times. *Practice will make perfect,* I thought. Would I be right?

Well, not only did our serving practice prove worthwhile, it was fun. We made a game of it; at first, the girl with the highest serving average at the end of practice would be put in charge of the school announcements the next day (an idea I'd gotten approved by Sister Fran Drake). I had also found something more challenging for Becky Chapman to do, and she truly enjoyed her role, with pen in hand, almost becoming my official "student assistant."

The girls were very fair to each other, but it had become apparent early on that the better servers, Megan, Karen, Lynn, and a few others, would win most of these contests. It was Becky who had come forward to point this out to me from the stats she was keeping. And she had suggested that the girl who showed the most serving *improvement* from the last practice should make the announcements. This way, a girl who made 20 of 30 serves could conceivably be rated ahead of a girl who made 24 of 30. Becky's idea was sound, and we used it. It created competition, teamwork, and gave incentive to both the high and lower-skilled girls, just what the coach needed to order!

After tonight's rousing full hour of serving drills, the girls were thirsty. I called for a five minute break, and they went for their sports cups, while I tallied the page from part one of our serving drills.

Twelve girls had served 20 times each. Of the 240 serves, 144 had made it safely over the net and fallen in bounds.

"Sixty percent!" I cried out to the girls. "Let's get to *70* by the end of practice!"

I had 80 percent in my mind, and that had been my goal heading into the season. Unbeknownst to them, I'd assigned each girl a target, with improvement in each subsequent practice. I'd made very clear to the girls my serving philosophy. Did they want to win? Were they tired of being the laughing-stock of the league? I again shared my research about past teams' serving records as they enjoyed their break. They had bought into the idea early; my presentations and preparation had paid off. They were eager to improve their serving, eager to see that line on the graph we made to track results, going up!

But, I told them, serving was only part of the game. Defense was vitally important, too. Good team defense could break the serve of a "hot" opponent. So defense we worked on primarily, *between* our two serving drills. Defensive drills were fun, if not as much fun as serving drills. I would serve from one side of the net to a team of six on the other side. It was their job to "pass" the ball to each other, "hitting" the ball no more than three times—the maximum allowed in volleyball—to get it back to their opponents. Each team of six girls would have five opportunities to achieve this goal. They would then rotate with the second group of six, and so on. In the beginning, even by practice number three, it was apparent that we needed to improve greatly. Neither team could get the ball back in three hits for over 30 minutes, and the entire team was getting frustrated. We occasionally paused for constructive criticism, but it was apparent that defense would need more time than I had at first set aside.

During defensive drills, I excused Becky from any participation, of course. She had no loose balls to track down; my ball rack held a dozen or more balls within my reach. One night, I'd casually suggested that she "serve left-handed against the far wall,"—and surprisingly, Becky went for it. Tonight I could see Becky in just the right corner of my eye as I ran the defensive drills. She was diligently serving with her left hand against the gray wall of our gym. Over and over she'd misfire, then run down each errant volley that sailed past the narrow wall and onto the floor of the giant gym stage.

It was actually comical to watch both Becky and the team of six—both seemed to be failing. The team of six kept getting no higher than two hits, and Becky Chapman kept missing with her barrage of shots.

As I was serving once more, coach Shea mouthed at me, "Seven-thirty!" pointing to her watch.

That left the final 30 minutes for the second part of our serving drills. I blew my whistle, signaling another five minute break, and the girls once more broke for their sports cups.

But Becky continued her torrid pace, serving left-handed. As they sipped their drinks, the other girls began to watch her and, cheer her on. Mandy Morrison led a few of the girls over to the ball rack, and they each carried two over to Becky.

The rest of the team gathered together, cheering Becky wildly as she valiantly attempted to serve one ball off the narrow wall (it was, perhaps five feet wide).

Several more balls sailed onto the stage, and the girls kept cheering. One of Becky's volleys barely missed clipping the corner of the wall, and a resounding "Oooh" rang from each girl.

I noticed five minutes had passed, and we needed to get back to our serving. But, I felt powerless to halt the proceedings somehow. Becky kept hitting, kept missing, but with fierce energy, and the girls kept cheering, completely tuned in to Becky.

I fumbled for my whistle, which dangled from a cord fastened around my neck. I was rooting for Becky, too, but it was time we got on with practice.

I squeezed my lips together, and the air in my lungs thrust forward, and just then the sound of a ball thudded against the wall. The girls roared, drowning out the sound of my whistle, which I immediately stopped blowing. The girls rushed over to Becky (who thrust her arms in the air), congratulating her as if she'd just made the winning serve of a championship game.

Becky was all smiles, despite her 50 or 60 misses; she wasn't in the least upset at herself over all the failures she'd just had; she was jubilant in her success alone. And I thought, ***What's important to this girl isn't how often she fails, it's the ecstasy she feels despite the face of failure, a kind of unshakeable sense of triumph.*** She had made only one serve out of 60 attempts that day, yet she felt as if she'd made them all!

I at last managed to get the 12 other girls back down to business, and we finished our serving drills, each girl serving 10 times. As before, Becky charted the numbers, tallied them up quickly, and handed me the clipboard.

I took a look and shouted, "Girls, you made 89 of 120 serves, that's *74 percent!*" As one, the girls leaped to their feet, clapped "high-fives" and hugged each other. As they did, I saw parents gathering at the door. I was glad the girls had done better than I had expected—and glad they were so pumped, pleased, and proud. *This* would be the perfect moment to present the patch to the girls. While I waited for Jane Modell to arrive, I killed time talking to the girls and, glancing towards the door.

Just seconds later, Jane entered the gym. In her right hand she carried a small gym bag, possibly an "overnight bag." She smiled as our eyes met and walked quickly towards the team.

The girls gave Jane their attention, and she waved all the parents also over to the middle of the gym, where the team had sat down. I then asked everyone present to listen to Jane. "She has a special announcement for you."

Jane's voice was halting at first, and she breathed rapidly, trying to introduce the patches to the team. I could see she was excited, tired, and nervous. Jane was not a public speaker, and she was having the usual struggles one encounters when facing this particular fear.

But I signaled her to relax, and she settled down at last and started over, as the girls and their parents listened to her with puzzled faces. She addressed Becky alone this time.

"Becky," she began, "the other night, that story you and your Mom told, it really moved me, it moved all of us." She took in the whole audience with her eyes, and I noticed all of the adults nodding agreement with her statement.

"So," Jane smiled, "with the permission of the school, and of coach Paul, I've stitched a simple patch with the hand symbol you gave us that night." She held out her hand, giving the signal she had sewn. Then she reached into the bag and, pulled from it 16 identical green and gold patches, each with a perfect left hand embroidered to a handsome finish.

Jane placed one on her upper arm, just below the shoulder. "Here's where you'll place the patches—there's just enough room on your uniforms' short sleeved jerseys for them."

"Awesome," came the lively Maggie Shea's voice. "Wow," came another, "Unreal!" said Katrina Glover.

Then, as Jane handed each smiling player a patch, the adults clapped with thunderous approval. Jane proudly emptied out her bag, but she saved the last patch for Becky. Jane's eyes were moist as she hugged Becky and placed the patch in Becky's left hand with her own. Becky looked up at Jane and said, "Thank you so much—this is the nicest thing anyone has ever done for me... thank you!"

Maureen Chapman, Becky's mom, had been standing silently in the far corner of the gym for a solid 10 minutes. As the girls got together and compared patches, Maureen came forward to Jane. She held out her hand and walked Jane to the far corner of the gym. There, they spoke privately for a few minutes, embraced each other with huge hugs, and walked back to the group, hand in hand.

This is even better than I expected, I thought. *What a day this has been!*

CHAPTER
11

A full week had passed since that memorable day at the cabin with Joshua Gibson, and I'd written my latest column to explore the history of the old deed, and ended with the question, "Where *IS* Deed 10-11?"

The column had gone to print and had been circulated throughout the county at the usual news-stands, convenience stores, and of course, to our subscription customers. Readers had sent dozens of "Letters to the Editor" responding to the column. Dozens more were still filtering through our in-house post office, a small booth operated by a little old lady I figured had been here at the newspaper since its day one.

Doris Thatcher, well past her useful days here, did struggle mightily, trying to keep up with the attention the column had received. Her job was simple, really: sort the mail, deliver it to the proper departments, and keep the postal area organized and clean.

But the ravages of age, namely arthritis, senility, cataracts, and brittle bones, taxed her ability to cope with this sudden onslaught of paper. The first few days following the column's publication produced the largest volume of opinions delivered to our humble Post. Mrs. Thatcher, accustomed to an afternoon nap in her quiet little room, simply misplaced the initial delivery, which was found at week's end by Mr. Charles (our singing janitor, who was at least Mrs. Thatcher's age).

Now, both of these people were wonderful characters, and their combined years at the paper spanned well over a century. But they had clearly lost their touch, their prime years of work well behind them. So it was now a rare sight to see the small trash cans empty at the desks of the 20 or more writers, columnists, photographers, and editors employed here, or the dust, which lent an opaque look to the place, cleared from the overhead lights. These two old warriors were responsible, everyone knew, for most of the lost letters, dirty bathrooms, and cluttered messes in the building. The daily sound of a reporter, editor, or photographer politely asking either of them for something missing, was simply part of the atmosphere.

The key word here is "polite." Everyone employed here was gracious and polite to the old two, even at dreaded "deadline" time, moments reserved for maximum chaos, bickering, and the release of adrenaline.

Our Publisher, Elroy P. Davenport, expected employees to treat each other in this civil manner. He was from the "old school," 65 years old, and running the same paper his father, and his grand-father, and his great-grandfather, and his father had since that first issue in 1847.

The Davenport family tradition had been passed down through the generations here at the paper, and it produced a wonderful sense of harmony and tranquility, deadline panics and all.

Mr. Davenport, just like his predecessors, treated the entire work force of 75 like one big family. Of course there were reprimands, occasional discords, some suspensions, but I can't recall a single firing. This Davenport tradition was in itself the reason Doris Thatcher and Mr. Charles were still gainfully employed, despite their obvious and routine blunders.

So, Mr. Charles had found the envelope marked

"Editorial Department" at the top of a trash bin located several offices away from Mrs. Thatcher's "Postal" area. Mr. Charles, a kind and obedient sort, personally delivered the package to our department, handing it to me with a concerned look of disbelief.

"Mr. Paul?" the janitor said politely, knocking lightly on the open door to my office.

"Yes," what is it Mr. Charles? Come on in."

"Found this package in the dumpster just now," he said. "Lucky thing I came along when I did, would have been tossed out, you know, if just one more piece of trash had gone over top of it. It's addressed to your office."

I thanked the gentle Mr. Charles, and listened for a moment to another sweet tune he had elected to whistle as he went about his business. How ironic," I thought, that this package was found by the man who most likely put it there in the first place. I got my letter opener from the black holder on my desk, and sliced open the sealed portion of the envelope.

Inside were 37 "Letters to the Editor," all dealing with the subject of the lost deed. Most of them were postmarked more than a week before. Now I needed to read each and every one. It was my duty, so I began to read.

The letters were full of the townsfolk's' passion. Incredibly, of the 123 letters received in response to the column, only three favored developing the land for new homes. I would lead with that fact in my follow-up column for Sunday's paper, our largest circulation day. Still, I knew that, even with the overwhelming majority of the people favoring non-development, it was all smoke. The courts had already issued a deadline for locating the deed, and developer Craft was waiting in the wings. He had won his cat-and-mouse game with the town, and with each passing day, the inevitable was approaching. The pristine wilderness was on its death row, and the date had been set for its execution.

A small miracle was needed here, and as I sorted through the letters, I silently hoped to discover one, even in the words of a stranger.

But the letters contained only the words of upset citizens, no clues that might lead me to the deed. I had turned down a dead-end road, I truly didn't know where to go next.

Then the idea came to me, courtesy of old Mayor Gibson. At my interview with him, he had said, "Whenever you're faced with a difficult task, your answer is usually right there. You just need to know how to read the signs."

Maybe those lost "Letters to the Editor" had been that kind of sign," I thought. But what did the sign mean? Thus far the letters breathed only anger and frustration, and gave me not a single clue. But I thought some more about Mayor Gibson's angle on things, and as I thought, I began to read the final, unopened letter from the lost envelope. It said:

Dear Editor:

"I am responding to your column about the lost deed of lot 10-11. It is something I am hearing people talk about wherever I go, and it makes me sad that this pretty land full of beautiful trees and wildlife might be ruined soon."

I read on:

"When I was younger, my father once told me that in the old days, if people had any valuables, like money, or jewelry, or even a land deed, that they would hide it somewhere where no one else would know where it was."

I read on with mounting interest.

"He told me lots of people would hide things behind walls, in the pages of books, or in the frames of pictures."

Very interesting, I thought, as I finished this brief letter.

"I don't know if this will help you in your search. Just thought I might try to help."

What if, I thought, ***the deed wasn't in fact lost, or misplaced, but hidden?*** And my eyes lit up as I read the three lines at the bottom of the page:

Signed: "Becky Chapman"
8th Grade Student
St. Luke's School

"Unreal," I thought, and I read the letter a second, then a third time. Of the 123 letters received on the subject, this was the only one to even hint at the deed being hidden, not lost. I pondered that truth as I neatly placed the letters into a drawer unit with the file simply marked "Lot 10-11."

We ran several more letters on the subject in the next edition of the paper. But I decided not to run Becky's...at least for now. The journalistic instinct one acquires from newspapering on a daily basis brought me to this decision. I played devil's advocate with myself.

If I ran Becky's letter, that would shift people's attention to searching in the obvious "political" places—the Mayor's office, the courthouse, The Police Station. They would occupy the community's full attention; also that of all the t.v. news reporters, and our own reporting crew. It would produce a "circus" atmosphere, bedlam in our small town—bedlam spawned from large crowds of people, and likely many strangers too. And some of these strangers would draw the low-life's, some, perhaps, interested in advancing more personal causes, namely, themselves.

And the lowest life-form attracted to the search would be A.J. Craft himself. Oh, he might not put in a personal appearance, but he'd be there, represented by a few "pay-offs" in the great search for the deed. After all, he had abundant dough, was as shrewd as they come—and had no conscience whatsoever. A.J. Craft had just the right combination of negative attributes, and in no way did we need to bring the hunter to his chosen prey.

So I would save Becky's letter for just the right time—if, the right time presented itself. If not, her letter would remain filed with the others, locked in that old file cabinet.

On the drive home that evening, I thought out my plan,

which now must include personally searching for the deed. I would begin with the Mayor's office, the logical place, and allow my search to take its own course.

I'll just follow the signs, was my last thought as I pulled into my driveway, *that's right, I'll just follow the signs*.

CHAPTER

12

I was certain there'd been only one letter written to the editor by a person as young as 13, and I found that in itself curious. I though back to when I was 13 years old, and in no way, shape or form would I have been the least bit interested in the politics of the town, nor would even have known a problem existed.

Over the past few weeks, I'd quizzed my daughters several times about Becky Chapman, asking if anything "unusual" had happened in her company. I asked them who she buddied up with, how her grades were, even if anyone had known Becky was writing a letter to the editor.

Of course Megan had more to say on the subject than Karen did, but it was Karen I turned to most for information this time, since she and Becky were classmates. By coincidence, the one time I asked it, something meaningful indeed had happened that very day at school.

"Today in school, at recess," Karen began, "a cat was stuck in the big oak tree by the parking lot, and they called the fire company to get her out."

"The firemen came quickly, got out a big ladder, and tried for the longest time to get that cat out of the tree, but she wouldn't budge an inch. We eventually had to go back to class since recess was over, but the men still stayed there, trying to call that cat down. We hurried upstairs to our classroom and kept watching what was happening." Karen paused for breath.

"Did they finally get the cat down?" I asked.

"No," said Karen, "it was Becky who got the cat out of the tree."

I felt my heart racing when I heard this information—I was eager to listen to the rest of Karen's report.

"So, *how did* Becky get the cat out of the tree?" I asked. "First, how did she get out of class to do it?"

"I guess the firemen gave up, cause they left, and the cat was still stuck in the tree. Then Becky asked Sister Rose if she could go to the bathroom. And the next thing we knew, we saw Becky standing under that tree talking to the cat. Old Mrs. Barnes, the cat's owner, was standing next to Becky, and she was hysterical."

"Go on," I said quickly.

"Joanne first noticed Becky was outside, and we all rushed back to the window, including Sister Rose. Well, Becky knelt down at the base of the tree, closed her eyes, and held out her arms—and that cat climbed right down the tree and into her arms!"

I shook my head a few times. *What power does this girl possess?* I thought. "What happened next?" I asked.

"When Becky came back to the classroom, we were all wide-eyed, in total disbelief," said Karen. "Becky just calmly went back to her seat, as if nothing unusual had happened at all. It seemed like no big deal to her, but it sure was weird for the rest of us."

"So, that was it?" I asked.

"Oh no," Karen countered, "Sister Rose asked Becky why she'd asked to go to the bathroom when what she really wanted to do was go outside and help that cat. Becky said she did go to the bathroom on the way out, and that she didn't know she was going to help the cat till she was halfway back to class, and the thought just came to her. And right then, Sister Fran Drake showed up and asked Sister Rose to step into the hallway."

"Yeah, and..?"

"While they were in the hallway talking, Janet Moore asked Becky how she was able to get that cat to come down the tree." said Karen, nearly breathlessly. "And everyone's heads in the whole class just turned towards Becky—like you see in tennis matches when the crowd follows the ball."

I told Karen to take a deep breath before going on, but she couldn't seem to get her words out fast enough. "Becky calmly sat at her seat," Karen said quickly, "and she simply told us she'd just closed her eyes, and pictured the cat safely in her arms—and it just happened! 'It always does, she said."

"What do you think she meant, *always?*"

"That's what I wanted to know—we all did," said Karen. "But Sister Rose came back into the classroom just then, and that was the end of it."

That's the end of it? I thought. I was disappointed. *There must be more to this story!* "Well, did Sister Rose say anything to Becky?" I asked.

"She thanked Becky for doing a good deed," Karen said, "and she told us to open our work-books. But she was acting kind of weird, too.."

"What do you mean, weird?"

"I don't know, but Sister Fran must have said something to her in the hallway, cause she'd gone out like a lion, but she came back in like a lamb."

I chuckled for a moment. This was one of my favorite expressions, and I felt flattered that Karen had used it, let alone understand its meaning. "Did you have a chance to talk to Becky after school?" I asked.

"No," Karen said, "she's always in a big hurry on Thursdays. Her mom picks her up out front by the buses, and she goes over to Chadwick Manor and spends the afternoon with the old-folks. She even asked me and the rest of the girls on the team if we'd like to tag along next week—and I'm thinking about going, if it's o.k. with you and mom."

This is Karen talking? I thought. *This shy girl wants to spend time with strangers six times her age? And at Chadwick Manor?* A memory hit me the minute Karen mouthed the words..

Chadwick Manor. Six years ago Millie Parker had provided me with a lead about some key information on some insurance scam that led me from County Hospital direct to the billing department at Chadwick. Apparently, several elderly patients from the hospital had ended up at Chadwick, and double-billing and other hanky-panky with bank accounts was occurring.

Millie secretly helped me develop the story, and the entire professional staff at Chadwick ended up being fired, arrested, or put on probation. It had been an ugly story to cover, and it had taken years for Chadwick to regain any semblance of its original reputation.

It had also been six years since I'd been to the Manor, and I wondered if old Millie might have any new and exciting information now, especially about Becky Chapman's visits to the old place.

"Going to see the old-folks sounds like a real nice thing to do," I said. "Not only do I think you *should* go, I *want* you to go."

"Awesome!" Karen blurted out. "And Becky says we can play volleyball on the big lawn out there, and she wants us to put on a show for the old-folks, maybe show them how to play and stuff. It should be *fun!*"

"Yes, it should," I nodded, "and maybe it'll make us a better volleyball team, too!"

CHAPTER
13

I tossed and turned in my sleep that night, over so many unanswered questions, so many little mysteries surrounding this girl, Becky Chapman. At some point during that restless night, I decided I'd become more aggressive in the pursuit of the truth about her. And I'd begin my search first thing in the morning with a call to Millie Parker...

A while later, I heard Millie's soothing voice curl through the receiver. "County Hospital, how may I help you?"

"Millie, it's Paul."

"Well, I'll be," Millie said, "first, I see you at the hospital, now a phone call. It's getting' to be just like the old days Paul, yes indeed, just like the old days!"

"Millie, I learned about Becky Chapman's father, " I began. "Most heart-wrenching story I've ever heard."

"Oh, yes indeed," she agreed. "And how has our little volleyball player with the broken hand affected your life so far?" I could hear an "I told-you-so" smirk in her voice.

"I'm not sure," I said. "How can I explain it? I just feel very... oh, *secure* when she's around—and so do the girls on the team. It borders on the bizarre."

I proceeded to tell Millie about the cat in the tree, and Becky's visits to Chadwick Manor, but Millie was, as usual, one step ahead of me. She said, "Uh-huh, I know she goes to Chadwick every Thursday, come rain or shine, both during the school year and summer vacation. The old folks just *love* Becky!"

"Know anything about her visits?" I asked.

"Do I know anything?" she snapped in mock disdain. "Old Millie knows this: that every Thursday at Chadwick Manor between three and five p.m., the quality of life for dozens of old and forgotten seniors improves ten-fold. And every Thursday night when Becky leaves, those same old folks sit around saying that a child of God's been delivered to their doorstep, and they can't wait till the next Thursday when she comes again. *That's* what old Millie *knows.*"

"Why do those old-folks feel that way?" I puzzled. "What is it specifically that Becky does when she's visiting these old folks that makes them think she's a gift from God?"

"Paul," Millie said, slowly and softly, "what is the one thing you've learned as a reporter all these years—the *one thing* that takes you to the truth more often than anything else?"

"Go directly to the source."

"That's right," she said with a confident swagger in her voice. "And where *else* other than me should you go for good information?"

I knew where she was leading me, but I knew I had to say the words to her, that was just Millie's way—and I truly enjoyed playing it her way. "Ask the old-folks themselves," I grinned.

"Right *again!*" she shouted, like I'd just answered the winning question on some game show. "And you can start with Irene Durella. She's the unofficial leader of the old-folks over there, and she hasn't stopped talking in her entire 90 plus years on God's green earth. She'll tell you everything you want to know about Becky."

I thanked Millie for her help, gathered my thoughts, and looked up the number for Chadwick Manor.

CHAPTER
14

Chadwick Manor *was one beautiful piece of property,* I thought. A winding, single lane dirt road led to the main door; the Manor was situated at the highest point in the county, overlooking the valley with a truly inspiring view.

The main complex was where I was headed. The ivy covered gray building shrouded the place with unruly growth, thick and hanging unevenly like giant tentacles from some unknown source. I pulled into the visitors' parking area and stepped outside my car.

The place looked the same as I last remembered it six years ago, and I felt a cold chill run up my spine, recalling the conspiracy that had infected the place. ***But things move on***, I thought, and I walked through the door and into a small waiting room.

I was quickly greeted by a young woman, to whom I introduced myself, and seconds later I was greeted by another young woman, who stood just inside an office, awaiting my arrival. "Hi, I'm Morgan Hennessy," she said briskly, extending her hand, "Director of Activities here at Chadwick."

"Paul Strong," I said, "nice to meet you."

Morgan had been my initial contact when I phoned Chadwick Manor. She was bubbly, "chirpy," and most importantly for me, willing to talk—the best combination one could ask for in my profession.

"So, I understand your Becky Chapman's volleyball coach," she said, catching me off guard a bit. "She speaks highly of you."

"You know Becky well?"

Morgan smiled faintly at me, she grinned hugely, and her pretty smile was all the answer I needed to my question.

"We all know Becky well," she said. "Why don't I take you over to the center so you can talk to the residents. I believe Irene Durella is waiting for you, with her whole band of friends."

We walked the 50 yards to the Activity Center, a nice building surrounded by pine trees. I noticed a volleyball net strung up between two trees in the great yard adjacent to the entrance. "Do the old folks play volleyball?" I asked.

"You never know with this group!" she laughed. "We've set that up for next Thursday—didn't you know? Your whole team is coming out here to play a game for us! The whole place has been talking about it, it's a huge event here. You should come out and be a part of it."

"Maybe I will," I said as we entered the Activity Center.

I confess I was shocked as we entered the building. My expectations for an Activity Center for senior citizens were a lounge area with a television set, surrounded by the smell of medicine, and hallways lined with wheel-chair bound invalids. What I saw instead looked more like a country-club.

I saw four pool-tables, two shuffleboard tables, and two ping-pong tables at first count. Sinatra music hung in the background, and I saw not one wheelchair lining the hallways, and every pool-table, ping-pong table, and shuffleboard table *was in use*.

"What do you think?" Morgan asked me, sensing my surprise.

"I had no idea it was like this out here," I said. "This is like a country-club."

"Oh, yes," she said proudly, "our members insist on staying active, and you'll find out why in just a minute—ah, there's Irene over there."

Standing near a large window was an elderly woman, probably in her 90's but looking 20 years younger, chatting with several other residents. Her silver hair was still fairly thick for her age, and her body language told me she was one very animated and passionate person. She smiled radiantly as the afternoon sun reflected off her slim shoulders.

"Irene," Morgan announced, "I'd like you to meet Paul Strong."

Instantly, all the ladies sprung from their chairs, as if some religious deity had just entered the room. I was flattered, to say the least, as Irene softly clutched my hand. "We've looked forward to your coming," she said brightly. "Why don't you have a seat right over here?"

"Have we met before?" I asked Irene, her face looking strangely familiar to me.

"I don't think so," she said, as she cocked her head to one side. "I'm originally from the area, but left when I was very young. I've been her at Chadwick for nine years."

I picked an empty chair by the window, the last seat in a circle of 16 chairs, all soon again occupied by smiling seniors and myself. Irene remained standing, however; there was no doubt about what Millie had said about her—she was in charge.

"Becky Chapman is on your volleyball team—how lovely," she began warmly. "We just love that girl—she's our gift from God, a treasure, that's for sure."

Fifteen nods quickly agreed with the smooth-voiced old woman's assessment.

"Ladies," I said, "I'd like you to try to tell me what you think is so special about Becky?"

Irene grinned and glanced at her seated friends, and they in turn, smiled back at her. "Where would you like me to begin?" she said matter-of-factly. *"Everything* about that girl is special—she's straight from God to us."

She held out her arms as if she'd just received a gift, while the others continued to nod agreement and chat quietly among themselves. *I needed to be in on this now*, I thought.

Then Irene caught me off-guard asking, "Did you happen to hear about the incident at St. Luke's yesterday, where Becky rescued the cat in the tree?"

"Why, yes, I did," I said, "but how did you find out about it so quickly?"

"Sister Fran is a very old and dear friend of mine," Irene said. "I'm sort of her sounding board, you might say, and she's well aware of Becky's connection to us."

"You don't look very surprised at the outcome of that event," I said with sarcasm. "I suppose you've already seen Becky rescue cats from trees?"

The old woman was sharp; I could tell she was picking up on my tone of voice. She paused for just a moment before continuing; then she said, her smile turning more serious: "Mr. Strong, the animals, all of them it seems to me, have some strange 'connection' to Becky. She communicates on some level with them, and they never show any fear around her. She tells us they don't fear her, and we can sense that's true."

I glanced at her with a "Come on, be serious!" attitude.

"Now, don't you be looking at us like we're a bunch of fruit-cakes," she scolded. "How do you know the animals don't communicate with her, just because animals haven't spoken to you? You come to the volleyball exhibition next Thursday, and there you'll see what I mean first-hand."

"Could you clarify what you've just said?" I was really puzzled now.

"Let's put it this way," Irene said, "I love animals, adore them even. I've been tossing nuts towards squirrels in bunches around here for years. I leave lettuce and carrots for the rabbits—I even throw bread on the lawn for the birds. The squirrels take the nuts, all right, but only when they think it's safe for them, when nobody's standing close. The same holds for the rabbits and the birds; they only come near the food when we're a safe distance away from them."

I was starting to sense where she was going with this, but I said, "Go on…"

"Becky's first day here, she came with me to feed the squirrels and the rabbits, and wouldn't you know, instead of tossing the food onto the lawn, she knelt down beside me, made a strange little animal noise, and instantly a squirrel walked up to her and began to eat out of her hand!"

"You're kidding!"

"No, I'm **not kidding.** Then within minutes, more squirrels arrived—then the rabbits—they started emerging from the woods, too. The squirrels and the rabbits both ate together out of her hand! Now that's something special—a true gift from God, don't you think so, Mr. Strong?"

I kept a straight face and stayed mum for a moment. I didn't know this woman well enough to be sure I should believe her—yet. I'm a reporter; I need to see things "up close and personal" before I believe them. Yet, Irene had a solid reputation, and was a personal friend of Sister Fran.

I felt adrenaline flowing briskly through my veins as I pictured Becky with the animals. I didn't answer Irene's question directly. Instead, I changed gears and went straight to what I'd heard about the bustling senior Activity Center. "Morgan, you're Activity Director, said you'd explain to me why this place is so active," I said, "I'll be honest with you, I didn't expect to see this level of action at an old-folks' home!"

"Well, this used to be a pretty slow-paced operation," said Irene, "that is, until Becky Chapman came along."

We spent the next hour discussing Becky's amazing,

almost "saintly" ability, to inspire *change* in people and their habits. Something about her boundless encouragement had made what once had been a typical Senior Citizen Activity Center come alive with enthusiasm. Clearly, residents' attitudes had changed, and "old" people seemed to be bursting with "new" ideas.

Irene told me about Becky's 30-minute readings from the Bible—something the group particularly cherished and looked forward to every Thursday, for the final 30 minutes of Becky's two hours spent each week at Chadwick. "Not only does Becky read the verses movingly," Irene said, "she has seemingly boundless knowledge of details and facts in the Bible. And her sense of timing is uncanny—she seems to know exactly what the people not only *want* to hear, but *need* to hear. She's made just all the difference at Chadwick Manor, and she's done it with an utter humility that's a small miracle in itself."

"How come I've never heard about any of this?" I said. "After all, it's a pretty small town, news like this travels fast, and I'm a columnist for our only newspaper."

"It's really not being kept secret," she said. "And *good things* just come to those who wait, don't they, Mr. Strong?"

She asked the question with conviction, a sad, almost distant look in her eyes.

"Yes—yes, good things do come to those who wait," I agreed, "I do believe the old adage is true."

Irene walked me to the door, her arm solidly wrapped around mine. "Goodbye, Mr. Strong," she smiled in parting. "And don't you dare forget to come next Thursday for the girls' volleyball demonstration!"

"I'll be there," I smiled, "I'm looking forward to it."

I walked towards my 10-year old Ford, and Morgan Hennessy, the Activity Director, ran to meet me just as I was unlocking the door. She said, "So, what did you think, Mr. Strong? Did Irene tell you what you wanted to know?"

"I *believe* she did," I grinned skeptically. "Let me ask you a question, Morgan, do you think Becky Chapman can walk on water?"

We both laughed, but was there any truth to my jest? Though Becky wasn't performing any true "miracles," her amazing relationship with the animals certainly bordered on the highly "unusual;" and the old folks, well, they seemed like sheep following a *13-year old* shepherd. "That Irene Durella sure is a feisty character," I said, jingling the keys in my hand. "She's the second 95-year old I've met recently who's so... so together, so alert and quick-thinking."

"Yes, she is at that," said Morgan. "And it's so hard to believe she never married, and has no family we know of. Her only real visitor is Becky."

"She never married? Seems a bit unusual for a woman like her, from her era never to have married. And her personality's so very attractive..."

Morgan nodded. "She's told me that she had her heart broken when she was 20 years old—that's 75 years ago! She said she could never again love someone the way she'd loved that young man, so she remained single. She dedicated her life to helping others, traveled the world, mostly third-world countries, helping the oppressed. Every now and then, she'll share some of her stories with me."

How sad, I thought, *and how inspiring, too.* "He must have been a pretty special guy, do you know what happened to him?

"Not completely," Morgan said. "I believe he enlisted in the Navy, also traveled the world at the same time Irene was. The story is that he never married, either, and we don't even know if he's still alive. Irene has an old photo in her room of them together. He was so handsome, and Irene was absolutely beautiful."

After a quiet moment, Morgan thanked me for coming, and we said our goodbyes. I got into my car, pulled from the lot, and slowly drove down the winding dirt road towards town. *Maybe I should run a story on Chadwick Manor, and especially a story on Becky*, I thought.

But something stopped me. My writer's instincts told me I should wait and first observe next week's volleyball demonstration. Then I might see just how real Becky's relationships and appeal were. Then I might let our community, and maybe the world know about a potentially great person here in our midst.

CHAPTER
15

During the next few days we held our final practices before our first game against St. Joe's, to be played at our gym. Anticipation was mounting as the team continued to jell.

Our serving stats for the nine practices were exceptional. Our 12 players had served 3,240 times, converting 2,689. That 83 percent success rate was even better than my original goal, and the girls sensed, along with all us coaches, that this team was prepared and ready to roll.

But games are won on the court, not in practice. Players often freeze, especially at these girls' age, when they're the target of fans' attention. Our small, tight gym, when packed with parents, grandparents, and classmates, might be a detriment to some of our players. But I knew others who would definitely ignore the noise, the comments and the failures sure to come with intense competition.

But I was soon to learn that this team was not one easily distracted. They were focused, they were hungry, and they were determined as a unit to play to their limits. And nothing was going to disturb their attitude.

So that final practice was more than just a practice. The girls selected their uniform numbers; each now had a patch on each sleeve, team photos were going to be taken, and we would announce our starting lineup. In addition, we would choose a team slogan to become our "cheer" and rallying cry for the entire season.

The cheer happens prior to every game, and directly after time-outs. The entire team huddles together, placing their hands in a circle in the middle, and they send up a loud cheer, representing that team's feeling about themselves. The girls knew it was important to have a cheer different from any other team's.

So when the team assembled for this final practice, we passed out the uniforms, each with a number emblazoned on the back of its green jersey. The gold shorts, with green verticals lining up each side, were stunning. And the green and gold patches matched perfectly, placed on the left shoulder area of the tops. We'd already taken requests by each girl for her preferred uniform number, so the handouts went smoothly, and the girls went behind the stage to change.

The coaches, myself, Emily, and Annie Shea, sported the school button-top shirts, with small volleyballs and the words "St. Luke Athletic Association" circling them. On our left shoulder areas, we too displayed the patches. *We look good!* I thought, as the girls emerged from the stage, fully dressed, and obviously pleased.

Now it was time for team photos. It was our school's tradition to hold the photo session on the practice the day before the first game, and today the gym was loaded with parents, all eager to fire off their loaded cameras.

We gathered the players and their families together in the stands, the players sitting in the first row, the parents and relatives sitting tightly behind them, occupying several rows.

But before any photo was snapped, we'd announce the two Captains, the team had selected. This was an annual event, and the selection process was strictly democratic. Each girl voted for three players, in order of preference. The top two vote-getters would be our Captains. Certain rules applied: No voting for yourself, and no voting for a best friend, unless they were a deserving choice. We made it very clear this was not to be a popularity contest, and if we coaches sensed the voting was shifting in that direction, we would toss out the ballots and make our own selections.

After the Captains had been selected and announced, the team would reveal the team slogan. We felt this year we'd pick just the right one, so it would serve for every season that followed. (And indeed, that year's choice turned out to be so popular and so "right," in years to come, future teams literally demanded that it stick). This was also a democratic pick, in that each player had been asked beforehand to submit a "cheer" choice unsigned, and each choice would then be voted on by the players.

It came that suspenseful voting time for the girls. It scarcely needs saying that to be selected as team Captain by your peers was a positive highlight of the season. Captains were expected to represent the team, first and foremost, not themselves as individuals. In my view, this also meant representing the school, the coaches, and each teammate. And given the full instructions we'd given the girls prior to the balloting, we had every confidence they'd made no mistakes.

The voting turned out to be one-sided. The girls chose my daughter, Karen, as lead Captain, and Lauren Carter, second Captain. As they were announced, the two came forward to rousing applause and were handed two gold "C" patches, to be sewn onto their uniforms. All us coaches were extremely pleased with the team's choices.

The "cheer" was voted in unanimously. It was an unusual cheer as these things go, not particularly long—and it embodied the spirit of this team like no other I'd ever heard. The rule was, the cheer's author would remain anonymous, so even the coaches were uncertain of its origin, and the paper ballots were unsigned. But I had a strong hunch who'd written it, because I had a good enough memory for detail to remember each girl's handwriting.

As I got set to read the winning entry, I looked each player in the eyes. They were eager to hear the winner and remaining very still as I spoke. "The winning entry, voted on unanimously, is the following."

I paused for a moment, grinning as I read the cheer to myself. Yes, I too, would have voted for it had I been a player. It was without a doubt the best choice—a simple, ten word cheer, and perfectly worded for this team. I read it aloud: "We're all for one, we're one for all...go Eagles!"

Immediately girls sprang to their feet shouting, parents clapped and cameras snapped like crazy. When things settled down a few moments later, I looked at Becky Chapman; as usual, her wide smile occupied half her face. She winked at me, and I winked back. *Just between us*, I thought. Nobody else happened to catch this exchange.

I knew the words were hers, and it was no surprise at all. Once again, she'd come up victorious, this time without saying a word. I had to remember, *She's still just 13,* as I watched her mix in with the other girls, as they all lined up for photos. She was so stunning, so lovely, and I wanted to ask her about her "Letter to the Editor." But this was "Team" day, and the news business could wait for another more appropriate time.

I took my place for the photos. We stood patiently, making sure each person with a camera had time to take enough shots. They clicked team shots, individual shots, "goofy" shots. Click, click, click, for the next half hour.

When the final shot clicked, we took fifteen minutes to go over our wonderful practice statistics. Then we sent the "troops" home until tomorrow. Opening day would be upon us—in less than 24 hours. Now we'd learn if all our tough practices would pay off; or if the St. Luke's varsity girls volleyball team would perform on a par with the others in our less-than-glorious past.

CHAPTER
16

Opening day is a banner event in the short, 12-game season of a girls' volleyball team. Before the game the team was allowed to decorate the gym with banners, posters, slogans, photos, streamers, and balloons. Our usually placid, dull, dingy and gray gym would be transformed overnight into a neatly designed "box" bursting with green and gold colors.

The school Art teacher, Mrs. Raymond, allowed the girls entry to her supplies (with Sister Fran's permission, of course). The girls readily seized on the offer and tore through the art room like hungry dogs through a meal.

When they'd finished decorating, the gym looked as if it had been remodeled. All four sides were filled with displays the girls had made. At the far side of the gym, where the concession stand sat, tucked into a neat little corner, a large green and gold banner, perhaps 12 feet long and four feet wide, read: "Home of the Eagles. Here's where WE nest!"

On the far side of the gym, which was reserved for the team benches, only a sliver of gray wall could be seen. Every inch seemed to be smothered by green and gold balloons, posters, slogans, photos, and streamers—an impressive sight indeed.

But what stood out most was a huge banner, hanging above all the others on the same side—20 feet long, five feet wide, with large block letters spelling out the words we'd chosen to represent our team: "We're all for one, we're one for all."

Ellen Anderson, one of the team's more quiet members, was an accomplished artist. She'd been chosen by the girls to put the finishing touches on the banner, and you noticed her work immediately upon entering the gym:

Ellen had copied the patch made by Jane Modell with precise detail. And the large figure of a golden hand, swallowed in a background of green, was awesome. She'd perfectly painted the index finger, pinkie and thumb, each member pointing to the sky.

And we all cherished the knowledge and understanding this symbol conveyed. Maybe the rest of our student body and all the visiting teams, referees and fans, might not know its significance and special meaning for us. But the sight of it would certainly arouse discussion among the people who attended our games. *That'll be good*, I thought. *What a meaningful symbol, positive and strong!*

I'd asked the girls to arrive promptly at 6:15, a full 45 minutes before the 7:00 starting time. We would perform our warm-ups and drills, and announce our lineups. The visitors, St. Joe's, would most likely arrive at 6:30, and I intended to make absolutely sure that we, the home team, would be on the court full force the minute our visitors entered the gym. I wanted the sight of our 13 girls, together performing calisthenics, their voices calling out in unison, "One, two, three..." to be intimidating "to the max."

Six o'clock came, and our girls began to filter through the door. By 6:15, all were present and ready to go. The entire team had conspired to paint their faces green and gold, like some Indian tribe from hundreds of years ago going to battle. And they all looked perfectly consistent with each other: three solid gold lines on one cheek, three green on the other, each girl's uniform number painted between her eyes, green and gold glitter sprinkled across hair neatly pulled back into a tight pony tail.

And the girls had planned still one thing more for this opening game. Lauren had gotten the idea for each girl to bring a "good luck" item with her, and to each game afterwards. When the games began, they'd leave these charms on the bench, to sit silently like guards, protecting the unoccupied seats of every girl who happened to be in the game.

Most of these items were stuffed animals, or bracelets of some sort. Lauren's idea was sound, I thought, creating even more of a "team" concept for us to wield. This night I counted a total of twelve stuffed animals and bracelets. ***Hmm.. either one item's missing, or one player forgot to bring hers in,*** I thought.

But I steered my attention to the team then. We had moved into jumping-jacks, and the girls were loudly sounding off as the St. Joe's squad, big and mean looking, walked boldly into our gym.

I went over and re-introduced myself to St. Joe's coach, Roland Wickersham. I had met him at the league volleyball organizational meeting prior to the start of the season. Veteran that he was, he'd been a bit cool to rookie me. Wickersham had coached volleyball for seven or eight years, and his teams were always well prepared. They'd never won a championship in his era, but they'd never had a losing season, either.

St. Joe's was an above average team, and one we had never beaten in our ten-year history. I'm sure Roland Wickersham was aware of that, I thought, as he led his charges to the visitors' bench, and began confidently running through their pre-game drills.

I tried to appear confident, too, but butterflies fluttered in my stomach. The girls looked composed and cool, but I was certain they were as nervous as I was, before this, my very first game. I did my best to hide my jitters as the referee,

Kevin Logan, caught my eye and strode towards me.

Kevin was known as the "graybeard" of the league. Everything, the old hands said, cycled through him—schedules, referee assignments, roster and league fees. Without the likes of Kevin Logan around, any league like ours would surely flounder.

Kevin gave me his hand and shook mine like someone who'd probably done hard labor for a living. We chatted for a few minutes, and soon coach Wickersham joined us. After a few more minutes of small talk, mostly between Logan and my rival coach, Logan said abruptly, "Let's get started." He blew his whistle to clear the court and quickly summoned the team Captains for the traditional coin-toss to determine first serve.

We won the toss and elected to serve first. The official scorekeeper reviewed the lineups and nodded back to referee Logan, who double-checked them and the rosters. He then rolled the ball to the Linesman and blew his whistle to officially begin the contest.

A decent crowd was on hand; each player had at least one family member at the game, and several classmates, teachers and visiting team boosters were present as well. I estimated the crowd at about 100 people—not bad for the small confines of our cozy little gym.

Karen had been chosen our number one server. Her practice statistics were amazing: Karen had served 270 times and missed only eight. And not only were her serves accurate, she hit *deep*, forcing back-line players only to handle her "knuckle-balls."

We were ready to play, with all the "trimmings" that should kick off a game and season. Our team "cheer" was solid, we looked like a team, and we had silently prayed our pre-game prayer just before the first whistle blew.

So now Karen toed the service line, took two giant steps backward, and got ready to fire. As per league rules, she'd have five seconds after the whistle sounded to whack the ball in play. Our other starters, Lauren Carter, Lynn Modell, Sharon Lee, Maureen Shea, and Janet Moore, held their positions, swaying back and forth, crouching like hungry apes in a cage, waiting to be fed.

Usually, a match would last about an hour, with the team winning two of three games played to 15 points the winner. But even if one team captured the first two games (thus winning the match), the third game would be played anyway, usually with the girls who played the least in the first two games. This was another good league rule to make sure all players got a fairly equal chance to play.

But on this day, the entire three game contest wrapped up in 23 minutes flat, due in large part to Karen Strong's stinging serves. The final scores of the three games' carnage showed St. Luke's winning by margins of 15-2, 15-3, and 15-1. In the six-minute opener, Karen served 12 successful points—even before many of the fans had settled into their seats. And Karen tallied 18 straight points over the two games she played.

We did more than just win convincingly, we got the "monkey" off our back, in two ways. For the first time in school history, we won the initial contest of the season and we beat the pesky St. Joe's squad to boot! And what immensely sweetened our feelings of pleasure was the fact that the St. Joe's roster was packed with returning eighth graders, and they'd been expected to challenge for the league championship.

The outcome from this particular contest would more than upset all the pre-season prognostications. And I noticed as the St. Joe's squad evacuated our building that the wall clock was clicking exactly 7:29. That number was beginning to stick in my mind—I'd been seeing it repeatedly. *Maybe I'd better start looking to see it more often,* I thought as I savored the winners' cheers we'd earned so soundly.

CHAPTER
17

They'd decorated Chadwick Manor as if they were cele-
brating a momentous achievement. They'd set out balloons, hand-made signs and a large picnic table, neatly covered from side to side with the whitest of table-cloths.
They'd neatly placed an ice-chest stock-full of soda and
snacks on the table set for 14.

The beautifully manicured great lawn, green and as perfect as any golf-course I'd encountered, was trimmed and
fashioned in great detail, as if to mimic an official-size volleyball court. Out-of-bounds markers were lined with lime
chalk, and the volleyball net itself was perfectly strung
between two giant oak trees.

Set against a background of the great woods on one side,
the valley on the other, the view was spectacular.

On both sides of the lawn they'd placed chairs a good 10-
feet outside the lime markers. I quickly counted three rows
of 30 seats on each side, 180 in all. The seats weren't filled
yet, though some of the old-folks had already taken refuge
in them. The volleyball team mingled amongst the crowd of
seniors, who'd given them all their attention. I was deeply
moved by the sight. *Two generations*, I thought, *one at the
end of their stay on this earth, the other, just beginning.*

The girls had all car-pooled this day, with several parents
taking part in arranging it. The team would stay here at

Chadwick for at least an hour, I guessed—the estimated time they'd take for their volleyball demonstration. After that, I figured they'd all leave, for their 20-mile drives back home. But I figured wrong this glorious fall afternoon.

"Mr. Strong, I knew you'd come today," Irene Durella said sweetly as she strolled to my side. "Come on over and make yourself at home. How's some iced-tea sound to you?"

I nodded eagerly, and the girls took notice of my arrival and greeted me as well. They were decked out in full uniform, and some had already begun to show various old-folks the proper way to serve a volleyball, underhand style. They all seemed so at ease to me, even my own daughters. They both had balls in their hands, and perhaps a dozen seniors were gathered around each girl.

Irene suddenly rang a little bell she carried, and the roar of noise 200 voices had raised began to wane. Two elderly men took Irene by the arm and lifted her up onto a small box, which I could see would serve nicely as a small stage. She stood two feet taller now, and rang the bell once more, after which a complete hush settled over the yard.

"Oh, we want to thank you girls so much for coming today," she began. "And thank *you*, Coach Paul, for allowing them to come, and for being here yourself."

I raised my hand to acknowledge her gracious greeting, and great applause from all followed. Then Irene said, "Why don't we all take a seat and let things get started? Mr. Strong, would you lead your girls in a few drills for us, please?"

The crowd quickly occupied the seats, and I took charge of the girls. They'd had a full week to prepare for this day, so I asked in a closed huddle, "What would you all like to do first?"

"We want to warm-up with our stretching exercises—and could we invite the old-folks to join us?" said Katrina Glover. "We've got it all figured out, Coach Paul, just follow our lead," she smiled.

Katrina, who had the loudest voice of the girls, and Becky, the organized one, spread the team out in perfect order before the seated seniors. Katrina nodded at me, and I announced, "The girls will now perform a few light stretching exercises, and they'd love it if anyone of you who's able and willing to join them!"

Immediately, a good number of folks got up from their seats (those who didn't feel able felt comfortable staying seated). For the next five minutes, the girls led neck, arm, and calf stretches—the first two fairly simple, the latter done only by the players. From the joy on the old-folks faces, I could see it had been a great idea to get them involved with the demonstration.

The next hour the team spent showing how to hold a volleyball for service, the proper hand positions for defense, and legal and illegal ways of hitting a ball. Just the basics, but the girls impressed me, because they patterned it all after our staff's coaching methods, and felt flattered to see them following our lead even though I was playing more of a spectator's than a coach's role that day.

A 30-minute, three-game slate wrapped up the hour; I refereed; Becky watched the out-of-bounds line as "linesman." The girls' playing was spirited, with many fine individual performances, and the seniors cheered after every great play. It all was uproarious fun, and I was thinking the entire time as I called the game, *This has to be one of the finest moments two generations have ever shared and it's going to profoundly affect every life here today!*

The session ended with Katrina Glover's team winning two-games-to-one over Mandy Morrison's. All the games were close—15-12, 12-15, 15-11—and the girls played hard enough for two practices, I thought, as afterwards the girls eagerly accepted the drinks from the ice-chest under the picnic-table.

Irene Durella once again mounted the two-foot box. "This has been wonderful, *just wonderful*," she told the still panting girls. "We thank you all so very much for coming here today! And you're all welcome to join us inside, where Becky Chapman will read to us from the Good Book."

She nodded to Becky, who beamed in return. I expected all the girls except Becky to pack up and leave then, as the crowd of elderly people began slowly making their way to the main complex—yet not one young person or parent headed towards the parking lot. Again, I'd figured wrong! *Charisma!* I thought. *That's what Becky has, Charisma. She was probably born with it,* I muttered to myself, as Emily and I followed the throng inside.

Sensing the overflow crowd of people was about to overtake the main building, Morgan Hennessy, the Activities Director, quickly suggested we reverse direction and go to the make-shift auditorium, which apparently held about 300 people. This great room was used primarily for large gatherings such as this one, and would quickly accommodate us comfortably.

This was a good decision, and we quickly entered the vast room, which needed little preparation from the Chadwick attendants. Becky walked to the stage area with Irene and Morgan, a microphone was set-up, and seats were promptly filled.

I thought, *how comfortable Becky looks up there,* as she began "testing" the microphone for sound. An attendant placed a large Bible onto a small desk adjacent to the microphone, and next to it, a wooden chair for Becky to sit in. Irene said a few final words to Becky, and now Becky's mother, Maureen, gave her daughter a big hug, before returning to her front-row seat next to Irene Durella. *I've got to talk to her*, I thought, as the place began to settle down.

Becky's incredible, perpetual smile glowed from that stage, as she patiently eyed the throng, waiting for just the

114

right moment to begin speaking. I took my seat about halfway back off the left side of the stage, with enthusiastic residents flanking me on both sides. "You're gonna enjoy this," the man seated to my left told me. "I've got my Bible here to look at—we can share if you'd like."

I nodded, thanked the man cordially, and looking around, noticed that most of the residents also had Bibles, some small, others full-size. "This looks like a Bible-study class to me." I replied to the man.

"Oh, it's much more than that, young man," he said. "It's not just a study of the Bible when Becky reads from it; it's more like an *awakening* to the Bible. She's a gift from God, you know, a gift straight from God to us." He leaned over just then and whispered into my ear, in a secretive way. "I think she's an angel myself."

I straightened in my chair, chuckling under my breath at the statement; yet at the same time, I was eager to hear Becky, who still scanned the crowd with her piercing blue eyes. Irene Durella now moved back to the stage and sat next to Becky in a second chair provided by the maintenance staff. They spoke to each other for a moment, hand in hand. Then Irene stood up, took the microphone in her hand, and said, "Shall we begin?"

An odd hush suddenly descended on the room, as the residents, who clearly knew what Becky's readings were like, paused in private thought. Their heads all bowed reverently, and I found myself following their lead. But I kept one eye open, and looking about, saw the girls on the team force a few little nervous giggles before also closing their eyes.

Suddenly, in a wave, people joined hands with those seated on either side of them, until an endless chain of hands, all linked as if for prayer, united the room. At last I closed both eyes, and though I felt a bit awkward, fashioned a personal prayer, or message, really, to my Creator. *Heavenly Father,* I thought, *I thank you for this opportunity to share in Becky's life, and I ask for your blessings, that I may be a strong teacher and example to her, and to all of my players. I ask for your guidance, and that I may remain open-minded. I thank you for all the good people you've sent into my life recently, and ask you to bless each of them. Amen.*

I opened my eyes, and it seemed my prayer perfectly coordinated with the others, for they had also finished, and as one, we were ready for Becky's reading. Becky "blessed" herself then, and the "congregation" followed her lead. After her "Amen," a loud "Amen" from the seniors resounded throughout the room. Becky placed her left hand on the Bible, closed her eyes, and stood up, and began to pace the stage, as if she were a veteran entertainer, but without an actor's "slickness."

"It is good, so very good, that all of you are here today," she began. "In this room two generations—one in your final stage of this life, and the other, just beginning the long journey. Together, we can learn much about life from each other."

I was stunned at her calmness, and the magnetic quality of her overall body language and delivery. She was only 13 years old, yet she **commanded** that stage, and her opening words had been perfectly thought out, said, and delivered. "Think about volleyball for just a moment," she continued. "Look how this simple game has linked us together today— it's been the **cause**, but the coming together of these two generations was its **effect**."

Dozens of encouraging shouts rose from the crowd. Numerous residents clapped, others smiled, nodded, and the attention of everyone, including the young girls from the team, was riveted to Becky.

"On this day, we have much to celebrate," she said. "Without giving it much thought, we've all performed the most basic of Christian duties, the most basic form of representing and distributing the **'Christianity'** in us. We've come together, not forced to do so, but by *choice.* And in so doing, we've shown ourselves to be not *little* people going through life without purpose, but *big* soldiers of faith, moving forward with *direction."*

As Becky paced from one side of the stage to the other, a huge volume of noise arose from all corners of the large room. Clapping, shouting, some weeping, elders stood and reached over to hug the girls. Moments later, people returned to their seats.

To say I was more than stunned would be an understatement. I'd had no idea about Becky's knowledge of Christianity. Much less her uncanny ability to put such incredible thoughts into words so full of in-depth meaning. I shook my head in wonder, wiped a few tears from my eyes, and followed her every move on that stage.

"If you ever look at your life, *really* look at it," she cried, "and you sense an empty feeling inside, and depression threatens to overcome you, or if you think you've failed while others have achieved, and you feel jealousy, or anger, or hate, or greed overcomes you, you've had a personal experience with your *human nature."*

"If you feel left out, alone, abandoned, tired, lonely, or afraid—these too, are part of your human nature, and though they're difficult to manage and overcome, there is a way to overcome them. When a loved one is sick, or dying, or a friend has suffered a setback, or you've been wrongly accused of something, the questions overcome you, like, 'If there really is a God, how could he allow these things to happen?' Or if you say a prayer, and it's not answered the way you want, do you feel betrayed?"

Around me people were nodding, and many voices in the crowd murmured, "Yes…"

"My right hand is broken," said Becky, holding up her cast for all to see. "My father passed to the other side when I was only nine years old. I've had personal experiences with setbacks. But I tell you, if there were no setbacks in our lives, if there were no calamity, or tragedy, well, we might think that would be good—but it would also be impossible."

Becky walked down from the stage and onto the floor, and she stood in the left aisle, no more than ten feet away from me, her gaze directed right at me. "You see," she said, "it's not that tragedy never happens to us Christians, and it's not that we will ever be able to explain tragedy fully; it's about how we gather ourselves together in the face of the storms of life, and how we move forward in this one life we're given to share with so many, and how we become *the difference* in this life, even amid life's tragedies!"

Something about Becky's emphasis on *the difference* sent a shudder up my spine. And around me a standing ovation erupted, yet all the while Becky continued to look my way with that perfect smile. Now people old and young were hugging her, smiling, crying, laughing. I watched even the girls from the team wipe tears from their faces. *This girl really is straight from God,* I thought, and I laughed to myself, *maybe she is an angel!*

After a short while, Becky returned to the stage and said, "Now I'll finish with a reading from the Bible. Romans, Chapter 12. That's a letter from Saint Paul," she added. Immediately I could hear the residents thumb through their Bibles. When the paper-turning subsided, Becky began to speak:

"Your love must be sincere. Detest what is evil, cling to what is good." I recalled the words, but I also noticed that Becky wasn't, in fact, reading from the Bible. I turned to the man at my left, and said, "She's not reading directly from the Bible!" And he responded, "Oh no, Becky doesn't read from the Bible, she *speaks* from the Bible. She's put it to memory. *Now*, do you believe she's an angel?"

Another chill ran down my spine as I turned toward Becky. *She has the Bible memorized?* I thought, together with a host of other thoughts. Becky went on: "Love one another with the *affection* of others. *Anticipate* each other in showing respect. *Do not* grow slack but be *fervent* in spirit—he whom you serve is the Lord."

Becky's emphasis on key words, and her apparent knowledge of the meaning what she was saying, and her wisdom, *yes,* her wisdom, spellbound her audience. I was stunned at the way she finished the chapter, with such vigor and conviction. And there was no doubt she had the undivided attention of a totally attentive audience.

"Rejoice in hope," she said, her face radiant, "be *patient* under trial, *persevere* in prayer. Look on the needs of the Saints as your own; be *generous* in offering hospitality. *Bless* your persecutors; *bless* and do not curse them. *Rejoice* with those who rejoice, *weep* with those who weep. Have the same *attitude* towards all."

"Put away *ambitious thoughts* and associate with those who are *lowly. Do not* be wise in your own estimation. *Never* repay injury with injury. See that your *conduct is honorable* in the eyes of *all.* If possible, live peacefully with *everyone.* Beloved, *do not* avenge yourselves; leave that to God's wrath, for it is written, 'Vengeance is mine; I will repay' says the Lord."

"But, if your enemy is hungry, *feed him*; if he's thirsty, *give him something* to drink; by doing this, you will heap burning coals upon his head.' Do not be conquered by *evil,* but *conquer* evil with *good."*

Cheers rang out twice as loud as this sized group should have been able to make. She walked off the stage, and being quicker, the girls were first to swarm around her, in all their youthful enthusiasm. I watched closely as, one by one, each girl hugged Becky, wiping away tears, big smiles on all their faces.

It was truly a remarkable experience, how this 13-year old girl had captured both her peers and her elders with her few spoken words. And most incredible of all, I thought, she'd been able not only to have held the attention of her 13-year old peers, they seemed not the least embarrassed, or jealous towards Becky. *Only time will tell,* I thought, *if this moment stays with them, or goes out the door quickly like most things do for girls their age.*

I tried to make my way towards Becky, but I couldn't get through the mass of people in the aisles, all lined up to pay homage to her. But eventually I reached the front, and would soon have my moment with her.

Up till now, I had viewed Becky as a volleyball player, a student, and a fairly normal 13-year old girl (though I must admit, my opinion of her "normality" was changing quickly). In my line of work, I had seen, or heard, or even written stories about unique individuals over the years, and as I approached Becky, I was already fashioning a story in my mind about her. But my mind, which was usually one step ahead when I had a bead on a story, once again held back.

If I ran a story about her, I thought, her life would change in an instant, and probably not for the better. There'd be talk-shows, other reporters, more interviews, all disrupting her life. I just couldn't be sure that would be right for her. So I made a mental note to ask Becky's Mother about it before we left for the day.

Now I was face to face with her. "Becky," I said, that was a most inspiring talk you gave." I engulfed her healthy hand in my two. "You moved me, you know."

"It's a gift," she said softly, "a gift from God. We all have them, some of us just need more time to discover ours than others. I've been blessed to know my gift at my age."

She looked at me calmly, and I wondered, *Does she know what my gift is?* Then several other people took her from me with their own greetings. And I wondered then, *Do I know my own gift?*

I walked outside, along with those who'd already

thanked Becky. Scattered throughout the parking lot, the residents were saying their goodbyes to the girls, and within ten minutes, the only people left inside were the parents of the players, Morgan Hennessy, and Irene Durella, who was walking out my way with a wave and a smile. "Was it all you imagined it might be?" she said triumphantly. "Didn't I tell you Becky's a gift straight from God to us?"

"I admit I was spellbound," I said. "I can't get over it— her delivery, her way with words. *And* her memory for the Bible so it didn't sound so sterile when she read that passage. I truly felt they were *her* words."

"Yes, it's an amazing phenomenon," Irene answered. "That girl is *pure.*" She took me by the arm as sounds of laughter came from the edge of the woods, perhaps 150 feet from where we stood. "Look," she said loudly, "they're feeding the animals."

I turned toward the laughter. The girls had all joined Becky, some squatting, others standing, all close to each other. Becky was in the forefront, bent toward the ground. She let out a quiet whistle.

"Watch," said Irene, "the squirrels will come first."

And sure enough, the squirrels shyly approached Becky, who now knelt on the grass. The pair scampered a few feet, looked around, then came closer in stuttered steps, till finally they reached Becky and instantly began to eat from her hand.

Becky motioned the other girls forward with her broken hand, and signaled them to reach into the bag of food at her side. "Kneel down like I am," she invited them, and they did, and seconds later, all of them had food in hand, waiting for even more animals to appear.

More squirrels appeared, tripping towards the girls, who giggled with glee at this turn of events. The squirrels ate from their hands—and now several rabbits hopped forward to join in the feast.

I walked slowly towards the action, so as to not scare off the animals. I quickly counted eight squirrels, four rabbits, and even two chipmunks as I finally reached them. This was another amazing sight: Wild animals, three separate species to boot, in harmony with each other, trusting enough to put down their guards and join together for an easy meal!

And at that moment my thoughts were also on the human species: How difficult it has been for those of different races, and religions, to do what these animals were doing, and I looked at Becky, and at that moment thought, *She will make a difference, a big difference, when she becomes an adult, because she's making such a difference right now.*

Irene pushed me gently from behind, and the girls waved me to themselves and handed me some food from the bag. "Here, coach Paul, here's some food!" said Katrina. "Can you believe how *tame* these animals are?"

I took my place beside the girls, and the squirrels and rabbits ate from my hand, too. *The girls think the animals are tame,* I thought. *Their 13-year old minds can't imagine Becky's role in this; they miss what's becoming clear to me now, that Becky Chapman is going to change all our lives. And the broken hand she suffered is no accident at all, but part of some design...*

Yes, I thought, *her broken hand was supposed to happen!*

CHAPTER

18

The "experience" at Chadwick Manor with Becky Chapman played on my mind every day for the next several weeks, and beyond. With the passing of each new day, my thoughts went to her words spoken from scripture, and, I found myself living out those spoken words in my day to day dealings with other people.

But I was still baffled by it all, and although it was my intention to seek out Becky's mom that day to talk about Becky, the distractions I encountered forced me to temporarily abandon the idea. However, I still needed to talk to Maureen Chapman, no, actually visit the Chapman residence, to get a first hand look at the way they lived, get a good look at Becky's room, find out what it's all about. I wrote down the words, "Visit Chapman's soon" on my planning calendar, and turned thoughts once again to the volleyball team—a winning team at that.

The next three games produced convincing victories for us. We'd never before achieved a season-opening record of four wins, no losses, so the team was sky-high—and tied for first place with perennial runner-up St. Cyril's, and perennial champion, St. Paul's, who were to be our next two opponents.

As might be expected, school spirit had undergone a dramatic "sports transformation." After all, our school was known more for producing spelling-B champions, and essay contest winners, and being tied for first place at this juncture of the season in any of the school sports was cause for celebration. The girls had become the darlings of their classmates, and everyone's heroes at this crucial junction of the season. The student paper, "The Voice," had produced one-sided stories about our team, which the entire student body now looked on with great admiration. After all, no St. Luke team, basketball, track, softball, or volleyball, had produced even a winning team in over a decade.

The "Deed" was also taking on a new life. Mayor Light had agreed to allow me to search during off-hours for it, in the obvious places where town archives might be kept, including her office and the library in there, and all the other known places where archives were kept.

But my search, though I was able to accomplish it without drawing attention to myself and what I was after, produced nothing. And though I also personally rifled through scores of books, photos, and pictures at the Police Station and Courthouse, in the end, I was still batting zero.

I searched very carefully, yet I knew I could easily have missed a hidden document, given so many possible spots where it might be hiding. Nor did I find the records very well organized among all the old archives. So I decided to change direction.

I turned my attention to the newspaper's archives. The Deed's last known sighting had been 1929. Perhaps I could uncover a clue in these old stories, if they preserved a mystery that could be unveiled here in 1979.

So I began. This extensive undertaking would take some time; I estimated I'd have to scan 10 full papers per day for a while. Some quick math gave me just seven or eight weeks, in which to cover a full year of 1929's issues. Then only two weeks would be left till the deadline required for finding the Deed.

But I was determined, motivated, and curious; plus, I had "hit the wall," and couldn't find my way around it. I slogged on.

January 1st's issue of the '29 paper had the traditional banner across the front page. I saw stories of a New Year baby, New Year parties, New Year pledges—boring stuff, but somewhat entertaining as I reflected on the writing styles of the journalists in those days. *Very different from today,* I thought, as I turned the pages with the blue handle of the microfilm machine.

By the time I'd gone through the January 9, 1929, issue, my energy was already spent. My bloodshot eyes were no longer responding to my weary brain's commands. I removed my glasses, rubbed my eyes diligently, then placed the glasses back on my nose. "Four o'clock," I whispered. "Time to go home."

But I didn't go home just then. Like some weary foot soldier some buck sergeant had barked at to "Go on!" I did just that. I even skipped dinner; I'd become more than just a reporter, I was a detective now, and it was somehow utterly clear to me that I couldn't stop till I'd unearthed the clue I needed.

By eleven o'clock, all my attempts to find the Holy Grail had failed. By the time I reached the February 6th issue, I'd hit the skids.

I cleaned up the area quickly, clicked off the lights in the small room and departed. I didn't feel I'd accomplished much, aside from having done a twelfth of the search in one night. And to top it off, I really had no idea what I was really looking *for.* Still, I'd been learning lately that clues come in all shapes and sizes, and are sometimes found in the most unlikely places.

As usual when I'm tired as I was, forgetting was easy for me. I exited through the back entrance of the paper, where my old Ford was waiting for me in the employee parking lot.

As I fumbled for my keys in my jacket pocket, I suddenly remembered I'd left them on the desk in my office.

Disgusted with myself, and growing more tired with each passing minute, I dragged my carcass back inside. I managed to approach a fast walk as I neared my office, its door still open, the lights were out.

The keys lay exactly where I'd left them hours ago. As I reached for them, I noticed a white envelope addressed to me, taped to the middle of my desk. Why hadn't I seen this before? Curiously, I opened it. Inside, a simple handwritten note read:

"Mr. Strong, will you please meet me for lunch tomorrow at Foster's Den, 1:00 p.m.?"

"Yours truly,"

"A.J. Craft"

"What does he want?" I growled to myself standing there in the doorway of my office. And that's the question that absorbed me my entire ride home—and for a full hour lying in bed, begging for the sleep fairy to visit me.

CHAPTER
19

I got virtually no rest that night, and the few hours of sleep I did manage to squeeze were low-quality. I knew I would pay for my sleep deprivation real soon. And this would be a lousy day to have lost any sleep; I needed to be sharp for this meeting with Craft. He was cunning, a master of chicanery, who got his way when he wanted his way, and the rumor was that he always wanted his way.

I had this information from reputation alone; this would be our first face-to-face meeting, and despite my long experience dealing with small-town politics, I felt apprehensive.

What did Craft really want? Did he know I'd been searching for the deed? If so, how had he found out? *Maybe he wanted to bribe me to quit searching*, I thought. *Maybe not. Maybe he wanted to negotiate a compromise with the town. Maybe not.*

I was putting more questions to myself than Craft would probably ask! *Just go to the meeting, stay calm, and don't reveal your hand,* I thought, and poured my first cup of coffee, grabbed the morning paper, and relaxed for 20 minutes.

My thoughts left Craft and turned to the volleyball team when I reached the sports section of the paper. Yes, this was an important day on two counts: Not only was I meeting with Craft, but the game tonight against St. Cyril's was a big one, tied as we were with them for first place. Usually after four games St. Luke's was occupying the league's basement—and we usually stayed there through the final game. I knew this match and the one two days later at St. Paul's would measure our club's true ability, and so did everyone else.

I got into my old Ford and began my journey to Foster's Den, a 40-minute ride on the outskirt's of the town. My thoughts bounced from Craft to the team to the Deed, back and forth, back and forth, until I finally reached my destination.

Foster's Den was the premier gathering club for our community's "elite" citizens. And I thought I could see as much "plastic" on the faces of Foster's patrons, as there must be in the wallets and purses they carried inside. The formality of the place chilled me a bit; it was way out of my league, fine cigars, fine china, fine manners, everything so aristocratic, so stuffy, so refined. *I'll be uncomfortable here,* I thought, as I drove my old Ford past the stunned valet, and into the farthest-from-the-entrance available parking spot.

I glanced at my watch. I'd arrived five minutes early for our meeting as I began the short walk to the restaurant's front door, manned by a stuffy attendant. I paused to admire the assemblage of Jaguars, Mercedes, Cadillac's, and some Italian-named cars I'd never seen before, only heard of. I glanced back at my old Ford, very pleased at the parking spot I'd chosen, and with my old wreck, nestled between a pair of high-polished Jags.

I wasn't intimidated by this sea of prosperity, I realized. I understood the power of money, and knew it inhabited these strange surroundings. I knew money talked here, and that as I passed through these great glass double doors shrouded in secrecy, I was entering a world of power, wealth, greed—and uncertainty. Here would no doubt be caviar and fine wine; cheeseburgers and good old American beer would certainly be missing items on the expensive luncheon menu.

The doorman wished me a "good afternoon" as I passed him and entered the realm of the rich. He shot me a peculiar look, but that did little to change my attitude. I could sense he thought of himself as one of the elite too, and of me as "one of those 'others.'"

I knew what tipped him off right away, aside the way in which I'd blazed my own trail in the parking lot, was my attire. I had one suit to my name, a 10-year-old gray rag that was outdated, tight, short, all wrong for this setting. And I had donned this old friend for this luncheon with Craft. I wasn't about to buy a new suit on short notice, just for this meeting. So if it was ridiculous looking, it was still my Sunday best, and it would have to do.

As I walked in I could see that my expectations of the place were right on the money, literally and no pun intended. A woman about 50 greeted me at the large coat-check area. I had no coat, but I noticed several fine wraps of patrons as I walked towards her domain—all the top designer names of the day were represented, I figured, each neatly hanging to make what looked like a fancy department store window display.

Inside the restaurant "proper," the maitre d' was directing waiters and waitresses like some air traffic controller at rush hour on a Friday afternoon. He was amazingly swift, composed and precise. His seating chart looked like a football coach's diagram, with x's, and o's. Waiters (it looked like there were a dozen or so in his charge) took his commands without question. ***There'll be no mistakes made here,*** I thought.

All told, I felt like I was looking into a "movie" world, where nothing appeared real to me. Cold sweat began to form under my arms.

"May I help you sir?" the maitre d' said icily, in a French-sounding accent.

"Yes, I'm here to see a Craft—he's reserved..."

The maitre d' snapped my sentence in two. "Mr. Craft is expected here in 15 minutes, Mr...?"

"Strong, " I said. "Paul Strong."

"Of course, Mr. Strong. Mr. Craft asks that in advance you enjoy the beverage of your choice in our lounge area. He says he will join you promptly at 1:15."

The man nodded toward the bar, and I made my way there, to the left of the dining area. It was fully glass-enclosed, and the stench of cigar smoke slapped me as I crossed the invisible border separating dining room and bar. Inside the enclosure, I sat down at the bar and was promptly attended to by the bartender, who introduced himself as "Phil." "What'll it be, pal," he snapped. His words caught me off guard; I was expecting an invitation somewhat more—well, more refined. This was "pub" lingo, or a variation of it. Rather pleased, I smiled and said, "I'll have a coke... if you have coke."

"Coke it is," he said with a nod. "Up or on the rocks?"

"Up," I said.

Phil poured my drink from a nozzle behind the bar, placed it in front of me, and said bluntly, "That'll be two dollars."

Two dollars for a glass of coke in 1979? *Highway robbery! Thirty-five cents would be more like it,* I thought. I'd began to reach into my pocket when a solid whack hit me on my left shoulder blade.

"Put it on my tab Phil," rumbled a man's deep voice. "He's with me."

I turned in my comfortable swivel seat, expecting to see a man about 60 in a three-piece designer suit, perfectly coiffured, with perhaps one or two "security" people flanking him. I'd pictured Craft plump, short and gray. He wasn't.

His trim, athletic figure, six-three, around 215 pounds, seemed cut from granite, and he held a huge hand out to me. I accepted it, and his fingers crunched around mine. I glanced down, and my hand seemed lost inside his. He was no older than 35, dressed in a sporty outfit, tennis or golf attire from come country-club, maybe. He was handsome, too, a full head of black hair, topped off with the Greek-God facial features of an Adonis.

He kept my hand trapped in his grip as he began to speak, very authoritively, very charismatically. He left no doubt who was in charge of this get-together.

"Paul, I'm A.J. Craft—but please, just call me Ted."

"Ted?" I said, puzzled. "How do you get from A.J. to Ted?"

Sitting next to me at the bar, "Ted" Craft said, "The 'A.J.' stood for 'Andrew Jackson.' "My father was a history buff, and for reason's known only to him, Andy Jackson was his main man."

"Now, I couldn't walk around all day as a kid being called Andy Jackson," he said. "When I was a sixth-grader, we had to do a report on one of the U.S. Presidents. Everyone thought I'd choose Andy Jackson, but I surprised them—I chose Teddy Roosevelt. After that, all the kids started calling me "Teddy." When I got a little older, it became "Ted." And over the years, the name's just stuck."

I got a kick out of his story and doubted that he'd shared it with many people. I certainly hadn't heard it, though Craft had been the center of enough discussions at the paper lately.

Craft got up and dropped a twenty on the bar for my two-dollar coke. Then he went into the dining area for lunch. *Heavy tipper,* I was thinking as he ostentatiously held the door for me. As we approached "Frenchy" the maitre d', the entire staff took notice of us and greeted Craft like some sort of King. With bows and flourishes, we were hustled past the main dining area, and into the private room, reserved for folks with "real" money, I figured.

The room was tastefully painted, with lime-green walls

and rich wood trim, and decorated with fine art, originals I presumed. A large chandelier lit the entire room, with just enough light to border on a "romantic" feel. One table sized for two graced the center of the room. The whitest linen cloth I'd ever seen fit the round table like a glove was set perfectly for two. Two magnificent cherry chairs were tucked neatly underneath.

An eager attendant pulled my chair out for me as I began to sit. I anticipated this move and politely allowed it to happen. **When in Rome...** I thought, as I pulled myself forward to within a foot of the table.

Once my luncheon partner was likewise seated, we were handed two menus, napkins were placed on our laps, and the very professional waiter recited the specials of the day.

Craft thanked him and asked him to return for our orders in five minutes. For my part, I had no idea what these fancy foods listed were, no idea how they looked, smelled, tasted, or whether they'd been spelled correctly. I was in trouble here. Despite my dislike of snobbery, I felt myself wanting to impress this obviously worldly man with some knowledge, at least, of food. So I decided I'd simply choose something from the "Seafood" side of the menu, and then live with my choice, like it or not.

Instead of reading the menu, Craft put it down and went right to his point. "Paul," he said, leaning as close to me as possible, folding his hands, with his elbows propped on the table, "I'm a man of vision. I can see things unfold, I can see the direction things have to take, even before they happen. Take this tract of land I want, for example."

He had my attention, and he went on: "To me, it's a win-win situation. The township is growing, it needs more housing, not to mention more property tax money in the coffers."

"Now, Paul," he said emphatically. "I really have no idea what the big fuss is over 200 acres of trees is. Thousands of acres of trees get destroyed every day, all over the world.

Hey, that's the direction the world's going in," he shrugged.

I nodded and he said, "Paul, that land needs to be developed—for the people of this town, and for our future generations..."

I finally broke in. "That's a fine and dandy speech, Ted," I said. "But what's any of it got to do with me?"

Craft smiled. "Ahh, I like a man who cuts to the chase! Yes, that *is* the question, Paul: What does a little old political writer like Paul Strong have to do with all this?"

That's right, I thought, *so let's hear it.*

Craft stood up slowly and glided to the window. He gazed outside for a few seconds, folded his hands behind his back, and walked toward the table. "Paul," he said briskly, "you know that Deed is lost. You know you're just wasting your time looking for it. I think you should put your time into something more substantial."

I was surprised and curious both. What was he getting at—and how had he learned I was searching for the deed?

He went on. "I've been admiring your work for some time now," he said. "Very nice writing style, nice flow to your words." He raised his hand, signaling for our waiter, who appeared instantly, carrying a large, rolled-up document. The waiter handed it to Craft and promptly disappeared.

Craft then rolled a portable bulletin board from a small closet in the corner of the room. He unrolled the document, push-pinned its four corners to the board and said, "Well, what do you think of *this?*"

It was an architectural rendering of his vision, I assumed, and he was obviously pleased with its three-by-four-foot spread. I didn't answer, and he asked me again what I thought of it.

"It's a lovely looking community," I said. "The homes are gorgeous, with nice, roomy-sized properties. It's picture-perfect, really."

I looked at Craft, who stood there admiring his work. He was getting off-track, I thought. I pushed things on. "But what does all of this have to do with me?" I said, more firmly than I had before.

"This composite is an artist's rendition of the 200-acre tract of land," Craft mused. "That's in your township. And Paul, as I mentioned earlier, I admire your work; you've built quite a reputation in these parts. Seems to me a man with your obvious writing talents would want to step up in the world, maybe work for a bigger newspaper, or maybe even *start his own publication.*"

Craft moved closer to me, smiling. I lifted a hand to stop him halfway. "Are you offering me a job?" I said.

"Oh, not really," Craft said, letting his words drift off as he drew a fountain pen and a notepad from a briefcase he carried in. He scribbled something on the notepad, and handed it to me.

I glanced down at a dollar-signed figure three times my current salary. I have to admit, my imagination reeled for a second with things I could do with that kind of money. Expensive cars, vacations, money for College. *So he's trying to bribe me,* I thought.

Craft cleared his throat and said, "That figure, Mr. Strong, could easily make you an Editor of a new magazine, of which I would be Publisher. I have all the confidence in the world that you could come up with just the right kind of magazine, and in a short time we'd both profit handsomely from its success."

He walked to the window again and stared out at the parking lot. "I noticed your car out there," said Craft. "Trusty old vehicle I'd say; a little worn, but nonetheless, probably very reliable, eh, Paul?"

"It gets me around," I said bluntly.

"Well, *my* editor would be driving a new car every year, you know—of course, completely paid for by the company."

My jaw dropped like a lead weight. In a matter of minutes my life could change completely. The ball was obviously in my court now. I had to respond. After a moment's pause I said, "I don't know how to answer. I'm flattered. If you've just made me an offer, it's quite a generous one. But let me ask you: Why is it that you actually seem to think I'm searching for that deed?"

"Oh, I have no proof, just a hunch," he said. "That old guy has lots of township property from his administration stored in that cabin of his. Totally illegal, but they've let it happen. No, I have no proof, Mr. Strong, but I believe that deed's there. Maybe he just doesn't remember where he stashed it—and my aim is to keep it lost for the next 10 weeks at least."

I looked blankly at Craft. No doubt about it, he was trying to bribe me. He had no interest in my writing talents; he'd wanted me to stay clear of Gibson. He was right, Gibson had a cabin full of 1920s items, I'd seen that for myself, photos, paintings, chairs and other furniture. And now A.J. Craft, this "enemy of the people," had openly provided me with my best notion yet about where that Deed might be.

"Why don't you go home and talk my offer over with Emily tonight?" he purred deeply. "But I'll need your answer tomorrow, Paul. Right now I can't afford to be a very patient guy."

Craft signaled the waiter again. The waiter entered quickly and quietly and stationed himself next to our table, ready to take our order. "Go ahead," said Craft, "you order first, anything on the slate."

I picked a seafood item from the specials. The waiter recommended a Chardonnay wine to go well with the meal, and I nodded my o.k. Then the waiter turned to Craft, and asked politely, "The usual, Mr. Craft?"

"Yes, a cheeseburger, medium-rare, and a Bud."

CHAPTER
20

I decided on my answer on the drive home from Foster's Den. Sure, the money sounded tempting. But repercussions and nightmares that would follow my casting my lot with Craft loomed first and foremost in my thoughts.

The townsfolk would have no difficulty putting two and two together. "Reporter quits job he loves, to work for the most hated man in the town's history." That would be the epithet on my tombstone, not the "Coach Paul" I was so fond of.

And even beyond that, life would become a real hell for my wife and daughters. "There's that two-timer's daughter," they'd whisper. "He's no Paul Strong, he's Paul *Weak*."

The decision was an easy one, really. I'd mention it to Emily, we'd discuss exactly what I'd just been thinking and put it behind us. That was my intention, and that was exactly how things went during our two-mile walk that afternoon.

Emily and I had been high school sweethearts, and we still saw eye to eye on such matters. The bottom line of our relationship was, any decision we made, we made together, and we made decisions with one thought in mind: If it's the right thing to do morally, then it's the right thing to do. That was our creed to each other, and neither money, nor property, or both, would have any influence on the decision-making.

I would break the news to "Ted" tomorrow—and pay my friend Joshua Gibson a visit later that same day. "But now, time to think volleyball," I said, as my wife and I entered our house, breathing hard after our walk. "Big game in a few hours."

Yes, this first of two big games over the next three days, was just about upon us. It was the talk of the school, and an overflow crowd of students was expected to more than fill our little gym this evening.

I took the last few hours before the game to review our team's impressive statistics. It had become clear who our front-line players were. But not much separated the top players from the second string. All 13 girls had contributed to each of our victories, including Becky Chapman.

Becky had become a true champion from the bench. Her willingness to just be there inspired everyone, even her St. Luke's classmates and the parents of the other girls. Becky had behaved like a real leader, even off-court. She was absorbing the details of the game, and did her best to encourage any girl who happened to be struggling with her game. Because of her hand, Becky might never play competitive volleyball, but she was a quick study who never used her knowledge to intimidate her playing teammates.

A few key players who hadn't started out among our best were developing nicely for us now. These girls we had rated "Group Three" to this point; that is, girls with less natural ability. But we'd had to change their rating after the game with St. Cyril's.

Mandy Morrison, and Katrina Glover, had been "Group Three" players. But in our four victories, each of them had improved on the court and on the bench. Taking their queues from Becky Chapman, they'd upped their levels of play quite impressively. Neither of them had broken into the starting lineup, but their inspired play off the bench was beginning to open some eyes.

I wasn't ready to elevate either girl to a starters role tonight. This game needed to start our top lineup if we hoped to compete with the mighty "Lions" from St. Cyril's.

But fate has a way of making sports complications, and fate was about to lend Katrina Glover a hand tonight. We headed for the gym, our family of four. Tension weighed in the car, as we and the girls thought about the upcoming game. We were all on new ground, and though this was "only" eighth grade volleyball, we knew it meant much more to our school's long-suffering sports program.

We were, just barely, the first to arrive. The rest of our nervous players soon followed; the key was retrieved and the doors opened. Cool October air flowed in to replace the damp air inside, creating a comfortable temperature for a game.

We went right to work.

Our drills had become routine, but we practiced them with considerable enthusiasm this evening. Our two Captains, Karen and Lauren Carter, led the calisthenics, while I zigzagged the lines of girls, shouting out encouragement.

A few moments later the St. Cyril's girls entered the gym as one, their equipment manager leading the way, followed by the players and coaches. *They're very small,* I thought as they paraded past our girls like they'd owned the place, *the smallest team we've faced yet.*

But I knew that in sports, size can be misleading. After all, we had pounded St. Joe's giants, so we couldn't let our guard down just because this team was a good four inches shorter across the board.

Soon I could tell from their warm-ups that the St. Cyrils' girls were quick, agile, and accurate. Check that—*deadly.* And they could jump, high enough to quickly erase any height disadvantage we held. I could sense that our girls were only keying in on their opponents small size. They were acting too cocky, and I didn't like it.

The gym was packed with people, probably 200

squeezed in, every seat of the metal bleachers filled. Game time was less than five minutes away.

At this juncture in the season, match number five of 12, I knew we were the talk of the league. People were taking notice, first, of our winning ways. St. Luke's had already matched our combined win total for the previous three seasons, and only three or four more victories would clinch a spot for us in the eight-team playoffs at the conclusion of the regular schedule.

But people found equally compelling the hand symbol all over our gym, and on the patches the girls wore on their sleeves. Everywhere "away" we played, too, you could hear the buzz pre-game about the "hands." Jane Modell, who ran our concession stand with two other mothers, typed up a little flyer explaining the meaning of the patch, and taped it neatly to each side of the concession stand walls. You'd frequently see groups of adults and children gather to read these flyers, and they always seemed to walk back to their seats smiling.

As I checked the rosters to hand in our starting lineup, I only counted 11 players. I quickly went over to the girls, gathered now at the bench, and asked the big question, "Where's Lauren and Sharon? I have to hand in the lineup right now."

"They were both out sick from school today," quipped Maggie. "They won't be coming."

We had a team rule: If you were going to be absent from a game, sick or otherwise, you had to leave word with the coaches. But apparently, Lauren and Sharon had forgotten this rule. I scratched my head as I thought, *How am I going to juggle our lineup?*

It wouldn't be easy. Lauren and Sharon, two of our top players, would probably have played most of tonight's contest. Their absence couldn't have come at a worse time in the season, and now I had less than a minute to pencil two non-starters into our lineup.

I looked up and down the bench, quickly wrote Mandy and Katrina into the lineup, retreated to the scorers table and handed in the adjustments. Then I returned to the bench to tell my anxious players our six starters.

"Listen up girls!" I said. "You all know how important this match is tonight."

I paused, and the girls fixed on me as one. "Lauren and Sharon are out, so everyone will probably play a bit more tonight. Here's the starting lineup for the first game…"

Announcing the starting lineup to a team of 13 year old girls is tantamount to taking only one dog home from a pet store with 20 cages full of canines. All the girls' eyes shone, "Choose me!" Might as well have been tails wagging, tongues panting, imploring me to "Choose me!" Glee always follows, so does disappointment. It's the same every time. Each and every time before each and every game. But on this day, two new "pups" would find a home.

"Karen, Lynn, Joanne, Megan, Katrina, Mandy," I said, rapid-fire. "Now, let's bring it in!" And we did: Hands piled on hands like a giant stack of pancakes, sticky palms all clamped together like glue. And our chant followed: "All for one, and one for all…TEAM!"

I'd made the replacements, and I could see they were nervous going on-court, and who could blame them? Now we'd see what we were really made of. I settled into my chair near the scorer's table, clapped my hands in support of our team, and barked out final instructions to our starters.

Fantasy—I closed my eyes for a few seconds, and in that brief span of time reserved for dreams, I envisioned a victory, with Mandy and Katrina the heroes. They'd each contribute big to the win, each stay cool under pressure. And we'd stay undefeated. *Nice thoughts.*

But now, eyes open. Reality. Whistle blows. Game begins.

It didn't take long for reality to conquer fantasy. We were

quickly handed our hats, 15-3, both over our stunned team and the crowd. The St. Cyril's faithful loudly and frenziedly cheered their Lions on, to what promised to be an easy two-game sweep.

Between the first and the second, long faces, stunned and embarrassed, dominated our team huddle. "It's only one game," I said, trying my best to rally my troops. "You need two to win—now go get 'em!"

A damp team cheer followed, and I suddenly pulled an unprecedented move—I called "Time out!" before the game ever began.

Silence fell throughout the gym. "You have only one timeout left," the referee reminded me.

I now had only one minute to deliver the most convincing pep talk in history to my bewildered team. I thought of Knute Rockne, the old Notre Dame football coach, and the legendary Vince Lombardi of the Green bay Packers. What would they say in this situation? Somehow, the "immortal" coaches like them seemed to be able to come up with the right "magical," energizing words to spark their teams, and I sure needed some for my girls.

Unlike Rockne's and Lombardi's minions, I wasn't going to pep up seasoned 30-year-old men playing out their livelihoods on some gridiron. These were 13-year-old girls, simply out for fun and competition, but 100 percent intense nonetheless. My words needed to be gentle, yet, at the same time, they needed to ignite their competitive spirit.

That first game had brought the girls to earth with a crash. We had lost, and lost big. We were vulnerable now; a crushing loss will leave you that way. And for the first time all season, I felt vulnerable, too, and nearly at a loss for words as we huddled together.

The girls eagerly waited for me to speak; I was on stage now; "lights, camera, action," all of it. No time for rehearsal, no time to practice my lines. As a journalist, I based my career on choosing just the right words. I was good at that—why did this seem so different?

Well, it **was** different. Different audience, different circumstances, different agenda. Here I was, though—time to deliver the goods. I began the way I always did, "Girls, listen up. I want you to look around at all those signs you made." They did, and I launched my version of "Win one for the Gipper!"

"Now I want you to look at all the people who've come to see you play tonight. I want you to think about all the practices and hard work you've put in."

I had their attention now, and I could sense the fire working in them. "Girls, now I want you to look at *me.*" They did, and I shot them all the fire in my open eyes, and just then the referee blew his first whistle.

Not much time left, and I made my last words their own. I pointed to the huge sign hanging on the far wall, and mouthed slowly, with all the determination I could summon, "All for one, and one for all…"

I wanted at this point a resounding yell of "TEAM" to reverberate from all 11 players. Still, I knew sometimes the best laid plans go awry. But sometimes, they go just the way you intend them to. Which would it be now?

I would know by these girls' reaction right now their true character. Winning, after all, covers up many blemishes; losing takes all the masks off. Either we were for real, or we were pretenders. It was much more than just wins and losses on this court; this was about character in the face of adversity. This was one of those moments in the season, where a coach knows the result of a game is secondary in importance. Sure, I wanted to win, the girls wanted to win. But right now the girls' reaction to my words, would mean more to me than being alone at the top of the standings in first place.

That instant, a louder blast of "TEAM!" than I'd ever

have dreamed 11 13-year-olds could muster nearly blew out my hearing. I had my answer—and the girls weren't even aware that I had asked them the biggest kind of question.

Now it would come down to truth and dare. The truth would surface during this next game, and the dare of my words' challenge to them would surface within that truth. I wanted to see it happen both ways, because in the games people play, truth and dare are sometimes one and the same.

Right then, I didn't really care who won the match; I wanted to see how the girls would play the game within the game. Regardless of who wanted to win more, St. Cyril's or St. Luke's, I knew St. Cyrils' was better than us at this point. But now we'd see a test of the human spirit, the will to succeed, to push forward, to face peril head on.

Katrina Glover, the girl I might have picked least likely to answer the call, the "Group Three" veteran who'd surged into our lineup only due to two starters' absence, turned the key. This twist of fate was one of many "coincidences" that would mark our season. And so frequent would these "coincidences" become, I no longer believed them to be coincidental. Things happen for a reason, I learned, whether broken hands, missed games or lost deeds. It was all a part of the perfect order something or someone was making of our imperfect lives. I was beginning to understand all this. I was beginning to "read the signs."

We woke up during that second game; raw emotion and adrenaline took over. We seized the early advantage, pulling ahead 6-1. The bench players, led by Becky Chapman, whooped it up something ferocious, prodding the starters with intense, encouraging shouts. The gym erupted noisily with every point the home team won.

But volleyball is the ultimate game of ebb and flow. We lost the serve, and in a matter of minutes, the lead as well, as the opposition reeled off 12 straight points.

Moments later, a huge defensive play by Mandy

Morrison returned the serve to us. It may have seemed too little too late for us, but another sports cliché reminded me, "It ain't over until the fat lady sings!"

We were trailing, 13 to six, with Katrina Glover at the serving line—the same Katrina Glover who in the past could send spectators scurrying with the league's most inconsistent and wildest serves. We had occasionally joked that "you'd better pay attention when Katrina serves—for your own protection!"

At best, Katrina's serve was like a coin flip—half the time "heads," half "tails." But this was no time for half-success; the weight of the game was clearly on Katrina's shoulders, however low our expectations.

Katrina took a quick look at Becky before her first serve. I saw Becky swiftly flash Katrina the "hand sign." Katrina smiled and returned Becky's loving gesture. Then the rest of the bench players followed Becky's lead, all, one by one, holding their left hands towards Katrina, each standing in place like volleyball statuettes. It was some sight, and the lump in my throat and the tear in my eye told me a touching scene was unfolding.

Now there's been lots of talk among the girls about the "hand," and the "patch," but this was the very first time they'd actually used the signal during a game. I marveled at the maturity of these kids. Instead of overusing this potent "symbol," and worn it out by now, they had saved it like some special "play," to be taken out under special circumstances only.

This was time for special, all right. Katrina proceeded to launch serve after serve hard liners, all, deep, strong, and straight. The missiles her hand shot totally befuddled the "Lions." With every point added to her total, the louder the gym rumbled with applause. Before long, Katrina actually drew us to within one point. We trailed, 13-12, when the opposing coach called a (wise) time-out.

Katrina, nearly hyperventilating now, was as surprised at her run as we were. She had been in a "zone," and this break in the action my coaching counterpart meant as a distraction to break her focus.

But Katrina's focus was trance-strong. Her eyes' pupils looked dilated, much larger than normal. Her mouth was open, feeding her pulsating lungs with volumes of air.

I tried speaking to her on the sidelines, but she wasn't there to hear. She didn't react to my 'one point at a time' speech. Jokingly, I waved my hand in front of her face, but her eyes stayed wide, never blinking once. She seemed to be in some kind of shock-like-state, standing there in the middle of our huddle.

But when the whistle blew, Katrina was the first back on the court. I raised my eyebrows at coach Shea; she just shrugged her shoulders. Hypnotized or not, Katrina was about to finish what she started.

Katrina's final three serves ripped untouched at the feet of the six unmoving girls across from ours. They stood stock-still, for Katrina's heat allowed almost no opportunity for reaction. Then it was over, we'd won the game, 15-13. Now we would play one more game to decide the match.

We lost the coin toss: St. Cyril's elected to serve first—a moral victory for the "Lions." We had just completed the greatest come-from-behind victory in school history, and the momentum was clearly with us. But St. Cyril's would have the ball first, and they most likely would grab an early lead.

I was right about that. Jennifer Irving, one of the league's best players, gave St. Cyril's a commanding 8-0 lead before an errant serve put us back on offense.

Karen, always our first server, equaled Irving's effort with eight points of her own. *So we're in for this type of game!*

Then things settled into a crawl—one point here, one point there, back and forth went the score, each team battling, sweating, cheering. ***Kind of game***, I recalled later, ***nei-***

ther team deserved to lose. But one of us *would* lose; there are no ties in volleyball.

The score stood now, St. Cyril's 14, St. Luke's 13. We had just held off game point; and again, as if by some Hollywood scripting, Katrina was at the serving line.

And Katrina was *hot.* She had nailed 10 consecutive serves, all under the highest pressure. I was beginning to envision this girl being mobbed by her mates in just a few minutes. She needed just three more good scrves—volleyball contests require winning by at least two points. She was set, this was it.

Katrina's right hand serve was powerful—too powerful. The ball sailed towards the ceiling, nearly taking out one of the lights that dangled precariously above, and landed a few feet from our bench, much to the delight of our grateful visitors.

Katrina's shoulders sank in disbelief. She held off tears as I shouted defensive instructions. Game point was at hand, and we needed to hold off one more serve and get the ball back.

St. Cyril's serve whistled deep into our end, clearly headed too deep, out of bounds for sure. As long as none of our girls touched, we'd have the serve again, and another chance for victory.

The line drive serve, shooting a good two feet above even our tallest player, headed in Katrina's direction. She apparently still had her mind on her errant serve moments earlier. She raised her hands high, leaped up with all her might—and the ball, though already behind her, tipped off the very ends of two of her fingertips, and landed several feet behind her.

Before the ball even landed, Katrina realized her error in judgment. Her hands went to her mouth, and her tears began to flow. The suddenness of it all overwhelmed her. I ached for her, standing there before 200 people, with nowhere to hide.

Such are the risks of sports—one moment you're king of

the mountain, the next, your crawling at its base. Katrina had felt all the emotions sports can bring in the last 30 minutes. How would she respond now? How would *we* respond?

We gathered at our bench, and I reminded the players games are not won or lost over one particular play, but I knew they weren't buying it. They consoled the devastated Katrina, who seemed paralyzed with guilt.

We went over and shook hands with the St. Cyril's girls, and I with their coach. They'd been the victors today, but I could see they were shaking their heads, as if to say, "Are we glad *this* one's over!"

Despite the loss, our fans stood unified, encouraging the girls. They were disappointed with the loss, but satisfied with our effort.

In two days, we'd be visiting the mighty St. Paul Crusaders—unbeaten this year as usual. Between now and then, I figured the girls (and Katrina especially) would have ample time to reflect on the game and put it behind them. During the next 48 hours, we'd see how this setback would impact Katrina. She'd gone from hero to goat in a swing of 20 minutes. Would she retreat, or would she charge ahead?

Well, time would tell if and how quickly Katrina's wounds would heal. She'd either let her personal anguish fester, or she'd begin the healing process. So young, so innocent, to taste life's bittersweet realities. I looked forward to seeing Katrina's choice.

For the team as a whole, the game with St. Cyril's had to be seen as a moral victory. We'd lost the match, but we'd gained a level of respect that we'd never had in our camp.

Still league standings don't depend on "moral" victories. From that standpoint, this had been a loss, pure and simple. Our perfect record was gone, and we faced our next game, against an even tougher opponent, just two days from now.

CHAPTER
21

A.J. "Ted" Craft was a peculiar guy. He never answered my phone calls, and he said he'd only meet with me in person. He apparently didn't trust phone technology, and feared his conversations over that medium would be taped.

But that was how he did things, they said—always on the edge, always some deal going down, always in control, and always getting his way.

I felt nervous as I pulled again into the parking lot of Foster's Den. I breezed past the valet as I had yesterday, located the parking spot I had occupied, and drove past it. I circled the lot once, then zeroed in on the perfect spot, between a black Rolls-Royce, and a black Mercedes.

I flipped my keys to the gaunt valet, who'd followed me to the spot. He was pale and yellow-skinned, from too many packs of Marlboros a day, I figured. His wrinkled skin looked like a dried-up creek bed under a scorching Sahara sun. I saw more cracks and lines on his face than in a jigsaw puzzle. He hacked three times behind me as I made my way inside.

Today I had left my old gray at home. I was dressed casually. After all, my sole intention was to remain just long enough to turn down Craft's job offer. Then I'd head up to the Gibson place at Rye Lake.

Inside the restaurant, I was motioned by yesterday's

waiter to proceed to the Back room, where A.J. Craft was waiting for me.

In the room, a bottle of champagne, cork intact, was chilling in a silver ice bucket, with a white towel folded neatly across its base. The table, empty of china and utensils, held only a lavishly decorated cigar box, lid open to reveal two long Havana stogies. An ash tray, also silver, rested just to the left of the open cigar box.

Craft sprang to his feet the instant the door opened. He welcomed me with his crushing handshake, his left hand overlapping my arm as he grasped my hand from both sides. This was congratulatory handshaking. But Craft was in for a surprise.

I pulled my hand from his abruptly. Craft, so wise to the world, read my gesture and spoke first. "Paul, have a seat."

"No thanks," I said. I wanted this to be over quickly and painlessly.

"Mr. Craft, Ted, as you knew it would be, your offer was tempting, might even have been very tempting if I were the sort of guy who'd take it. But I gave it some thought, and I'm staying with the job I have. I'm sorry to disappoint you."

Craft's rage made his voice tremble. "You're being ridiculous!" he barked. "Where in your flat life will you ever make that much money in a year?"

Sure, I knew he was right about that. But I wasn't about to alter my decision. "Like I said, Craft, thanks for the offer, but I'm staying put."

Like a great giant cherry, Craft's face lit up the brightest red I'd ever seen skin turn. Rudolph the Red-Nosed Reindeer himself would have been jealous. Craft was angry, and now I had to manage my way around the next few minutes of what I knew would be a venomous outburst.

"All *right*," he said. "All right." He was obviously trying to calm down before continuing. "If it's a question of job security, don't worry about it. If you come to work for me, you come for life. You don't get fired, you don't get laid off."

I'd known he'd try to be persuasive, and I'd prepared myself for such tactics. I knew I was on his "turf." This was his home court, I was the visitor. He knew how to manipulate to gain leverage and ultimate victory. This was a game to him, and he was used to winning. He was St. Paul's volleyball coach, standing there so sure and confident. I was St. Luke's, unsure and easily trampled. Or so Craft thought. "I've made my decision," I said. "I'm staying put, I like my job."

"You pathetic loser!" he snorted at me. "Take your measly little joke of a job—stay a hick the rest of your life, I don't care."

He seemed like a once-calm dog that had suddenly gone rabid. I could hardly believe one human being could turn on a dime as quickly as he had. I knew beyond any question at that moment that I'd made the right decision, turning down this egomaniac. Now more than ever, I wanted to find that deed and send him packing. Now it was "personal," Strong vs. Craft, St. Luke vs. St. Paul, David vs. Goliath.

I handed Craft the flyer he had given me, and he swatted at my hand as if it were a disgusting insect about to inject it with some nasty blood-sucking stinger. I dodged his hand in plenty of time.

I knew Craft would need to have the final word, and he took it. Yesterday, he'd made me a bribe; today it'd be a warning. "I'll let you go now, you sorry excuse for a writer. Go on, look all you want for that deed, you'll never find it now. That land *will* be cleared, it's just a matter of time. So consider this a threat—*DON'T* put your nose in where it doesn't belong!"

I turned to leave, but kept an eye on him. He was a mad dog, and mad dogs will attack from behind. I walked away slowly, my backside bristling. I breezed out of the room, past the coat check lady; I pushed the double glass door open before the doorman could even react.

Outside, the valet flicked the last stub of his Marlboro into his personal ash tray, a four-foot-high container with a round lid of sand. This particular nub found its way into the outer edges of the sand, one more of perhaps 40 that poked up like markers for the dead. *He'll be joining them soon,* I thought, but I politely asked for my car keys.

The valet hacked again, straightened up, looked me up and down, and proclaimed, "It's valet parking, I'll get your car."

I was in no mood for games, I simply wanted out of there. I stuck my face within a few inches of the man's and tried to keep from gagging at the stench of his pungent and revolting tobacco breath. "Just give me the keys, please," I said. "Just the keys."

He didn't budge, he repeated himself. *Real testy, this one,* I thought. He knew I didn't "belong," so he was eager to take this little game of his all the way. About 20 feet to my left sat the key panel, each set numbered, hanging in place, so neat and orderly. I quickly spotted my key holder, trimmed with a dangling replica of a volleyball, given to me as a gift from the players. So I shifted my feet and strode briskly past the valet towards the key rack.

Now, maybe I should have allowed this annoying valet to retrieve my car, slipped him a few bucks, and just escape back into the real world. But this walking chimney of a man represented A.J. "Teddy" Craft to me—everything about this place did. So I wanted my car, and I wanted to get it myself.

As I got to the rack and reached for my keys, I took notice of the nail they hung from. It was in row seven, slot number 29. "Seven twenty-nine again," I mouthed—another strange "coincidence." *I'll be,* I thought.

The valet, out of breath from his short walk to the rack,

cursed me out as I grabbed my keys and started for my car. I knew Craft was probably watching. At last my car would provide me with the shield I craved. This 10-year-old friend's security was soothing. I cranked up the engine, hit the pedal, and went on my way back to the comforts of my middle class world. Next stop, Rye Lake and the old mayor.

CHAPTER
22

The ride North was therapeutic for me. I knew the tranquility of Rye Lake would soon be mine to enjoy—a perfect way to put the ugly earlier events of the day behind me.

I had called Joshua Gibson in advance to clear my short-notice visit with him. And he'd welcomed me to visit his retreat again. "I'll take you fishing for some lake trout," he'd said. Sounded good, the sweet smell of fillet stirring in some country pan.

The day was more perfect than the one we'd met on. October's leaves, their crimson and orange colors flanked by shades of red, made for a picture-perfect Autumn day. Like some giant invisible rake from the sky, the Fall winds had blown thousands of leaves together, organizing what nature had originally dropped and scattered. The sky, blue as blue could be, stretched out cloudless and pure.

But something broke that purity as I snaked my way through the long dirt road leading to Rye Lake. Puffs of gray were filtering through the magnificent blue—and they were coming from the general direction of Gibson's cabin.

I paid the gray puffs little attention at first, but as I neared the road leading to the cabin, the gray turned to black, and mixed with the smell of old wood, now smelled like a giant bonfire. ***These aren't clouds,*** I thought. ***That's smoke.***

I felt a sense of urgency overtake me. I sped well past the posted limit of 15 miles per hour, and dropped left, then right, then left again with every bump in the road I managed to cross. Finally, I saw that in the short clearing leading to the Gibson cabin, my worst fears were being realized.

Local volunteer firemen milled around, their makeshift pickups circling the cabin like it was a wagon train under Indian attack. Hoses, some no larger than the traditional garden variety, weakly sprayed the old structure with a steady stream of water pushing from a portable pump inserted into the nearby well.

But I could see that the structure itself appeared intact. The smoke was diffusing, and I saw no sign of flames. The worst had passed already. To the left of the main action, Joshua Gibson stood with his niece, Rosemary. He turned toward me as I pulled into the nearest parking area and slammed the door as I exited.

"Paul," Gibson said, "I'm glad you're here! I have something to show you."

I found it rather intriguing, that the old mayor was more interested in showing me something though the cabin was both under both fire and water. "But what about the cabin?" I said. "What's happened here?"

"We'll talk about that later," he said. "It's under control now, not a lot of damage, mostly water. Your buddy Craft probably did this."

I paused, then said, "What? How could he? How are you so sure?"

The old man gave me a look that said "experience." He'd been around the block a few times in his day, seen it all in his 95 years. He wasn't stupid, he was street-smart and plenty so.

"That Craft can't outsmart me," Gibson said, pounding his thumbs on his chest with the certain pride of a victorious senior citizen. "This cabin may be as old as dirt, but it's got some hidden secrets inside."

"How's that?"

He started walking toward the back of the cabin. I followed, and he pointed at each corner of the structure. "See those tiny disks?" he said. "Security cameras. Got 12 of 'em around the place. They run 'round the clock, never stop unless I shut them off. Any secrets in this old cabin don't stay secrets for long."

"Oh, and there's more," he said. "See those cameras? Mounted inside fire retardant boxes, and can't be destroyed by fire. Should give us some interesting viewing later on, don't ya think?"

"Yes," I agreed, "should be very interesting, indeed."

About then the Fire Chief, a middle-aged man, called us back to the front of the cabin. He was dressed in the traditional fireman's yellow parka and matching, unlaced boots.

"Mayor," the man said, "everything's under control now—good thing you have that sprinkler system."

"You have a sprinkler system?" I asked Gibson.

"Of course I do," said Gibson. "This is an old wood cabin. You take me for a fool?"

The chief and the mayor completed the appropriate paperwork as we surveyed the damage inside. The smell of wood smoke clung to the air, but broken windows were allowing the pungent odor to slowly retreat. Things were a bit of a mess, but "we'll have no need for hotel rooms," the scrappy former mayor said.

In a little while, the crisis past, the firemen packed their gear. They left together, each truck kicking up dust that blanketed the area with a fine dirt mist. Along with the ash that had accumulated on certain areas of the cabin, the old place looked like it had been covered by the fallout of an erupting volcano.

Well, the fire had been turned back, but there was much work to do. Hours of cleaning were in the Gibson's immediate future. Dust, ash, water, broken glass—all fire's left-overs requiring attention.

But the Gibson pair had no neighbors to assist them. They would need to tackle this project head on, a daunting task even for two people in their primes. The local Sheriff would pay a visit tomorrow, followed by insurance company representatives, and possibly arson specialists. Gibson would be busy hustling about with these intruders, his valuable time stolen from him. He'd need to contact glass companies to install new windows; the roof would need inspection; so would the building's superstructure. The mayor was still spry as a spring chicken, but he was 95 years old, and would need some help.

"Tomorrow is Saturday," I told him. "I'm off, and so is Emily. We'd be available if you'd let us both come up here and help you out with this mess."

I figured there'd be ample time to make the trip, get as much as we could accomplished, and head back home for the game at seven. "If we get here by eight a.m.," I said, "we can stay until about two."

I half expected this proud man to wave off or scoff at my offer. But he was a man full of surprises. "That'd be nice Paul," he said gently. "Very neighborly of you. Sure would like to meet your Mrs.; she's got to be pretty special to put up with the likes of you."

We laughed, standing together in the middle of the damage. I'd put my search for the deed on hold for now; it could wait a few more days. Anyway, the old deed was probably somewhere right in front of us, and my Saturday might involve both helping clean up *and* finding the deed.

"Coincidence" might again lead me on.

I stayed on at the Gibson's for *seven* more hours, filling 40 gallon trash bags with ash and dirt, over and over. I told Gibson about my encounters with Craft, the job offers and Craft's reaction. He told me about his life in politics, his life in the Navy, the secrets of his family. But he spoke not one word about the woman in the picture, though he saw me clean it off and place it back in a box for temporary storage.

But we bonded, shoveling, sweating, talking. I belonged here, on their side, I knew. We boarded up the broken windows with slabs of plywood that had been stored in a nearby shed. We built a huge blaze in the fireplace, to ward off the plummeting temperatures Autumn nights in those parts bring to the woods. We filled up 25 bags with the day's debris. At last our bodies had taken as much as they could, and we were done for the day.

I had stayed on much longer than I'd anticipated. It was nine p.m—seven hours had passed, just like that. I needed to get home, get some rest, and return with Emily, and start anew.

My long ride home was silent; not once did I touch my radio dial; the silence felt like my ally. I had phoned Emily earlier, and she'd told me she was ready and willing for the upcoming day's challenge. I knew all her cleaning instincts would already be surfacing. I pictured her neatly packing cleaning supplies, bags, brushes, and brooms for the day. Emily was like that—she was quiet, but her feelings for humanity equaled mine in every way. She cared for what was right, and helping the Gibson's was more than right in her mind.

I arrived home at one a.m., and walked into the house like a church mouse, hoping I'd wake no one. I quietly undressed, climbed into bed next to Emily, and fell into a deep sleep.

CHAPTER
23

The alarm clock sounded. "Not possible, I just went to bed," I moaned, squinting at 5:55 on the clock.

But the sound of the shower quickly convinced me I was wrong. Emily was up first, as usual. She'd expect me to follow soon after, so the shower's pulsations were my signal to rise.

By the time I got ready to enter the same shower stall, Emily was already dressed, apparently eager for the day. She hugged me on the way in. *She's a whirlwind of a worker,* I thought with pride. *The Gibson's will certainly take to her.* She was quick in all she did, and I knew a fine breakfast would be ready the minute I turned off the shower, dried off and got to the table.

And it was: toast, eggs, pancakes, coffee—a smorgasbord of breakfast foods—Emily never cut corners with breakfast, and glad I was of that!

But the surprise of the day was seeing Karen and Megan, both dressed, both alert, already there, eating hearty breakfasts. "What's going on?" I said. "Are *you* girls going with us?"

They nodded, mouths full with selections Emily had prepared. That they were going with us, giving up a sleep-in Saturday for hard labor at some stranger's house, this woke me up fully, as I sat down to join them at the table.

Quite impressive for young girls accustomed to enjoying the pleasures of Saturday mornings, I thought. They would usually sleep until eleven, lounge about in their p.j.'s till noon, then begin to contact friends. "Why are all of you coming? It's going to be a lot of work, it's a long drive—and we have a game tonight."

Megan spoke first. "We heard Mom talking to you on the phone, and we just want to help. Mr. Gibson sounds like a neat guy, and we want to see the cabin and the lake. So we're going with you, and we'll make it *fun.*"

"Great," I beamed back. "The more workers we have, the less time all the work'll take."

The girls giggled then, as if they were hiding something from me. From knowing them all their lives, I had to figure they were also plotting something else, beyond just joining us for the work today. I looked quizzically at Emily, but she just shrugged her shoulders. *For sure,* something's *up,* I thought.

We briskly finished our breakfast, cleaned our messes and packed the car for the long ride to Rye Lake. It was still dark as I looked out the back window toward the apple orchards. Mother Nature had frosted them last night, and a fine sheen glared off the apples. It was a cold morning, but I'd heard the weather forecast, and it was promising. It would be a good day to clean cabins—and do whatever else they might have up their sleeves.

"Let's pack up and get going!" I shouted.

We all grabbed tools and other items we'd need and opened all four doors to the family car, and its trunk. With the precision of experienced packers, we soon placed all items perfectly, leaving not an extra inch of space.

The girls were giggling again as I pulled the car out of the garage, and into the street. I looked both ways, and noticed a long line of cars and vans, lights on, all parked in a row, off to the side of the road across the street.

Peculiar for a Saturday morning, I thought. Maybe it was a funeral procession, forming their perfect lines, organizing themselves. ***Couldn't be anything but that,*** I thought. "Look across the street," I said aloud. "Did someone die around here?"

The girls answered by opening their doors and waving at the rows of vehicles. At once, doors opened, people poured out of their cars, and they all made their ways to our car.

The sun wasn't yet up enough for me to clearly identify any one who was approaching.

I quickly opened my door and eased out to get a better look. The girls got out, too, and walked halfway to meet the group. And now I noticed they were exchanging hugs with girls their own age, several of whom I now recognized.

"That's Janet and Mandy," I said to Emily, and here come Katrina, and Lauren. And there's the Shea twins."

The whole volleyball team was there, coming out of the morning fog. And now their parents—all of them—crossed the road like chaperones from the wings.

"Morning, coach Paul," hailed Charles Moore, Janet's father.

"Morning to you," I said. "What's going on?"

I didn't really have to ask—I knew what was going on—and Charles Moore just grinned. Somehow, the whole team had organized, overnight. They would be taking the trip with us, it appeared, giving up a beautiful Fall Saturday, just to help an old man and his niece, total strangers. Another huge surprise in a season full of them.

Within seconds, they were all standing in our driveway, filling up most of the area, which could hold eight full-sized cars. As the group gathered, the girls on one side, adults on the other, the large driveway literally swallowed up the whole crowd standing in it.

As I mixed in with the other adults, I noticed that everyone looked amazingly alert for the hour, as if a long, overdue vacation had finally arrived for everyone. "Now, do my eyes deceive me, or is this what I think it is?" I said to the assembly of girls. "Are you *all* going with us to Rye Lake?"

They nodded, looking eager to get going. I felt something like awe overcome me, and I turned to the adults. "I don't know what to say—this is so incredibly generous of all of you..."

I turned back to the girls and I counted heads. *Thirteen,* I thought, *they're all present.* I wheeled back to the adults and quickly counted 23. Adding Emily and myself, the full contingent of 25 were here. Not a single person was missing. "No need to take attendance," I said, "looks like the whole team made it."

A group laugh followed. Charles Moore looked at his watch. "Better get going, coach," he said, "it's almost seven."

He was right. The usual three-hour trip would get us there by ten. But this was a Saturday, and there'd be less traffic than normal at this hour. We'd arrive by nine-thirty giving us a full five hours to get the place in order.

Just seconds later, it seemed, and we were on the road. Our car led the convoy of vehicles, 13 in all, all packed with supplies for the day. With 38 of us working, I thought delightedly, we'd come close to completing our task in a single day. I smiled to myself: Mayor Gibson and Rosemary were in for a real—pleasant—shocker!

We got there in exactly two and a half hours, making no stops along the way, and never once did a car in the convoy get separated from my view. The trip had gone as smoothly as I could have wished.

Our winding crawl on the dirt road leading to the Gibson's afforded us spectacular views of the lake and woods. The October fog was still lifting from the trees; the lake looked as smooth as glass, except when lake trout made occasional splashes, leaping for meals, insects buzzing near the water's surface.

I saw a family of rabbits foraging near a clearing, and squirrels darting in and out of trees, curious about our presence. Hawks circled silently above, targeting any movements in the grass by the scores of chipmunks and mice foraging as well. A doe and her fawn drank at the lake's bank, no more than 100 yards from where I drove.

All of this I observed in less than a half mile on the twisting dirt road. Nature was going to play out its own day for us, like some theatre created by the animals themselves. This seemed like heaven on earth to me; I belonged in this place, so rustic, so secure.

We turned at the fork in the road where Gibson and I had first met. And though this was my third trip, the vivid memory of that meeting came on me like a vision—the coin flip, Gibson grabbing it from the air, the right turn in the road. (I would always cherish this particular memory, each and every time I came to Rye Lake.)

As we approached the cabin, 200 yards from me I spotted the mayor and Rosemary, rocking on the deck. The cabin was still slightly covered with a clayish color from the ash and dirt, but the overnight frost seemed to have nearly self-scoured the giant structure.

As we drove even closer, the old mayor and his niece rose from their rocking. Mayor Gibson held his hand above his eyes to shield them from the sun's glare and get a better look. Beaming, he walked down the four giant steps to meet us, Rosemary at his side.

I parked first; the others followed. There was plenty of room for all of us; the vast clearing could hold three times our number. I got out, and Gibson and Rosemary approached me, embraced me, then surveyed all the cars and people.

"Paul, who *are* all these people?" Gibson said, as we watched the volunteers start carrying in a steady stream of supplies and tools. Moments later, I lifted my hand to halt progress and motioned everyone to gather at the foot of the steps leading to the cabin. I could see by the looks on the faces of our contingent that they were awestruck by the place. "Everyone," I said, "I want you to meet Mayor Joshua Gibson and his niece Rosemary. Please don't forget to introduce yourselves while you're bringing in the supplies!"

The big crew did so during the next 15 minutes, while they continued unloading. The mayor and Rosemary bowed to each of them as if he or she were the guest of honor in some wedding line. I could easily see the glint of joyous tears in their eyes.

The last girl to introduce herself was Becky Chapman. *She always seemed to choose to be last*, I thought. I had told the mayor about Becky at our first meeting, basically telling him all I knew about her life. He kissed her hand as if she were a princess, and Becky blushed.

I said proudly, "Mayor Gibson, if you haven't already guessed, this is our volleyball team—all of 'em—and we're all going to fix this place up for you!"

And with that, we went to work. Seeing I was expected to take charge of the work, I gathered the adults together so we could organize this considerable crew. We went inside, surveyed the damage and shortly thereafter began what must have been the greatest one-day cleanup in the history of mankind!

Gibson and I had removed the broken glass yesterday, so it was safe to move around inside the cabin; but it was very dark in there, since the windows were boarded up with plywood. We needed to have every light on as we went about our business.

Soon, the talents of certain livelihoods surfaced from the group. Phyllis Glover, Katrina's mom, cleaned houses for a living. Brad Cross, Joanne's father, owned a window replacement company. George Morrison owned and ran a hardware store. The Lee's owned a deli.

We put the girls in charge of cleaning the outside of the cabin. This included scrubbing the logs to remove any debris left by the fire. We'd brought ladders, buckets, gloves, and solvent for their use. Within minutes, all 13 girls scattered around the cabin, some on ladders, some on the ground, some leaning over the great awning.

And the adults went right to it; Phyllis Glover took control of the cleaning, instructing the women of the group to assigned stations. Brad Cross removed the plywood and measured the windows with precision. George Morrison distributed hardware and tools to the men, as he took charge of those operations.

We were soon busy as beavers building a dam, not pausing an instant in the action. We worked hard and we worked together. Outside, the girls were singing along to contemporary rock and roll, which they blasted from radios positioned in each corner of the cabin. They scrubbed, sang and sweat—a team both on and off the field of play—as they were getting the job done.

At noon, Steve Lee and his wife Julia added to the day's surprises. They went to their car and brought dozens of hot dogs, hamburgers, chips, sodas, paper plates and bags of ice—enough of all to feed and "water" a small army, which is exactly what we were. Steve fired up the giant barbecue pit with Gibson's approval, and transformed himself into a chef, donning an apron, and even a chef's high hat.

My mouth was soon watering at the smell of the meat sizzling on the grill. I knew we all must be hungry, and needing the energy such a feast would provide. We hadn't gotten all the work done, but we had put a major dent in our task, and we could see light at the end of the tunnel.

By twelve-thirty, the first line of food was ready. We shooed the girls in first, and they plunged at the food with the same vigor they'd employed on the job. They took their plates and sat under a huge, ancient pine, all 50 feet of it shading them from the sun overhead.

We adults sat together on a giant picnic table that Gibson had built for just such occasions as this. The large group fit comfortably around it, even its whole surface spread thick with paper plates, condiments, and delicious food.

As we ate, we got more familiar with each other. Both work and our meal had bonded us like the girls, and I thought, *We too, have become a team!*

After a while, Mayor Gibson and Rosemary excused themselves from the table, and together they took their plates and drinks, and went over to the circle of girls, and asked if they could join them. The girls nodded as one, and the Gibson's sat down in the dirt, under that great pine, and ate the rest of their lunch, eating and chatting with the girls.

I noticed the girls laughed at each and every thing the mayor said. They were enjoying his brand of humor; and at the same time, he was earning their respect.

Gibson sat between Katrina and Becky, and they paid particular attention to his words. I found it fascinating, the way he could reach them, all the way from his perch 82 years older than they, and bring them such enjoyment.

We finished eating around 12:45, leaving us about 90 minutes to finish our job. And not a minute did we waste. During that final 90 minutes, Mayor Gibson and Rosemary stayed with the girls, advising, instructing, and admiring their work. He even danced with them, to the beat of a current pop hit. Obviously, he was having the time of his life, as were the girls to his buoyant presence. If there was any such thing as a "generation gap," the old mayor had bridged it and demolished it behind him in record time! I thought, *he's been away from people for so long, maybe this will help get him back into circulation.*

Still, it was apparent, if you looked closely, that he'd especially taken to Becky Chapman. You could see that during the 10 minutes he spent with her. He nodded with every word she spoke, as if a young Jesus was holding court with elders in a church of the elders, and old Gibson himself was a master being taught by his prize student.

Becky said one last thing to Gibson, excused herself, and went into the cabin. Whatever it was she said last, Gibson suddenly gave all his attention to Katrina Glover. *Maybe Becky had told Gibson about the night of anguish Katrina had survived*, I thought, *maybe not*. I waited to see Katrina's reaction to Gibson as he spoke.

He spoke, she listened—then she lit up like a firecracker on the fourth of July. She spoke, he listened; he laughed, she laughed. I couldn't quite make out their words, but it was undoubtedly an exchange for the ages. How wonderful I felt, that this great old man had impacted the girls as deeply as he had me!

I excused myself from the table for a moment, went into the cabin, curious as to the whereabouts of Becky. As I entered through the great door, she was standing in front of the fireplace, and she was admiring the picture of the young woman from 1904.

"Beautiful, isn't she?" I said, startling her.

"Coach Paul," she said, "I didn't hear you coming. Yes, she is *beautiful*. Do you know who she is?"

"No," I replied, "but she does look familiar to me."

"She looks familiar to me, too," said Becky.

We went back outside to join the others, and at two o'clock, we broke camp, our jobs completed, except for one remaining item, installing new windows. We'd re-nailed the plywood to the framework, and Brad Cross had promised to deliver the windows as soon as he possibly could.

I'd had no time to search for the deed on this day, and it would have been inappropriate for me to do so, I thought. I'd need to return in the very near future for that crucially important search.

We packed our vehicles and gathered once more to say goodbye. The mayor was ready for us—he had slipped inside and returned with an old Kodak camera, the kind with the bulb attached. We lined up for a group photo at the base of the steps leading to the cabin. Rosemary insisted on taking the photos; she wanted her Uncle to be a part of this memory more than she did herself.

During the commotion of placing people in just the right spot for a photo, Rosemary signaled me over to her, as the mass of people moved about.

"What is it?" I asked.

"Do you remember the day we met, and your aura was very clear to me?"

"Sure," I said.

"Well, I've never seen such an aura that that girl has," she said, nodding her head in Becky's direction. "There has never been a stronger aura in any of my experiences before. That girl is *special*."

"That's what I keep hearing," I said, looking at Becky.

At that moment, Mayor Gibson stepped to the top of the porch as I took my place for the photo. He raised his hands and said, "May I please have your attention!"

We all hushed and we turned to face the mayor. Tears spilled from his eyes, and he fumbled for the right words.

"I want you all to know that—what you did here today...well, it's the nicest thing anyone's ever done for me in my long life."

He paused to collect himself, then he said, "I want you to know that you girls, and your parents, have...have restored my faith in mankind. You know, I moved out to this lake to escape people. I'd had enough of them. Rosemary can tell you—I resisted going into town even for a visit."

He paused again, moved beyond words. At last he was able to speak, through sobs, "I can't tell you how much I enjoyed your company today. I-I want to thank the parents who brought the food, the tools, all the equipment." He smiled warmly at the girls. "And I want to thank you girls...for—making me feel like a young man again."

Then he spread his arms wide, turned to the cabin and cried triumphantly, "And just look at what you've accomplished here!" Turning back to the small crowd, he said, "Now, just one last thing. Next Sunday, I'm inviting all of you back up here—for a day of *fun*. No work, not a lick of it—just fun!"

Heads nodded and faces gleamed approval, and the mayor said, "I know it's too cold to go swimming now, but we have a rowboat. There's fishing, trails, and a horse farm up the road here a bit—you girls can go riding. Now I know it's a long drive and all, but we'd love to have you for the day."

The girls belted out in unison a long, "Yea!!!" turning to their parents for approval. We glanced among ourselves and moments later gladly accepted Gibson's offer.

Hugs and handshakes in plenty followed, of course, and afterwards, as the crew broke up into families again and got ready to leave, Gibson took me aside, amid the sounds of car doors opening and closing. "Paul, come on up here tomorrow, can you? Gonna be a beautiful day, and I owe you a fishing date. Plus, we need to watch a little 'show,' don't we?"

He pointed to the security cameras. Oh yes, I would certainly be interested in this little show! And I'd enjoy the fishing and the company—and we could search for the deed. "It's a deal," I grinned. "I'll be here tomorrow."

I joined our family and got behind the wheel of our car. And our long line of autos began moving out as one. Our windows down, we waved goodbye to Gibson and Rosemary. And I could hear him yell faintly, as we put some distance between us, "You show that St. Paul's team who's boss tonight!"

CHAPTER
24

The twists and turns of that dirt road to Gibson's cabin reminded me of life itself, so full of the unexpected. One minute, you're on the straight and narrow, the next, you're fixing a flat tire on the side of the road. Sometimes in life, you just get no warnings. Sometimes, you just don't read the signs.

And so it was with our game that evening in the vast, well lit confines of the St. Paul Crusaders—the **undefeated** St. Paul Crusaders. The rafters of their gymnasium were full of championship banners from the previous eight years, hung like warning signs, with dark crimson backgrounds and old English gold lettering etched and raised. One side of the gym's wall was plastered with the names of past players, professionally printed on a crimson, wooden background. Each player in the past eight years who' tasted the sweetness of winning a championship was listed. We were in awe at the mere sight of it. ***They take their volleyball seriously,*** I thought.

Everything about St. Paul's was top of the line. Their uniforms were crimson and gold stitched, their net, tight and straight. Their court looked like it was newly waxed, the overhead lights reflecting images like a mirror.

And at that moment their girls, amazons all, were undergoing a strenuous warm-up, under the supervision of coach

Daryl Reed, the coach of all coaches in our league.

Coach Reed was the dean of our league's coaches, and all work, no play. He was tough on his girls as a buck drill sergeant pushing marines. His crew-cut hair, square jaw and broad shoulders suited his personality well.

Coach Reed not only expected victory from his girls, he expected *demolition.* It wasn't enough for them to easily sweep three games from an opponent. The results of their games were easy to predict, but Coach Reed was rarely satisfied if an opponent scored more than 10 points in those three games. That was his goal, he said, to allow less than 10 points, and he would allow his girls a smile only if they gave him such results.

His amazing won lost record in ten years was 145 wins, and only five losses. His team had won the league title eight straight seasons, and had built an incredible 124 game winning streak. They were the Harlem Globetrotters of grade school volleyball—they just never lost. And we were next on their list.

We had received word before we came that just last night St. Paul's had slaughtered St. Cyril's—the same St. Cyril's team that had handed us our first loss. I'd tried in vain to keep this information from the girls, but dozens of handouts, printed after each St. Paul game, were placed on every seat, table and counter in the building to tell the tale.

"Coach Paul!" the girls cried, "Look, they beat St. Cyril's 15-2, 15-2, 15-0. And look at the headline!"

I glanced first at Mandy Morrison, who was reading the flyer aloud, then at the rest of the girls, all of whom had copies in hand. I grabbed one from the table; the headline read, "Lackluster effort lands Crusaders in first place."

"Lackluster effort!" I said aloud. "They only allowed four points *total.* What do they think constitutes a good, or an excellent effort?"

I tossed the paper back down on the coach's desk and

urged my girls to do the same. "Forget it, it's just what they want us to see," I said, "a little pre-game hype to get us scared."

I noticed Coach Reed fast approaching me. He'd heard me, and wasn't hiding the fact. ***He's arrogant, pompous, and has no business coaching,*** I thought. ***Sure, his teams won, but where was the fun, and what exactly was he teaching his players?***

He reached me, but gave no handshake, no welcome, no "good luck" exchange coaches usually make prior to a game. Instead, he just wanted to show me his chest puffed up like a rooster who'd successfully completed a mating conquest. His graveled voice bit at the air between us. "It *was* a lackluster effort. Took a whole 28 minutes to complete three games, usually takes 24. Need to do it in 20 tonight, that's the goal."

And with that, he spun off, to lead his team in another grueling warm-up exercise.

I'd known we were going to have our work cut out for us this game, but I hadn't expected this kind of crude psych job. This was damage control time, and it was up to me to pull it off. How after this strutting display of his could I deflect the pre-game distractions, get the girls focused? I tried to remind them that a victory tonight would put us back into first, tied once again with St. Paul's and St. Cyril's.

But all the joy that we'd felt at the cabin that day was dashed not long after we hit the court. Coach Reed made his goal, turning us into victim 125, scoring 15-2, 15-3, and 15-0 wins. Twenty minutes flat of play turned his goal into reality, right to the minute. Yes, death came fast, like a poisonous snake striking its victim a lethal blow.

But the loss itself wasn't what upset me; it was the way Coach Reed went about his debacle. We played the third game, meaningless in the standings because the victors had already won the first two games, with our-non–starters. That was the unwritten rule in volleyball. But just to fulfill his prediction, Coach Reed kept his top six in—a fact that both our players and the fans noticed. There was even some rumblings from the St. Paul's fans.

Our bench issued its own rumbling as the scoreboard began to scroll his top six's numbers at the start of the third game. During that game, even the referee asked Coach Reed if he wanted to send in substitutes, but he declined. "They'll finish what they started," he growled. This cold-blooded coach wouldn't even allow his second string to pick up the scraps from this feast. Did he really need to let us know like *this* that he wouldn't allow us to even get a distant sniff of first place? No, first was their sole domain, and we were trespassing. Coach Reed was teaching us a lesson.

But lessons like this, you don't soon forget. A good team they were; sportsmanship awards they'd never win. We didn't like taking a licking that day; but we knew that in sports—and in life, eventually—"what goes around, comes around." Maybe their time would 'come around' if we happened to meet again in the league playoffs.

CHAPTER

25

I spent a splendid Fall afternoon with my friend Joshua Gibson, fishing in a small boat built for two, hauling in lunkers from the deep. Within two hours, we had our limit hanging from stringers off the stern of the rowboat, and we headed for shore to prepare our catch for an afternoon feast.

The two hours with Gibson produced more information on our township, the deed and his life than I'd gained in my original interview with him. He opened up far more this time, which I attributed to the more relaxed setting, his greater comfort level with me, and the working visit by the girls and their parents.

We spoke at length about the volleyball game we'd just played, and compared Coach Reed to A.J. Craft. They were equals, we agreed, and they were the bad guys. I wanted badly to somehow beat them both, each at his own game, I confided.

Life had taught Joshua Gibson many lessons. He had battled the A.J. Craft's and the Daryl Reed's of his day; he was keenly aware of how these types operated. He also had been quite successful in head-to-head matches against these kinds of self-serving piranhas.

"Believe me, those two are like all the other bullies," said the mayor. "They have a history of winning at all costs. They believe in themselves and in their tactics, there's no other way, you see. For them, it's not just the winning that matters, it's playing the game under their rules."

"How do they get away with it for so long?" I asked.

"Because of the way they build power," he said, making a fist and flexing his muscle like some body builder on display. He went on: "Take Craft, for example. He starts out his career with a bang, closing deal after deal, making his reputation, doing things *his way*. Then one deal feeds off another, along with the history he creates with the deals, and his reputation is born. Guys like him get to believing nothing can stop them, that they're above everything. They don't know it, but they become victims of their own tactics. Just nasty bullies, that's all they are. The same goes for that coach. He wins a few titles, builds power. 'Who could replace me?' he thinks. He's convinced the people of that school, that his way is right, and like a herd of sheep following a Shepherd, they trust him."

He was right on the money; he'd described both of 'em, yet had never met either one. "How do you take them down?" I said.

The wise old mayor smiled at me through those thick glasses, took me by the arm and held up the index finger of his free hand. "Paul, it began with one deal, one win. That was their beginning. It can all end the same way, one deal gone sour, one loss, and the questions start to come."

He made it sound so easy, but I knew it wasn't. First the deed needed to be found. St. Paul's needed to take a whupping. Neither possibility looked very promising just then.

"Sure, that's the *idea*, I said. "But what about the *reality* of it all? I can't find the deed, and that team plays like professionals."

Gibson now pointed to his head and tapped on it a few times, to make yet another point to his new student. "It all starts up here," he said. "Sure, you've been looking all over the place for that deed, but *think* Paul, *think*. Have you read any of the signs? Far as beating that team goes, *think.* Every team has a weakness, even teams that have won 125 games in a row. You need to exploit the weakness—or, recognize what makes them so good and *mimic them.* You need to assess your teams strengths, your weaknesses. You need to evaluate everything about that loss, and practice with that in mind. If you do, Paul, well, as they say, anything is possible, you just have to believe it here, and *here."*

He pointed to his heart with one hand, his head with the other—a simple equation coaches at all levels used, yet only a few had mastered its answer. And what about "reading the signs?" I believed the signs had directed me to the archives of the paper, to the meeting with Craft at Foster's Den, which had then led me back to the cabin with Gibson. I believed Becky Chapman's letter to the editor was also a sign. But what was I missing? Where was I going wrong?

I told Gibson about Becky's letter, how her father had told her about the hiding places people used in the 1800's. I let him know about my search of the old photographs in town, and the archives from the paper, all of which had turned up nothing.

I said, "Well, if you want me to read the signs, not just follow the directions, could we search those old photos on the mantle—and specifically those of the original town?"

"Sure," Gibson agreed, let's get right to it."

We spent the next two hours carefully pulling the old backings off each photo and picture from the mantle. One by one, we painstakedly handled the old photos with kids gloves, putting each one back together as we went. Finally, when the last frame turned up nothing, I sank down into the chair I was sitting on, disbelief and frustration clouding my face. I'd been sure I'd find the deed in one of these photos, but I'd come up empty. *Now what? Guess I'll go back to the archives, turn the pages one by one, finish that diligent, needle in a haystack search for this pot of gold at the end of the rainbow.*

Slumping there, I quickly found despair replacing my zeal; and the old mayor looked just as downcast. I looked across the room at that old upright Grandfather clock. *Stuck on 7:29,* I thought. *Why is such a beautiful piece of time-keeping stuck on the wrong time?* And at that moment, I also noticed the old photo of the young woman from 1904, hidden behind all the others on the mantle.

"Mayor," I said, "there's one more photo we forgot to look at—that one there—the photo of the girl from 1904."

"I assure you, it's not in that photo," he said glumly.

I got out of my chair and arranged the picture in its usual spot. "Who is she?" I asked. "She's simply beautiful."

As I turned to the old man, I saw his hands cover his face. I had never before seen such raw emotion overcome him. A barely audible sniffle slipped through his hands. I approached him, placed my arm around his shoulder and said, "I'm sorry, did I open an old wound?"

"Oh no," he replied. "Would you mind getting me a glass of water, Paul?"

"Of course not," I said.

I went to the kitchen and poured a tall glass of water for him. Just then, in the corner of my eye I saw Rosemary appear.

"Hello, Paul," she said.

"Rosemary, you startled me a bit; I was getting a glass of..."

"Sit down, Paul," she said firmly. "It's time I told you something about the woman in that picture."

I set the glass down on the kitchen table, looked out into the great room where Gibson sat, and turned back to Rosemary. "What is it?" I asked.

"Paul, have you ever wondered why Mayor Gibson never married?"

"As a matter of fact, the thought *has* crossed my mind," I said.

"The photo—the one of the woman from 1904—that's why he never married," she said.

"Why, did she marry someone else?" I asked.

"I don't think so," she replied. "We don't know for sure."

"I don't understand," I said. "You don't know if she ever married someone else, yet he never married at all? I'm confused." Now nothing about this woman in the picture made sense to me.

Rosemary went on: "Soon after that photo was taken, the mayor went off with the navy, spent a few years in different countries, learned even at that young age how politics worked in other nations. He and the woman in the photo were an item at that time, and they had talked of marrying when he returned home, they loved each other so very much."

"So, what happened?"

"The mayor wrote to her every day, sometimes twice a day, but never once did he receive a reply. He was heartbroken, and when he came home and called on her, she had already left—joined a Christian missions group who were traveling in Third-World countries, bringing Christianity to those nations. This group was the first of its kind at the time, and she apparently loved the adventure of it."

"Why didn't she answer his letters?" I said, "Did they ever get in touch with each other again?"

"No one knows why his letters went unanswered. Rumor was that she never received them, with her moving away and all. But he's a proud man you know. He just felt that since she'd never responded to his letters, he'd stay focused on his navy duties. He stayed with the navy all the way through World War I, sort of retreated into a shell during that time. He was never interested in another woman again."

Sad story, I thought.

"Irene was a remarkable woman for those times," Rosemary said. "She was what you'd call a real go-getter."

"Irene?" I said, remembering the image of the woman in the photo, which now seemed to be even more familiar to me. "Do you remember her last name?"

"Oh, yes, of course," she said. "It was Durella, Irene Durella."

I sat motionless for a moment, and though Rosemary was still talking to me, I couldn't respond. *This is nuts,* I thought, *another unbelievable coincidence.*

"Mr. Strong! Are you all right?" Rosemary asked sharply.

"Uh, sure, I'm fine," I said, snapping out of my reverie. "You know, I think I'd better go back in and see the mayor. Thanks for letting me in on this—though I'm sure you'd like me to keep it between us."

"Please do," she said softly, and she got up and left the room.

I composed myself before re-entering the great room. My head was swirling with all kinds of new thoughts as I carried the water out of the kitchen. The mayor was standing now, in his trademark arms-behind-his-back, admiring from a distance the old Grandfather clock.

"Mayor," I said. "What's with that clock—why are the hands always at 7:29?"

The old man turned to me, then back to the clock. He looked at it quizzically, as I had the first time my eyes caught sight of it. He stared at it for a solid minute, then dropped his head, then looked up again. He turned to me and motioned me to join him, and together we walked towards the great old timepiece.

We stood together, man to man, admiring the craftsmanship of the clock. The handwork and carpentry was impeccable. Clock makers took their time in the day, that was for certain. I read this as I studied the thickness of the wood, the perfection of the grain. There was no denying that this was more than a clock. It was a work of art.

"Paul," Gibson said, "it's *not* at 7:29—come a little closer."

When I'd come as close as I physically could to the clock, Gibson pointed to the area in the middle of the time piece, a small, round cutout of numbers, no bigger than a compass.

Looking more intently, I then noticed two sets of numbers over each hour, one through 12. One set of numbers was black, the other, red. Clearly, the black numbers signified "a.m.," the red, "p.m." "What is this, a military clock?" I asked.

Gibson nodded, looking as greatly relieved as a man whose life had just been saved. Then he said, "When I came up here in 1929, I brought that old clock with me. Been in the family for a very long time."

He touched the fine grain of one side, stroking it with a smooth, gentle touch. "All the men in my family were navy men,"he went on. "My father, God rest his soul, used to always give out the time in military time, you know, one o'clock p.m. would be thirteen hundred hours."

He stretched out his arms, touching both sides now, literally embracing the old clock as one might a living person. "Now, I may be pretty sharp, Paul, but I am 95 years old," he said. "Sometimes, the old wheels get stuck, just like this old clock, and need a little push out of the mud."

"In 1929, as I was going out of office, the new mayor, Grover Ward, came in. He wasn't a man I trusted, ran a nasty campaign, lasted only one term. He was a land baron—developed the land, like your buddy Craft. The times back then, they were changing; but it would still have been easy for a man like Ward to manipulate that deed—Deed 10-11—into land that could be developed, with himself as the top beneficiary."

"So I took the original—as a matter of fact, the *only*—copy of that deed, and brought it up here, for safe keeping against just the likes of Grover Ward."

He paused and I said, "All right, that's quite a story. But what does any of it have to do with the clock? And what made you suddenly remember that you do have the deed—and where is it?"

"One question at a time, Paul," he said, gesturing me to sit with him on one of the two giant rockers. *"I* set that old clock at 7:29, but in military time, it's *19:29.* That's the year I came up here, so I set the clock to that time, 19:29. And, the deed's number is 10-11, right, Paul?" I nodded, and he said, "To further assist my old memory about where I hid that deed, I played some math games. I love playing with numbers."

There was no rushing the old mayor; he was taking his time, telling the story so clearly, almost as if he was waking from a long sleep. "Take those numbers, 1929. The first two digits add up to 10, the second set, to 11. See? The number is 10-11, the lot number for the deed!"

Incredible—he'd played a math game with himself long ago, then forgot he'd done it until this very moment. "So, where is the deed?" I prodded. "Is it somewhere in the clock?"

He didn't answer, but rather walked over to a drawer, took a long screwdriver from it, walked back to the clock, bent down to the base and turned two screws till they slowly gave way. He handed the old screws to me, paused for a moment, then slid out a hidden compartment, a drawer of sorts, from the foot of that old clock.

He reached into it, then handed me an old, brown metal box, the size of a shoebox. I tried to open it, but it was locked. I noticed a keyhole on it, but no key. Raising a curious eyebrow, I handed it to the mayor, He fumbled in the top of the drawer and finally located an old key that had been hidden somewhere in there.

"Here it is," grinned Gibson, "clamped to an old magnet,

just where I left it. "Adios Mister Craft!"

He placed the key into the hole, cranked it to the right, and the lid popped open like a jack-in-the-box. Inside, one single, aged envelope, yellowed and thin, lay, sunlight about to fall on its contents for the first time in 50 years. A gold seal held the envelope together, and on the front, in faded black ink, I could clearly read the numbers: 10-11.

The mayor handed it to me. "You open it," he said. "Honored," I said, and so I did.

The two page document was dated March 5, 1875. The writing was eloquent, in the speech of the day, and made it more than clear that the 200 acres of Lot Number 10-11 would remain in God's hands until the end of time!

It was signed by Mayor "Arnold Jackson," and embossed with the official gold seal of the township. "This is it, all right," I beamed at Gibson. "Sure looks authentic to me."

I handed it to the mayor, and he took his own turn studying the old Deed. "Yep," he agreed. He looked up with a wild grin, shook a mischievous fist and yelled, "We got him now! Time to send that big bully away for *good!*"

So the great search for Deed 10-11 was over, just like that. I felt incredibly relieved, as if some giant pain had been lifted from my back, plus a feeling of immense pleasure.

Smiling, we sat down to plan our next move. All right, we had the document, but we knew Craft wouldn't go down easy, that was for certain. We needed to do even more.

"Tell you what—let's watch the video tape," Gibson said slyly. *"That'll* put the last nail in his coffin."

The mayor walked gingerly into the back room, retrieved the security tape, and inserted it into a Beta tape player, that alone surprising me.

"What's the tape player for" I asked him.

"Old westerns," he said, pointing to a shelf on the wall of a miniature library, where perhaps 20 tapes I hadn't noticed were nestled in a among the books. "I love John Wayne movies." He pushed "Play" on the control box, and we settled back to take a good look at some great home video footage.

To tell the truth, it was far from edge-of-your-seat exciting to start with. The footage of the back area of the cabin showed nothing but the changing winds distributing leaves and debris across the vast acreage. But then the mayor pushed Fast Forward, till some real action might break out on the tape.

After several minutes, we finally noticed some movement in the nearby woods. The sensitive camera had picked it up, too, and turned its primary focus toward the slight movement.

We watched the figures of three men emerge from the deep woods, one from the far left, one from the right, and the middle man, who crouched down near the edge of the woods, a metal device protruding from his hands.

The three men wore kaki fatigues that blended in well with their surroundings. The two on the flanks acted as sentinels, one covering the rear, while the other weaved back and forth between the front and his side. Their movements looked "experienced," like they were mercenaries, perhaps paid henchman out to do someone's sinister bidding.

When it seemed the coast had appeared clear, the man on the right waved the middle man forward, and the latter wasted no time, scurrying forward to the back deck of the great cabin.

"Look at the time on the screen," Gibson noted. "Eleven-thirty," I said. "Right," said Gibson. "I received a phone call at about 11:20. The voice told me there was an emergency at George Butler's cabin, 10 miles up the road, then just hung up. Old George has just as many neighbors as we do, so I got in the truck with Rosemary, and headed up his way."

"A diversion," I said. "Oh, yeah," Gibson agreed.

We fixed our eyes on the screen again. The man on the

back deck peered inside, evidently looking for any human movement. Then he stepped back from the windows and looked around once more.

Abruptly, Gibson paused the tape. Just where he froze it, the man's face was turned toward the camera, as handily as if he'd been posing for a snapshot. He looked roughly 30 years old, black beard, dark eyes, thin build.

"Hey, he was at Foster's Den, both times I was there!" I said.

We leaned closer to the screen to watch the rest of the tape. We saw the middle man ignite the device he held, then toss it through the back window. And at the first sign of fire, then smoke breaking out, we watched all three men high-tail it out of there and disappear into the woods, stealthily as a cougar fleeing with its prey.

Gibson snapped off the machine. "I've seen enough," he said, and I nodded my agreement. We weren't 100 percent sure these were Craft's men, but we were 99 percent sure. And we now had both the deed and the tape evidence to back us up. "Life is good," I smiled to Gibson.

Right then, I wanted in the worst way to drive to Foster's Den with a certain package for A.J. Craft. In it would be a photo copy of the Deed, and a copy of the video tape. I could see myself marching to that stuffy back room where we'd met for lunch, hand the package to Craft, and smugly say, "Here Teddy, I want you to look at these items, think about what you see, and let me know just what you intend to do about what you see. But I'll need your answer by tomorrow—sorry, but I'm not a very patient guy."

Gibson and I discussed the whole business over the next hour, and he persuaded me that it would be better if we stayed our hand for now. We still had time to devise a perfect plan. And we had what we needed most, our 104-year-old little ace in the hole.

I reflected on all that had happened this afternoon. I

could only interpret the signs that had eventually led me to the deed, and allowed me to learn the story of Joshua Gibson and Irene Durella had certainly been divine in nature, I reasoned. Invisible forces were drawing a "map" for me that was strong and straight. I felt kind of like a little lost boy in the woods, dropping stones along the way to mark his path—only by reading those signs, might another person be able to walk the same path.

That's how it had been, with the number 729, the lost letters to the editor, Becky Chapman's letter, the luncheon with Craft, and now the story of Irene Durella. It was as clear to me now, as it had been blurry when the search began: I was being used as an instrument of higher forces in all of these circumstances.

Gibson and I parted warmly not long afterwards, and two things I knew, driving back to town, one for certain, the other a strong hunch. First, *the* deed, Deed number 10-11, was now in our possession, and that beautiful 200 acres would remain pure as it had been hundreds of years ago. And second, a reunion between two old lovers who'd lost contact with each other for 75 years loomed in the near future.

CHAPTER

26

A quirk in the schedule had us playing only one game the upcoming week, a Friday night tilt against Our Lady of Sorrows. While we were losing two in a row, they'd been winning four straight—and catching us at third place in the standings, with an identical four wins, their only two losses, to St. Cyril's, and St. Paul's.

I scheduled two practices prior to the contest, exactly what I knew my team needed at this point of the season. We were halfway through now, and though our record was impressive by our standards, we were beginning to sink in the standings, and I could feel the team's confidence wavering. Another loss would drop us to fourth place, if victory, so easy to come by earlier, escaped us again.

The free night before our first practice I spent with Emily, reviewing the loss to St. Paul's. As we spoke, Joshua Gibson's words kept hanging over me, like some great puzzle. "Every team has a weakness," he'd said. "You need to either exploit that weakness, or recognize what makes them so good, mimic them. And you also need to recognize your team's strengths and your weaknesses. So, evaluate that loss and everything about it thoroughly, Paul, and practice with all you've learned in mind. If you do, as they say, Paul, anything is possible; you just have to believe."

With that, I started to chart a new course. I was improving at reading the signs, becoming more and more conscious of their mysterious phenomenon with every coincidence, every encounter with seeming chance. First, I hit the scorebook. I drew four lines on blank white paper, two lines for us, two for St. Paul's, column "A," strengths, column "B," weaknesses.

Our strengths? Serving! We'd been clicking in at a league-high 83 percent success rate. That part of my analysis was easy. Our weakness stood in contrast with St. Paul's greatest strength. Their serving was good, but not great, just 75 percent. But their defense was something else—each girl on their team held ground staunchly against enemy fire; their defense was almost impenetrable. No wonder we'd walked out of their lair with our tails between our legs in just 20 minutes.

By comparison, our defense was second rate. I noticed that the teams we'd beaten were poor defensively, so our record was skewed a bit in that regard. So it was obvious that we could trounce teams with poor defense, but we'd fend poorly against the likes of a rock-solid defense like St. Paul's.

St. Paul's servers weren't as accurate, percentage-wise, as ours, but they consistently served the ball to the back line, tipping the scales to their advantage: The deeper they served, the farther back they forced us to bring the ball back, and the higher our chances of failure.

But strong as they were, St. Paul's side of the page did have weaknesses, though few. They could handle the ball on defense, no question. But despite their serving's depth, it was suspect. Seventy-five percent wasn't particularly impressive for a team with their dominant history. Clearly, our plan of action to defeat them was on this page. We would focus on team defense, apply the skills we developed to our upcoming games and hopefully peak at playoff time. With good luck and play, we'd hopefully meet St. Paul's again in the championship game.

I set our practice plan: Tomorrow we would begin new drills designed specifically for St. Paul's. I realized that to do so involved considerable risk; introducing new tactics midway through a season could backfire. You usually conducted practices like the ones I was planning in the pre-season, not now, mid-season. Well, we'd soon find out how the 13 girls would react to this new plan.

I had read the signs, but had I followed the directions? ***I'll live with my decision,*** I thought, ***that's all I can do.*** I wanted "Coach" Daryl Reed's scalp as badly as I wanted A.J. Craft's—and I'd met that goal halfway. I kept reminding myself volleyball was only a game, but it had grown into something personal, too—Strong vs. Reed.

CHAPTER
27

Our team's plate was full that week, despite only one game on the schedule. The new defensive drills bored the girls, but they hung in there, realizing we needed them if winning was to be our goal.

The girls were reluctant to change when we began, but they performed well in the end. They got both tired and energized, the drills' frequency accounting for the former, the drills' success, the latter.

While the rest of the girls were taking their game to the next level, Becky Chapman continued to serve off the narrow wall with her left hand. And I noticed she was charting herself, like someone might on a diet. I found her diligence astonishing, since her results continued to show only moderate improvement.

Again, how she dealt with failure was extraordinary. And though her zeal and energy seemed to be doing little to take her game to the next level, her willingness to try hard energized the rest of the team. All they needed to spur them on was to look at Becky, banging that ball nowhere near her target, chasing down ball after ball, like an eager young puppy playing fetch. She never seemed to tire of this game, almost as if she was truly expecting her effort to pay off in some way or other, some time or other.

The new practices were only part of that fast moving

week. The game on Friday, the picnic at the lake on Sunday, the plan to eliminate A.J. Craft, from our lives, and what exactly to do with the tape—one day flowed into the next, but like a huge old clock stuck on the same time.

When a general makes new plans before entering the field of battle, he always feels great trepidation. We had plans for the team, and a plan for Craft as well. My experience as a writer had prepared me for failure; editors disposed of my fine prose by simply wadding up paper and tossing my words into the nearest waste basket with a grunt. So I'd tasted both the sweet and the sour of life, and was equally prepared for both as our seventh game played out.

The tremendous victory we achieved against Our Lady of Sorrows that Friday night did everything to restore our confidence—and make me look like some volleyball genius. Of course it's players who win and lose games, but the girls thought differently. Sure, they played a defensive game like St. Paul's, but they were crediting their coach for the plan. For the first time, I truly felt this was *my* team, and I could sense that they felt I was *their* coach.

We enjoyed the picnic at Rye Lake that Sunday, spending a glorious day fishing, trailing, and riding. And after that, our season really took off. We spun together win after win, each coming easier than the last. We performed so well, in fact, we ran the table, taking our final six contests by an average score of 15-3.

This wasn't only the longest winning streak in school history, it represented outstanding individual achievements, by 12 players and one cheerleader. Each victory produced a new hero or heroes: Lynn Modell against St. Peter's, Joanne Cross against Assumption, Ellen Anderson against St. Joan of Arc, Karen and Megan against St. Lucy's. Along the way, Lauren Carter amassed 76 successful serves in succession, only missing at last during a meaningless moment during another rout. And that wasn't all: The girls played defense every bit as eagerly as they'd concentrated on serving during the first half of the season. They learned to position their bodies correctly on defense, read the opposing server and adjust like professionals. They achieved real excellence at all this now, and in addition we established a rotation that counted, utilizing all our players in the games. They weren't just a team now, they were a juggernaut.

Even the school's team bulletin board reflected the desire burning inside the girls. They circled November 7—the date of the league championship game—in red, and above the date, they wrote the words, "All for one, and one for all," in crimson and gold, St. Paul's colors.

And I didn't read these seemingly overconfident gestures as negatives. The girls were still taking each game one at a time, and they'd need just two playoff victories to match up with the once again still-unbeaten St. Paul Crusaders. St. Paul's had captured the regular season with a breezy 12-0 record. St. Cyril's followed, in second, having also run the table since our game with them, finishing 11-1.

Our 10-2 record gave us third place, and assured us of at least one home playoff game, taking on sixth place St. Joe's the team we'd defeated on opening day. But St. Joe's had won five of their last six games, peaking at just the right time.

During the 25-day stretch since we found the deed, I kept the information about the deed to myself; only Joshua Gibson shared that secret with me. I was ready to burst with it, but Gibson and I had prepared the final details of our plan, which we'd reveal in the courtroom on November 6th. That date would mark exactly the six months Judge Meredith Sloan had given the town to turn up the deed.

I noticed that Mayor Light was becoming increasingly emotional as that crucial date approached. She was apparently suffering anxiety attacks, growing subject to mood swings and was getting very little sleep from what I heard. She phoned me on a daily basis, always with the same question:

"Anything new, Paul?" she'd ask, the despair in her voice pleading for an encouraging reply.

"Nothing to report yet," I said. Is wasn't quite a white lie; I didn't have anything I wanted to report. We were going to give Craft no edge whatsoever in this game. But it was painful to watch Mayor Light seemingly age overnight, as the timetable shortened with each day. I sensed her health was beginning to become a serious mater, but we needed to stick with our plan, despite the anguish she was experiencing. I wondered how Joshua Gibson would have handled this kind of pressure, but I already knew he had endured a world of it in his time.

I hadn't heard a single word from or about A.J. Craft since our meeting at Foster's Den. He'd evidently gone to a low profile hiding after enduring his failure to burn out any evidence at Gibson's cabin. Craft made no phone calls, no letters, nothing, to anyone connected to the case. Maybe he was scheming to destroy another small town's wilderness, I thought, and gain another notch on his gun, a trophy on his wall. I didn't know, no one else did, either; but it was certain he must be counting down the days, but with opposite hopes to Mayor Light's.

So there we were: A great volleyball season winding down, the court date approaching, and the conference championship, all happening within 24 hours of each other. *No coincidence here,* I thought. ***Right now, coincidences just don't exist for us.***

CHAPTER
28

My combined work and coaching schedules made it feel like I had two full-time jobs. Time was always a factor in everything I did, but it also prevented me from visiting Maureen Chapman yet, to find out more about Becky and what made this remarkable girl the way she was.

But as luck would have it, Becky happened to leave behind at practice a favorite sweater of hers, which I picked up and brought home with me. I could have given the sweater to my daughters to give to Becky at school, but I took this as my chance to personally deliver it to her home (also a client I was scheduled to meet with lived near the Chapman's).

I picked up the phone, reached Maureen Chapman and found it would be a good time to come over there and drop off the sweater. Maureen gave me directions; it was maybe a 15-minute drive from the paper. I grabbed my coat and went out the door in a flash.

The Chapmans' neighborhood was very modest, middle-class, which pretty much describes the majority of people in our township. The homes in the Chapman's neck of the woods were a bit older than those in many of the developments that had sprung up in recent years; but they had a dignified quality about them which captured the essence of our community.

The Chapmans' lived at 26 Clark, a beautiful tree-lined street, one quarter of a perfect square shared with Laurel, College, and Maple Streets. Like a wedge cut from a large cake the whole neighborhood was, with all the adjoining streets forming perfect blocks of squares.

I passed the Chapman property once, searching for a place to park, since there were no driveways on their street, it was street parking only, and all the spots seemed to be taken. I looked at my watch; it read 1:15 p.m. *Odd, that there's no place to park this hour of the day,* I thought. I circled the block once more, and finally found an opening several houses up from the Chapman's, and parked my 10-year-old Ford there.

I wasn't in any particular hurry to approach the door; I wanted to take it all in, study the property, get a good look at the surroundings. I wasn't sure what feeling overcame me as I began to look around, but decided it must be comfort, the instant I laid eyes on the Chapman house. *It's happening again,* I thought, *that peaceful feeling of inner warmth that always seems to accompany anything to do with Becky Chapman.*

The green paint on the two-story home needed a new coat, I thought as I scanned the scene. The front porch, shaded by a green awning, looked very cozy. The small front yard to my right was full of leaves, as were all the properties on this thickly laden tree-lined street. A statue of the Virgin Mary, perhaps three-feet high, was neatly tucked into the far corner of the property. *No surprise there,* I thought. A Page fence in the back yard separated the Chapman's property from the one next to it. I could see that thousands of leaves had blown back and forth between the two properties.

"Hello Paul!" came Maureen Chapman's friendly voice from the front porch. "Come on up here."

Seeing her put an immediate smile on my face. I turned and waved to her heartily as I made my way up the four brick steps and onto the porch.

"I see you had a bit of trouble parking," she said, laughing. "It's tough to get a spot around here, even in the middle of the day. There never seems to be an open spot."

I particularly admired her just then; after all, circling your own home for a parking spot could easily get frustrating. *But good cheer's the Chapman way,* I thought, *always under control and very much at ease, regardless of the circumstances.*

Maureen led me into the foyer, quickly hustled my jacket off me and hung it on a hook of the upright-coat hanger positioned in the corner. The house gave off a very warm feeling, as I glanced around each first floor room. "I thank you for bringing Becky's sweater over," Maureen smiled. "Becky'll be disappointed she didn't get to see you here, you know."

"Is that right?" I grinned. "I'm kinda fond of Becky myself."

"I'm sure you can't stay long, seeing that you have to call on a client," Maureen said, "but if you could take just a few minutes, I'd like to show you something."

"Of course," I said, "I can spare a few. What is it?"

Maureen showed me to the kitchen and unlocked a door that led to the basement. She led the way down some winding stairs, and I followed close behind her, eager to see if what she was about to show me would have anything to do with Becky, and could at least offer me a clue as to "who" this girl was.

The dim basement smelled like an old cellar. *Too much humidity,* I thought as I whiffed the damp air. Shadows danced on the far wall as Maureen reached for an overhead light, immediately changing the perspective of the room.

I could see that the small room, perhaps 10 feet square, was a makeshift library. Columns of books, neatly organized on all four walls of the room, loomed quite impressively.

Family photos, several I assumed were of Becky's father, Jack, lined the tops of each shelf, intermixed with plaques of cheery old sayings and inspirational verses.

I glanced at Maureen, who simply smiled and gestured, urging me to move toward the books. I hesitated momentarily, then took a few steps to the first column of books, off to the left. Now I could see that each of the four walls held six columns of books. I quickly guessed about 50 books would fit across each row, meaning over 300 books lined each wall, over 1,000 total, by my quick estimate.

But not just the volume of books impressed me, so did their content. The group on the left wall were clearly labeled in black marker above. "Middle-Eastern Religions," "Hinduism," "Middle-Eastern Philosophy." The second wall held topics such as "European Beliefs," "Ancient Religious Cultures of the World," and even "Mysticism." The other two walls were full of Christian titles, such as "The Crusades," "Christianity in America," "Legacy of the Popes." I saw a section marked "The Peace Corps," and a solid collection of books on Judaism, including the "Torah," and "Survivors of the Holocaust." In all, dozens of topics sprawled the shelves, each dealing in one way or another with the world's religions, literally from A to Z, I guessed.

"I'm beyond words," I gasped. "Is this **Becky's** collection?"

"Oh, yes," Maureen said matter-of-factly, "922 books and counting, all collected in just over four years. Interesting hobby, wouldn't you say, Mr. Strong?"

"Hobby?" I said, thinking not only of the great collection, but of the sheer *cost* of the books themselves. "I've never seen the likes of this anywhere. There may be more books on these subjects here than there are down at the public library. Where did you get all this stuff? Does Becky read it all?" I reached out and thumbed clumsily through a 600-page volume on Jewish customs.

"Just one at a time," she laughed. She took a quick breath, then said, "We've only purchased a few of these books. Becky's on so many publishers' mailing lists, I don't know how, but she gets these sent to her, almost daily. And yes, she *has read* all these book, all in four years' time."

That's more than four books a week, I thought, *four books a week—FOR FOUR YEARS!*

"Mr. Strong," Maureen said, "do you recall when Becky spoke to the people at Chadwick Manor?"

"Of course, I'll never forget it," I said.

"Good. Do you also recall that she quoted from memory, didn't need to look in the Bible for the verse?"

"Yes, that simply amazed me," I said. "I've heard the girls whisper that she has the *entire Bible* memorized—is that true?"

She smiled again, her eyes piercing my soul. "Well, I can't say she's got it all memorized, but she can pick any verse or topic out just like that," she said, snapping her fingers. "It's one of the truly amazing gifts she's received from God."

"And these books," I said, "922 in four years' time? You're sure she's read all of them?"

"Yes, she has," Maureen said without hesitation. "Becky spends almost all of her free time with these books, taking notes, cross-referencing one book to another. She even writes letters and comments to the authors. Look, here are some of the responses she's gotten back."

Maureen pointed to several manila folders stuffed with correspondents from around the world. "Those are mostly letters and cards from the authors of these books—intriguing responses to Becky's equally intriguing comments," she said. She handed me a folder, and I thumbed through it quickly. I was astounded at the sheer volume of letters this 13-year old girl had received.

I shook my head several times from side-to-side as I read

the notes. "Where does she find the time?" I said. "And why is she so obsessed with all this?"

"Please, Mr. Strong," Maureen frowned. "Don't call it an **obsession.** I prefer to think of it as her **passion.** There's a difference, you know."

"I suppose there is," I replied. "I wouldn't have thought of it that way. But you must admit, this is a bit out of the ordinary—no, a *lot* out of the ordinary stuff for a 13-year old girl to be interested in."

As I waited for Maureen's reaction, I thought, *I don't want to sound out of line here. Maybe I'm sounding too harsh.* Maureen raised her eyebrows at me and said, "You know, Mr. Strong, Becky has had no ordinary life, not by any stretch of the imagination. Yes, you know that her father died when she was nine, leaving us alone to face the world together. But through all the trials we've faced without a husband or a father, we've always had each other to cling to. So perhaps, Mr. Strong, this is Becky's way of feeling closer to him, by learning more about where he might be, and what happens to the immortal spirit. No, I don't believe she's obsessed at all. She's *interested,* she's hungry for truth and meaning, and to share and give back. That's all, nothing more. And by the grace of God she'd been granted a truly amazing gift to share the knowledge she's gained, together with the ability to put it all into words, meaningful, powerful words, to make people feel good about themselves, help them heal and grow, gain confidence, and yes, to even help them get closer to the truth themselves."

Maureen reflected a moment, then said, "I know you know about Becky's 'aura.' She's read all about them too. All of this, everything she's done with people and animals, I believe it's all tied into her father's passing somehow. The moment he died, I believe, I could see a transformation begin in her. It's simply a miracle, all this, Mr. Strong. Now we all just sit back and watch what happens next with her. Isn't it exciting?"

I could see the excitement gleaming in her eyes. ***Whoa, what a speech!*** I thought. ***She really...needed to let me in on all this.*** But she wasn't finished. "You know, Mr. Strong, since Becky's dad died, she's become so strong in her beliefs, yet she never 'throws' herself at anyone, she never abandons that innocence 13-year old girls should have. You are the ***only person*** except for Becky and myself to even know of this room and what it contains, what she insists on learning about. She never brags about any of the knowledge she's gained from these books. She's very private, Mr. Strong, very private in her beliefs; but she's probably, no, she ***is,*** the strongest and kindest person I know in this world. She is my ***angel.***"

Amazing as it all seemed, I couldn't disagree with a word of what Maureen had said. Yes, Becky kept her knowledge to herself, that was for sure. Yet from the seniors at Chadwick Manor, all the way down to Millie Parker—they all knew in one way or another about Becky Chapman's gifts.

"Maureen," I said softly, "I will certainly keep this room a confidential matter between us, I assure you." I paused, rubbing my hand across my chin. At that moment I wanted to tell Maureen how I was feeling about being smack in the middle of a part of Becky's life—at a sort of crossroads— and of the real warmth I felt whenever Becky was around me. I wanted to let her know I was sure we were only see-ing the beginning of what was to come, for Becky. But I couldn't. Maureen turned toward the stairs, and I simply fol-lowed her up, plucked my coat from the rack, and headed for the door.

When I got there, Maureen said, "Mr. Strong, I respect your judgment. I'd like to know how you feel personally about all this—you know, about the things you've person-ally experienced with Becky."

Though all of this had just crossed my mind, I wasn't expecting the question. Nonetheless, she'd asked me, and I felt I had to let her know some of my feelings on the subject.

"Boy, that's the question, isn't it?" I said, fumbling for just the right words. How could they flow smoothly, though, since I would be revealing for the first time to anyone my feelings about Becky Chapman?

"Well," I began "that day during practice, when Becky broke her hand, I was overcome with emotion, kneeling next to her, watching her go through the pain. But through it all— and especially when she raised her hand with the 'sign,' I somehow felt very much at peace, very relaxed. Almost *too relaxed.*"

Maureen smiled and folded her arms across her chest.

I went on: "Then at the hospital, talking to Millie Parker, the conversation in the parking lot about your husband's death, the story about the animals, the stage presence she had at Chadwick Manor, even the way I saw the girls on the team respond to her and adore her—it all began to make sense. It seems she has a way of bringing out the good in everyone she's around."

"And I'll tell you one more thing," I said, looking side-to-side to see if we were being watched. "I've had many other strange things happen to me lately, so many...coincidences. I'm beginning to think I'm part of some grand scheme, and that the reason is wrapped up in Becky. I feel...well, that her broken hand was the first event in a chain of events, and it was *actually supposed to happen.*"

"Amen!" Maureen said in a kind of awe. "You *do understand,* don't you?"

"I don't know," I said. "Understand what?"

"You understand, coach Paul, that everything that happens, happens for a reason, and that we are all players on life's great playing field. Some people, *most* people, they have no idea why things happen. They haven't learned to *tune in.* You, on the other hand, have had the window opened to you, and now you understand, because you've kept that window open, and you've learned to *read the signs.*"

CHAPTER
29

Our playoff game against St. Joe's was the school's first venture into league playoffs. In our ten-year volleyball history, regular season play was all we knew. But we broke virgin ground this late October day, and our fans gave the girls a welcoming salute to remember.

This would be our final home game of the year, and the final home game in ten young players' lives, since they'd be graduating to high school next year. So this day was set aside especially for them; this was the only school most of them had ever attended, and this would be the final athletic event in most of their careers at St. Luke's.

The events prior to the contest played out in line with tradition. Each of the ten was introduced by Monsignor Sean Cahill, and the scratchy sounds of our old public address system cracked with every word of his Irish brogue. Upon hearing her name, each girls was on display for a few moments at center court, and each girls's parents presented her with a bouquet of flowers. Then Sister Fran came forward and fastened a school pin on each jersey, a little old relic of a thing, a cross in the middle bordered by the "St. Luke" logo.

This touching tradition, was attended by entire families, including grand parents, siblings, past players and faculty. Attendance for this contest bordered on breaking the fire code laws for people allowed in the building, and the heat from so many bodies was intense, to say the least. Able-bodied men had hustled in extra chairs; 50 or more were neatly lined on the stage, which was usually open for our games.

People were asked to slide in right, to make room for others—kind of like church at Christmas, we were full to the brim.

I knew this atmosphere would lend even more excitement to the game itself—a special air of intense excitement in the place. And our fans had more than just tradition to look forward to; a game was to follow these festivities, as there always was; but this one had special meaning.

The one true surprise during the pre-game presentations, came to Becky Chapman. I'd been wondering who, if anyone at all, would take her father's place at the presentations. School tradition called for a man and a woman to represent each girl on this night, and Becky was the only girl of our 13 to be part of a one-parent family.

The presentations took place alphabetical order, Ellen Anderson first, Lauren Carter next, then Becky Chapman. The school had arranged for photos to be taken as each girl came forward. (The ceremonies would add up to a good hour before the contest, and build up the game's excitement hugely).

Throughout the season, each of this team's girls had each kept a lucky charm of some sort, and now they carried them out for the photos. Most of these "charms" were stuffed animals from bygone days, scruffy looking critters, some torn and aged. But I remembered seeing during the regular season only 12 items actually brought to the games. One was always missing, but I'd forgotten to ask the girls where number 13 was.

Becky Chapman's name was called, and she walked to center court, greeted by gentle applause. Father Sean droned his message: "And now, presenting Becky Chapman, her mother, Maureen, and a 'team' friend, the former mayor of our town, Mr. Joshua Gibson."

The old man hobbled out from amid the throng, Maureen holding his arm tightly. The two made their way to Becky, and I could swear Gibson looked proud as a father giving his daughter up for marriage. Becky greeted them with bear hugs, and Joshua Gibson politely handed Becky her flowers.

On the bench, the girls *aahed*, as surprised as I was. When Becky's turn was done, each other girl on the team came over and gave the old mayor a tight hug. They loved the old guy, we all did, and we were deeply touched by the mayor's incredible gesture, standing in for her dad.

During the commotion, I now noticed it was Becky who carried no stuffed animal or charm with her. I quickly asked a few of the girls, "Where's Becky's lucky charm?" Several shrugged their shoulders. One said, "Oh, she has what she needs." A voice to my left said, "She has her lucky charm." But this made little sense to me; Becky had nothing with her, at least nothing in sight, so I decided to forget about it.

The ceremonies finished with the usual group photo. The team's parents returned to their seats, and a huge rush of noise spilled from the multitude of voices. It was finally game time!

I could see the tension built up over the past hour only on the St. Joe's girls' faces. They looked nervous, and their warm-ups looked slow. In contrast, we looked sharp, quick, and each of our girls' faces wore a determined look. We were ready.

I could have predicted the outcome from those determined looks alone. St. Joe's went down easily, as had all the others in our current seven-game winning streak. Our Karen buried them with sizzling serves early on, and her skill, combined with our huge home crowd's reaction, took our foes out of any rhythm they might have generated. The final scores, 15-3, 15-2, evidenced dominance we showed this day.

A party, still another of the many cherished school traditions for this day, followed, but it, too, was unlike other past ones. The girls talked about winning the second playoff game in two days—and of meeting up with St. Paul's in the championship game. Little clusters of adults surrounded each player, talking championships, their pride in the girls, the "hand" signal and its meaning.

There would also be talk of the deed; questions about that would be directed to the star of the show, Joshua Gibson. And Gibson would be careful with his answers; after all, he was a politician, and so he knew the fine art of answering questions with appropriate rhetoric.

I knew he must be as eager as I was to announce to the world what we knew. But we were holding our tongues and doing our best to direct out attention to the business at hand—our league playoffs.

So things were fairly simple; I stayed in one place most of the night, taking the same questions from dozens of our fans. They wanted as much as we did to get to the championship game, but they weren't aware of a particular little detail: St. Cyril's Lions were our next opponent. That game would be a whole different affair from the massacre we'd enjoyed tonight. For one thing, we'd be traveling to their gym, which would be full of *their* fans. Our home advantage comforts would be only a memory. We would need to play above the pressure that always follows teams on the road in playoff games.

But I had unwavering confidence in these girls. We had just won out first playoff game in school history, and looking at it from that standpoint, our season would end well if that was as far as we got. After all, you might say we had "no business being in" the semi-final game, as one of just four teams left standing in a 13-team league. Even if it had ended tonight, our season would have been a success. If the season were to end at St. Cyril's, the same would hold true.

Still, nothing would be sweeter than to beat St. Cyril's—and then match skills with St. Paul's, assuming they, too, won their semi-final game.

Yes, I could play mind games like these because this evening had been such a rousing success. But I knew deep down that we'd need a miracle of sorts to beat one of these teams, let alone both of them.

So I mingled with the crowd, finally reaching Joshua Gibson whom I found surrounded by excited people. I could see he was loving the attention, and that people were loving him in return. Getting his ear moments later, I seized a short conversation with the mayor, during which he promised he would attend our next game, and, if we were victorious, the championship game, too.

"Looks like I'm good luck," he quipped. He'd enjoyed the game immensely, he said—from the "Hand" banner, the girls' play, and the people's enthusiasm. "From this game on, I'm hooked," he said. "Paul, you've got a *very good* team here. Very focused and talented, they all played well."

He went on to tell me how proud I should be of my team, and how glad he was that Becky had invited him to come that day. He left me humbled, telling me how proud he was of me, how happy and privileged he felt that our paths in life had crossed. "This was all destined to happen, Paul," he smiled knowingly.

Just then another group of parents came to greet the mayor, so I excused myself and mingled some more. Mulling over Mayor Gibson's comments, I realized: *It's I who feel privileged—privileged to even be in the same company with this man, privileged to be coaching this group of girls, privileged to have had Becky Chapman's path cross mine. The mayor's right—this is all destiny!*

CHAPTER

30

O f course, all the news about our smashing victory spread throughout the school like wildfire, the girls told me later. Maybe we'd won just a single playoff game, but it was big news. Sister Fran herself led off the following morning's school announcements by honoring the team with the game's results. She was throwing kind of a curve, because she'd never before included sports in her announcements, other than sharing when tryouts would be, or any cancellations of after-school practices. This was a first, and showed us that even Sister Fran had now gotten caught up with our team's success.

Though she tried to conceal her newfound zeal, you could hear the note of pride in her voice: "And in volleyball playoffs last evening, our young girls showed St. Joe's a thing or two, by winning with convincing margins of 15-3, 15-2. Now, our girls will be playing at St. Cyril's tomorrow night, so let's all get out there and support them. Congratulations, girls!"

She then clicked off the microphone—her only announcement that day. All down the halls of the school, each classroom erupted in a spontaneous ovation, 270 hands clapping at once, and 270 voices chirping, even through all the brick walls.

On the work front, I had other matters to attend to. I

learned that Mayor Light had fallen ill and been rushed to County Hospital. *A panic attack, most likely,* I thought. It turned out to be my assignment for the day. I was to check on her condition and report on it in my next column.

I had to admit, as I prepared myself for the short trip to County, that I felt partly responsible for her distress. She was undoubtedly in a knot over the issue of the deed. I'd sensed this from the tone in her voice when she'd phoned me like clockwork each and every day. She'd been losing weight, too, her stout figure turning first to svelte, then plummeting as if a cancer had invaded her body. She looked frail now, her cheeks were gaunt, her skin sagged; and her eyes looked as empty as her body seemed wasted.

There'd already been talk in town of sending her on a leave of absence, or even of calling for her resignation. I paid little attention to these rumors; my job was to assemble the facts. I closed the door to my office and rang up Joshua Gibson. We had decided that under no circumstances would we divulge the information that we now had the deed in our possession. But now this story had taken a new turn, and I thought we needed to extend our little secret to Mayor Light.

Though the door was closed, I still spoke softly into the phone as to not draw any possible attention to our exchange. We were still weary of A.J. Craft. He had remained silent for some time now, but we were cautious of his "reach," even choosing our words carefully over the phone, should the line possibly be tapped. If so, any listener would suspect nothing from the contents of this short chat. I felt as if we were plotting a perfect crime, and felt confident we were thinking everything out with utmost care.

It was a short drive to the hospital. As a formality I pulled my press credentials from my wallet on the way through the front door, but that wasn't necessary. Annie Shea, my assistant coach, was working this particular shift, caring for the mayor.

When she saw me, Annie took me into a small waiting room, away from some of the other media types lurking in the hallway.

"I'm glad to see you Paul," Annie frowned. "The mayor's been repeating your name, and saying, '200 acres,' and talking about resigning. She's not making much sense, I'm afraid."

"What's her physical condition?" I asked.

"She's suffering from dehydration and exhaustion—and she's anemic. They're taking some more tests," Annie said, "cause they think she may have developed ulcers, too."

"I really need to see her," I said. "Can you get me in there?"

She looked toward the group of other reporters. They'd be a problem. Camera crews from the local stations were setting up equipment down the hall from Mayor Light's room. One, plain-clothed assistant was assigned to her door. "Only family and hospital workers are allowed inside," Annie sighed. "No cameras, no media."

My big break came at that moment. A spokesman for the mayor arrived on the scene and announced that he would field questions from the reporters in the conference room two hallways down. The anxious media broke their little camp and began hauling cameras and microphones toward the big room. Soon they'd vacated the hallway, and the coast was clear, except for the mayor's assistant.

"I've gotta get in, somehow Annie," I said. "What can we do?"

"You come with me," boomed a voice behind me—Millie Parker's.

"Millie, I was wondering where you were," I grinned. "Am I glad to see you!"

"There's no time for pleasantries," she growled, "just get over here!"

She hustled me into a storage closet where dozens of white lab coats hung. *Aha!* I knew what was about to happen; I'd seen it several times in the movies.

"Here, put this on," Millie said. She seemed totally unconcerned about possible consequences. "Then come with me and ask no questions."

She tossed a stethoscope around my neck and pushed a clipboard into my hands. She placed a green cap over my head to help shield my identity, and we were on our way.

As we approached the room, I kept my head buried in the clipboard, to look like I was concentrating on a document I in truth knew nothing about. I took a quick glance toward the assistant, to see if he would recognize me. He didn't. I was glad of that; my face was well known, because a head shot of me sat above every column I wrote. I may have gained easy entry into the room, but it was one of the most heart-pounding episodes of my life—both exciting and nerve racking. When I'd cleared the assistant, a rush of extreme exhilaration engulfed me.

"We did it," I softly to Annie as we both entered the room. I peered down at the mayor. She was hooked up to intravenous tubes and monitors, recording data flashing numbers and lines. She looked woozily sedated, but she evidently saw through my disguise, and she waved me over to her bedside.

I sat on a chair next to her bed. And for the first time in months I noticed a faint smile on her face. *The sedative?* I wondered.

"Paul," she said monotonously, "I don't know what to do. That deed will never be found, we've lost, that land is as good as gone."

I shushed her with a wagging finger. Her eyebrows stretched, she nodded. I took my notepad and wrote, "Say nothing, the room may be bugged." In the corner of my eye I saw Annie, staying close to the door, acting as a lookout. I could still hear Millie Parker doing her best to keep the assistant occupied, so I hurried on. I quickly scribbled the following: "Sorry it's come to this. I'll explain later. Have something to show you."

When she'd read this, the mayor's eyes signaled me to continue. I pulled a photocopy of the deed from my pocket. (Of course, Gibson and I had hidden the original in a safe place, making two copies, one for each of us.)

I placed the deed copy into the mayor's hands, and just then the sound of voices began echoing through the hallway.

The mayor's eyes darted over the document. As she read, her breathing shifted from shallow to super speed, as if she'd just run a great race, and crossed the finish line out of breath. The voices drew closer, and Annie whispered frantically, "We *have* to *go now!*"

I grabbed the deed from the mayor and folded it back into my pocket. She raised her arms and muttered, "Hallelujah!" I said, "You swear you'll keep this a secret until the court date?" "No problem," she said, and we high-tailed it out of there.

We were turning left after walking out the door just as the throng of media hounds approached from the right. I felt like a great thief who'd gotten away with the loot.

Down the hall I removed my costume, gave great thanks to Annie and Millie, and headed for the mayor's spokesman. I apologized for my tardiness and asked for all the details of the press conference he'd just given. All business, he filled me in on the mayor's condition very matter-of-factly. Then I admired his carefully chosen hype:

"Mayor Light is simply suffering from slight exhaustion. We are certain she will be released in one or two days. There is no cause for concern over this matter."

I returned to the paper armed with both the official announcement and the truth. The column I would write would be only the frosting on the cake. The real truth would have to wait until next week's court date, when A.J. Craft would face the beginning of the downfall of his little empire.

CHAPTER
31

"The Dungeon," was an apt name indeed for St. Cyril's gym. It was located down a flight of 15 creaky wooden stairs in a building adjacent to the old church, situated on a slab of old linoleum, cracked and brittle. The ancient place smelled as old as it looked: A musty odor of a closed attic hung on it like a fog that never rises. The wooden chairs wore splinters, seat cushions were torn, the walls and windows were smudged brown as can be.

The volleyball court's dimensions were considerably smaller than other schools'; in fact, they failed by a long shot to meet the standards, but it seemed the officials never measured them. The ceilings were no more than 30 feet high, dangling lights hanging from the rafters. Every visiting team knew what they were up against playing in this building. If any team in the league enjoyed a home court advantage, St. Cyril's did. They had a grip on the trajectory they needed to serve accurately and the soft passes they'd have to make. But for everyone else, playing here was a nightmare. But play here we had to, and we understood the great challenges that lay ahead of us. We'd been warned of all the hazards, and we'd set our practices accordingly.

Our girls worked on serving as straight as possible, and eliminating almost all "arc" from either our serving or passing. Still our preparation in our own gym was no comparison to our warm-ups now, in front of a huge crowd from both schools.

St. Cyril's was as used to being in championship games as St. Paul's was at winning them. They'd achieved the "honored" distinction of being league "bridesmaid," as the perennial second-best team they'd been. They'd gone to the finals six of the last seven years, always only to lose to Daryl Reed and his mighty Crusaders. So I knew they had to be as sick at finishing second as we were to finishing last, but they fully expected to get to the big dance once again with a victory tonight.

Joshua Gibson once again came as our guest; I let him sit next to me on the bench. He seemed reserved as game time approached. "Pay no attention to me, I'll just watch," he said, as we were about to begin our pre-game prayer. (Prayer was another of our traditions. Each girl took a turn before each game, offering God a few words before we met our present challenge. On opening day I as coach said the first prayer, beginning with a line or two of thanks and of encouragement, to show the girls the way.)

This would be our game number 14, so every girl had led the team in prayer once, except for Becky Chapman, whose turn came tonight. The "usual" prayer might be something like, "Keep us free from injury," or, "Protect us during and after this game." The girls didn't pray from books or bibles; their prayers were personal, each girl's coming from her own heart and mind. I had looked forward to this turn of Becky's, knowing she wouldn't speak ordinary words. We knelt together at the side of the bench, huddled in a tight circle, and joined hands. I announced that Becky would lead, and we bowed our heads as one, waiting for her to speak.

Her clear voice began her prayer clearly and precisely. "God, I thank you for the opportunity we each have to be a small part of this great team. I thank you for coach Paul, coach Annie, and coach Emily. They've been great teachers, patient and understanding. They've been fair and kind-hearted. I thank you for the great friends I've made this year, such great teammates, on and off the court."

As Becky went on, she glanced at each girl: "I just thank you for Karen and Megan, Lauren, Lynn, Sharon, Joanne, Mandy, Katrina, Maggie, Colleen, Janet and Ellen. Amen."

Becky lifted her head, and her look swiftly turned from piety to fierce intensity. She said, "Ready?" and the girls shouted, "Yes!" then she led us in the team cheer, louder than I'd ever heard it in all our previous 13 games.

Our six starting players took the court; the others returned to the bench. Becky, seated on the furthest chair from me, led the cheers, her voice somehow soaring above all the incredible noise echoing off the tight corners of the old "Dungeon."

The contest that followed starkly contrasted our first game with St. Cyril's, which we'd lost in a three-game heartbreaker. That "coming out" game for Katrina Glover had been sticking in her craw, I knew, ever since that last ball skimmed off her fingertips, and rolled out of bounds. This was her get-even game, and I'd planned to play her from the start, to get her nerves settled right away.

As it turned out, this move was wise—Katrina served, passed and bumped like an all-star. She glided, slid, dove, leaped, cheered, in every way playing beyond herself on this night. We'd have no need for late game heroics or game-saving plays tonight, and Katrina would be the star.

We needed only two games to stun the hosts, 15-6, 15-8, vaulting us into the championship game. Pure bliss flooded our veins as the final ball fell at the feet of a dejected opponent. Joyous bedlam ruled on our side of the net, as the girls mobbed each other, jumping with joy.

I could only imagine what the scene would be like after one more victory as Annie and Emily buried me with hugs. This feeling was special, but it wasn't *final,* and I recovered my composure and made my way toward St. Cyril's coach Allyson Buchek, for the traditional post-game handshake.

Allyson and I met halfway, as we battled the dozens of people on the court. Allyson was all smiles on her approach, holding her hands out like a mother to a son. I returned her smile, managing to hold back my glee somewhat. In no way did I want to gloat; I was as happy as my girls were, but I was greeting a coach who'd gotten so close for so long, and had just lost a game she'd expected to win.

"Your girls played great, simply great," Allyson said with grace, embracing me and patting me on the back. "Where did they learn to play defense like that?"

I began to mutter something, but Allyson didn't want to hear me. She leaned close and set her mouth near my ear. "I want you to kick his sorry behind!" she yelled against the din around us. "I'll be there for *that* game—we all will."

She leaned away and looked me in the eye, winking. Then she retreated to her bench to face yet another of her teams to have fallen at the end. I watched her for a moment. She did this difficult task very well. I tried to put myself in her place for a moment. One week from today, I, too, would either be standing as a winner, or squatting as a runner-up. I decided I wouldn't speak the term, "loser," in any way, shape, or form before or after our upcoming game, regardless of the outcome. This team was a *winner.*

After the game, we headed for ice cream at "The Cold Eskimo," our town's most popular after-dinner spot. We honked our horns along the way, waved to total strangers, and did silly other things, things expected from victorious 13-year-old girls, if not their coaches and parents.

At least 100 of us converged on the 200-seat building. Danny Blair, the owner, announced the result of the game to the 100 or so patrons who'd gathered before we came. Free ice cream followed for the 13 girls and their coaches. Danny Blair was generous that night for a reason: His daughter

Carol, had played for St. Luke's some time ago, and suffered through two dreadful seasons of losing. Danny, too, was tasting victory, from his perspective, so he bustled about, scooping ice cream and whistling a happy tune.

That evening, I thought about that very phenomenon: A team is *your* team, no matter how separated by years or distance you become. My dad rooted for certain teams when I was young. In turn, those teams became my teams, win or lose, regardless of how many players retired or were traded, eventually replacing the one I grew up with, with a whole new team. None of that mattered; they were still *my* team.

So this was Danny Blair's team, too, and the team of all the other parents who'd paraded their children through our school. No matter if their kids played volleyball or not, this was a proud moment for all at or affiliated with St. Luke's.

I wondered how many of our fans, past and present, would be attending the championship game. News travels fast around here. The game itself would be played at a neutral sight, the local 2,500-seat college gym would host the event. Would 200 attend? Three hundred? Maybe more? Surely not less—we had enjoyed such fine support during the season, maybe attendance would be as high as 400. Time and the event would tell.

The upcoming week would prove the most emotional and memorable of my life. Things would be played out on two courts—one in a court of law; the other inside a gymnasium. What I'd originally regarded as personal had now gone far beyond that in my mind. No, this wasn't just Strong vs. Craft and Strong vs. Reed anymore. This was an entire township vs. Craft, and an entire league facing Reed. Both bullies were about to face Judgment Day; the repercussions of their past actions were about to catch them. Joshua Gibson's prediction would be, I thought, accurate to the word: "It can all end the same way—one deal gone sour, one loss, and the questions start to come."

CHAPTER
32

Mayor Light was released two days later, looking alert for the first time in months. She soon again tackled tasks that had been hanging over her office, apologizing to the public for her recent absence from effort. This was a risky strategy for her political future, but she'd been renewed by my sudden, great news.

I met with her mid-week at her office, and, as constant interruptions by her staff gave us no private time together, we decided to duck out for lunch. We went for takeout at a local hamburger stand and ate in my car. I could see her appetite had returned with a vengeance; she swiftly downed two cheeseburgers, a large fries, a large shake, and a hot apple pie, washed down with a large diet coke.

As she ravaged through the meal, she paused now and then to discuss how we'd found the deed, how long I'd had it in my possession, and what the next step should be. It was great to see she was "alive" again.

During those moments, I reflected on how powerfully the human thought process affect a person's physical well being. Mayor Light had struggled for months with mental turmoil, landing at last in the hospital. Then she'd heard encouraging news, and that alone had healed both her mind and her body. Her position was a difficult one, I knew, requiring a very special person who could take its daily blows well.

But, I thought as I watched her rummage through her food, this woman wasn't made for this job, and she should by no means seek a second term. I hoped she'd just walk away come next November, while she still had her health.

Immediately, though, I felt a pang of regret. I should, as a neutral observer to any campaign, include my opinion in future columns, but I wouldn't relish that part of my job. After all, Mayor Light was a friend of mine. Still, if I were to remain impartial and show no favoritism toward any candidate, maybe that would end our friendship.

This was the very quandary no longer having to decide about the land put Mayor Light in: She was safe now from being turned out of office for deciding wrongly. She had dodged that bullet...

With these thought of mine in the background, Mayor Light and I reviewed the strategy Joshua Gibson and I had planned. She seemed almost giddy and eager with glee, contemplating how the tables would be turned on A.J. Craft, on November 6, 1979, at noon.

Back at city hall, I dropped off the mayor at the rear entrance. She waved back at me before entering the building, to resume her business. The hop in her step struck a grin in my mind. I wasn't to see her again till the formidable team of Strong, Gibson and Light met to take on A.J. Craft and company.

I decided to return to the newsroom the long way; taking the extra few miles to St. Luke's school would cost me no more than 10 minutes, and I was well ahead of schedule. It was a crisp Autumn day, the kind of day where the scent of Winter lurks, but that Old Man still waits his turn. It looked like it might snow, but no flurries flew this day. The thermostat read 32 degrees; the wind spun the remaining dead leaves like miniature tornadoes; the life and death of each flashing like fire flies, instantly disappearing, reappearing, disappearing again.

The school's brick building already wore the signage I expected to see, a huge "CONGRATULATIONS!" banner covering the entire length of the façade, clearly visible from a quarter mile away. "Go Eagles! All for one, one for all!" underscored the headline in four-foot green and gold letters, the "hand" symbol trailing the final letter.

It's starting, I thought, *all the pre championship hype is beginning, the school's totally absorbed as one, from the janitors to the women in the kitchen, to the five-year-old kindergarteners.* This would be the most "involved," the most "together" time, in the old school's history.

I pulled into the school's parking lot. Curiosity had gotten the better of me, for one reason: The league had allotted 200 advance tickets for the championship game to both schools, for sale to the students, faculty, and parents at half price. This was common practice for the league; the 200 tickets were usually just enough, or a few too many. With walk-up sales on game day, a crowd of 600 might be expected for the finals.

That would be a good crowd, I thought, but we'd probably do better this time. St. Luke's alone had 270 kids enrolled, and all of them, from kindergarten through the eighth grade, were team boosters now.

The glass door to the main entrance of the school opened into a small waiting area; a small window was cut into the left wall alongside it. A black buzzer was situated to the left of the window, prompting visitors to "Push for Attention."

Nellie Nelson, the school secretary, would undoubtedly answer if I pushed the buzzer, but not quickly. She never seemed to notice any activity in this partition. I thought of Nellie with affection. Her half-eye reading glasses, firmly planted at the end of her nose, were a facial fixture. Her 1960-era typewriter, rusty and brown, always clicked away, like some ticker tape machine stuck on "run." Her attitude when she heard the old buzzer would be as consistent as her general attitude: She was indifferent to all and everyone; and always, *always,* when she got around to opening the small window, she'd peer through the open glass like a guard at the door of Emerald City in "The Wizard of Oz," and announce with one word, and one word alone, "Yes?"

Now, I may not have been the most frequent visitor to the school in the past, I figured I had been through this routine 20 or 30 times in the past nine years; yet the exchange between us had never wavered. It was truly comical —from my perspective, of course. Nellie probably found my intrusions rather annoying...

But I quickly found out how amazingly a winning team of 13-year-old volleyball players can change the attitude of even a person set in her ways. I reached for the buzzer, but for once Nellie was way ahead of me. She'd already pulled herself out from her sliding chair, smiled, waved, and removed those plastic spectacles. She slid the window to the right, and said in a high, excited voice, "Coach Paul—come on in!"

I confess I was startled. I couldn't get my body to move at first, my brain didn't seem connected with it. Nellie stood her ground and waved me in once more. My mind at last caught up with Nellie's unusual actions, but I didn't think to make a joke of it, I simply said, "Well, o.k."

When I got inside, Nellie met me as I rounded the short corner to the office. She took me by the arm and led me down the hallway towards Sister Fran Drake's office. My, was this usually reserved prototypical secretary of the 70's ever transformed! She acted more like a guide, I thought, as we hustled down the hallway strewn with green and gold banners everywhere in sight.

Sister Fran's door was open. "Paul," she said. "What brings you here today?"

Nellie said goodbye and briskly walked away. I nodded my head toward her. "What's gotten in to Nellie?"

"Volleyball!" Sister Fran said without hesitation. "It's just what the doctor ordered, don't you agree, Paul?"

"Yes," I said unthinkingly. "It sure is gratifying to see what winning can do to a person."

"Now that you're here—you stopped in at a perfect time. I just left a message at your office. I have two things to tell you." She pulled from the top drawer of her desk a manila folder marked "VOLLEYBALL LETTERS." She handed it to me and said, "Would you sit down for a moment?"

"What's this?" I asked, puzzled. I opened the clasp on the folder. Inside, a quick glance showed me letters of congratulations from the 10 other schools in the league. (Of course there was none from St. Paul's). Carbon copies were addressed to "Coach Paul Strong."

The letters were signed by each school's head coach, athletic director, Monsignor and Mother Superior. Handwritten notes of encouragement had been penned to Sister Fran; all these "old buddies" of hers wishing her the best. So even the old religious guard were aware of our achievements, and they, too, were rooting for us as one.

The letters' tones clearly reflected their writers' mood. "Beat St. Paul's!" was their underlying message, carefully omitted from the texts, yet more than clear from their spirits.

"They want us to win, Paul, purred Sister Fran's firm voice. "And they all want tickets."

Sister Fran then told me that all our 200 tickets had been snatched up in 20 minutes, and she had ordered 600 more from the league secretary. This was unprecedented in league history, and her request had been quickly granted; the tickets would be delivered later in the day.

I then asked, "Are you in charge of distributing tickets to the other schools? I mean, are some of those 600 tickets ours, or are they all for the other schools?"

She wagged a finger. "Oh no, I'm afraid you don't

understand. We took a count this morning after the first 200 tickets went like hotcakes. Those 600 are for our school *alone*, Paul. We've had requests for nearly 800 tickets!"

I slumped back into my seat. "Wow! That has to be some sort of record, don't you think?"

"Indeed," she nodded, smiling broadly.

"What about the other schools? Are they getting more tickets, too?"

"Each of the 10 other schools need 100 each," she replied. "Every coach wants to be present for this game, and they're all bringing their teams with them."

I did some quick math: 800 from our school, 200 from St. Paul's, 100 each from the 10 other schools. "That's 2,000 tickets!" I cried.

"*Advance* tickets," said Sister. "That doesn't count tickets that'll be sold on game day as well."

Whew! The hottest ticket in town—eighth grade volleyball, I thought. *Two thousand plus people for eighth grade volleyball.* "Sister," I said aloud, "I'd like to have a good old-fashioned pep rally on Friday night, after school. And I'd like to send what you've just told me home with all the children today. We need your o.k., of course..."

"A pep rally?" she said. "I haven't been to one since I was a youngster. Splendid idea, coach—the perfect way to send the girls off to their great battle."

"I'll let you know more later in the week," I said. "We have our final practice Thursday after school."

We said a few parting words, and I walked away as if on air. What a schedule I had before me: practice on Thursday, pep rally Friday, courtroom Saturday, championship game Sunday night! It was like a great symphony building to a crescendo, each day striking a new, mighty chord. A true championship week was set for me, the girls and the mayors, its tunes destined to be stored in our minds' great memory vaults forever.

CHAPTER

33

B y Thursday, ticket sales for the game were official: 2,000 tickets had gone out, all of them had been sold. Five hundred remained for general purchase on game day, and the college had been notified to install another 300 "emergency" seats.

This was unprecedented for any girls' scholastic sport back then, though we knew well the underlying reasons for the great throng ready to converge on our community college in a matter of days.

Of course, more than a third of the tickets had been snatched up by our school, which in itself surprised me. The remaining seats, purchased in blocks of 100 by each team in our league, had already swelled the usual count by 1,000. Letters received by Sister Fran indicated all 1,000 of these people would be rooting for us on volleyball "judgment day." *We need to give them what they'll be coming to see,* I thought.

At the same time, of course, I knew we were up against it. Daryl Reed and his volleyball machine had won 132 straight games, nearly all of them easily. They'd won eight consecutive league championships, and lost only five games in 10 years. They'd be expected to win this year, too—and win handily.

No, those thoughts never left me, not for a minute, neither

did the memory of our loss to them earlier in the season. Like anyone coaching a huge underdog, my expectations should have been "stay close and keep the score respectable." But they weren't. My only thoughts were these: *Ignore the past and the odds, concentrate on the present, exult in the future.*

I'd take these words with me all game day, for to me these inspiring words symbolized our great 1979 team, sharing billing equal indeed to "All for one, and one for all." And I'd carry them forward for future teams to learn and be inspired by, too. They were words spoken from the heart, and words spoken from the heart carry truth discernible to anyone searching for it. they were words answering questions, short verses on inspiration, that would be spoken and written to guide many through uncertainty, for the message they carried was every bit as powerful as any new drill I might have taught on the field of play.

I gave the girls this as my final message at the conclusion of that final practice on Thursday afternoon. I was satisfied that this brisk 90-minute practice had produced our sharpest results all season. Only a few of the 240 marks we charted were misses; our defense was equally sharp, passing and bumping with precision and accuracy. And I could see the players' moods were boosted by the results—each face showed intensity, eagerness and solid preparation. Every girls knew her part, every girl knew she'd take part and give her all. This team was ready for that last battle.

I was pleased especially with one footnote to that final practice; Becky Chapman's hard cast had been removed earlier in the day, and replaced by a soft, more flexible one. Her hand had healed nicely, and she wore her new contraption mostly for added protection during her shattered bones' final healing process. Becky could move the hand freely now, though it was still tender to the touch. In my mind, her hand's freedom, its bondage was sort of like our season in miniature, and that irony I took as still another sign. Now, I thought, I was reading "the signs" with more clarity and vision, almost like I had a sixth sense.

But Becky's serving at practice was the one thing about the team that truly showed little signs of improvement, even on this final day when everything else was clicking. Still, Becky continued her determined assault on the gray wall. Her left hand followed through each ball, though she still failed on close to nine of 10 attempts. I figured the right side of her brain had never clearly gotten through to her left hand; it was something like a bad telephone connection. Her brain gave the command, but the action failed with persistent consistency.

But her refusal to be discouraged was a clear sign to me, too. Becky, like the whole team, would not give up. Surrender to failure was out of the question for her, for any of the girls. Despite Becky's disabilities, her will always won. She was a fighter, and the whole team deeply admired her unending desire to improve.

As I'd watched Becky serve ball after ball during that final practice, I'd reflected—no, *really* pondered—on our entire season. I had grown spiritually over these four months, and I looked at things from a much different perspective now. My life had become filled with important stepping stones on life's path, and now I could read the signs. Better yet, I could *interpret* them; and now I was convinced that nothing, *nothing*, happened in life without a valid purpose, whether I could figure it immediately or not.

I had opened myself up to God's Spirit, and like an electrical cord now plugged in, I'd found the outlet, and the light had come on. I felt secure and confident, humble yet proud in a good way—proud of my team, proud of Becky, humbled to be included in her life, and Joshua Gibson's too. I felt so alive with both of these people in my life, and I was thankful beyond words that the two had crossed my path, and that the three of us formed a unity on several fronts: the team, the community, and the very future of our little corner of the world.

I smiled to myself, thinking again about what a life might have been like filled with the "riches" I might have harvested from the job A.J. Craft had offered me. But it would have been harvesting under false pretences. Instead, I'd been guided by unseen spiritual forces, and I knew that in the end, when the final chapter of life would be written on each soul, that I would have made the right choice, and I rejoiced in the power of my spirit, that it had been stronger than the selfish part of my will.

So I was at peace with whatever lay ahead, for the ded, for the game. Win or lose, I only needed to read the next sign, and follow the road to the next stop. And I knew my life would unfold that way from this point on.

Tomorrow, I planned to drive to Rye Lake and pick up Joshua and Rosemary. They would be guests at my house on Friday and Saturday night. They would attend the pep rally, the deed meeting, and the championship game. *Maybe it's time I told Mayor Gibson what I've learned about Irene Durella, too,* I thought.

I wondered, *Is Joshua Gibson himself an agent of the spirit world?* And I answered myself, *Yes, he is.* I had little doubt in my mind that our relationship had been driven together not by the mere circumstances life presented, but by the events the Spirit had brought to birth. I was glad to know that there was a difference, and that I was in on it now.

I was alive now with life breathed into me with a new meaning. But I'd be facing the lower side of life, too, over the next few days, and often the lower side seemed to come out ahead. A.J. Craft, Daryl Reed—they represented that lower side, and they'd been winners, at least in an outward sense.

And they'd also had an opportunity to see the signs, I was

sure of that. But I was also convinced that they had ignored what I had accepted, because they were prisoners of their own agendas, not the Spirit's.

That's the way it was, I supposed: Some people read the signs, others ignored them. There was a world at war out there, the eternal tug-of-war between spirit and flesh. Only a few answered the call. I had answered, and was now in the Spirit's network, like a conductor of energy from the Spirit's world.

What a comfort.

CHAPTER
34

Pep rally. Remember back to one. A good team, about to do battle with a formidable rival. Energy, beyond the norm, synchronized. A student body, pulling as one giant will, a unified body of individuals. Loud and strong, hopeful and confident, double-power: St. Luke's fans, hungry, eager to see us take apart St. Paul's mighty volleyball machine.

That's how it was Friday night at our little gym. The festivities were so perfectly prepared and handled, a great send-off for our girls, a 90-minute display of passion, power and hope. I watched the faces of the older fans, and the students and the teachers, committing each to my memory. All the eyes were so alive with admiration for our young girls, who'd accomplished so much in such a short time.

I felt no need to rush any of the upcoming days. Along with learning to read the signs, I'd learned to take one day at a time; I knew each one would take care of itself, though there were no guarantees included. So the anticipation was controllable. So many things had happened to change my life recently, each day had become one to look forward to, with more signs, more events, big and small, filling the voids of my past ways of thinking.

I was experiencing a great surge of energy that absolutely affected the things I was writing in my column as well. In past columns I'd been unconcerned with others' feelings, to a point. I had my favorites, my adversaries, my connections. But writing had somehow lost its luster. Now, though, my new passion for truth above all else was even affecting my position at the paper. Not that truth hadn't guided my decisions in the past, but truth was priority number one now. Still, in politics, truth is a word that can come wearing many disguises.

My position in the community involved reporting political dealings with little regard for their repercussions. Often, so often, I saw lives affected by my written words. In my opinion, it was the politician's own words that did them in. I simply recorded their words, and through the power of the media, their actions got circulated.

As I spoke through that microphone at the pep rally, I felt a peaceful serenity engulf me. As each girl came forward to a thundering ovation, the serenity only increased, great waves of peace surrounding me like a huge tide.

After the rally concluded, while the rattle of chairs being folded and put away echoed throughout the gym, three words pounded away in my brain, over and over, like an invisible message being sent: *"The Good News."* I couldn't discern the significance of those three words just then; nonetheless, they wouldn't leave me, much as I kept focused on other things. For whenever my mind cleared itself out, *"The Good News,"* was still there, visiting.

Thinking about it a little, I found I could easily connect the message with my life's recent experiences. But did *"The Good News"* simply represent a culmination of the volleyball season, the finding of the deed, new friends in Joshua, Rosemary, and of course, Becky Chapman's everyday doings? Yes, those were easy connections—but were they *too* easy? My old reporter's instincts led me to suspect there was still more to this message. "Now you've got to keep reading the signs, following the path, figuring it out," I told myself.

What greater challenge can there be than to solve a difficult puzzle? I couldn't quite dismiss the three-word thought altogether, or chalk it up to an overzealous mind now full of *"The Good News"*...

"Fine job today." Sister Fran's voice broke my reverie. "I do believe our girls are ready for the challenge; don't you agree, coach Paul?"

"Yes," I smiled. "I sure do believe they're ready, Sister."

"Fine," she nodded. Sister made a kind of reverent gesture, almost like a blessing. She lifted her head, turned towards the door, and said over her shoulder, *"That's* the good news I expected to hear from you."

I smiled. Message number two had come through loud and clear; *"The Good News"* had issued from her lips before the paint had even a chance to dry in my mind. The seed had been planted. I needed to understand the message of *"The Good News,"* much as I needed to get hold of the 7:29 message I'd followed earlier. I had decoded that message, though it had taken me some time to decipher. But now I bought into the possibility that messages are sent from beyond our understanding, and like a great beacon signaling a lost ship, the transmission was coming at me loud and clear.

Later that evening, Joshua, Rosemary, and Mayor Light enjoyed dinner at our home. The two mayors, Emily and I remained the only souls in on our little secret of the deed. We had protected our information, and we were ready to strike in just 18 hours.

After dinner we let Rosemary in on the plan. We discussed all the details fully for over two hours. Rosemary, in her usual spiritual way, insisted we close our meeting by the holding of hands. Hands, she explained, were connectors to the soul, the bridge between prayers, strengthening them by numbers. The power of numbers would be more readily heard by the unseen, she said, and a group prayer, she explained, "Will get to the Big Guy much faster."

Ours was a simple prayer, really; we asked for nothing more than the strength to guide us through the courtroom proceedings. We made no mention of anything beyond what we'd prepared for. *The day would take care of itself, and a little prayer sure wouldn't hurt,* I thought.

Our meeting broke up around eight p.m. Mayor Light, who looked the picture of health, gave us a strong "thumbs up" sign as she drove from sight. After she left, I spent a few more delightful hours with Emily, Rosemary, and Joshua. He exercised his uncanny ability to carry the conversation. He knew so much about everything, yet never seemed to come off as a know-it-all. And he seemed to find no special pleasure in hearing himself speak. In fact, he was a fine listener, not the least bit disagreeable, and very respectful of others' opinions. It seemed to matter little if you agreed with him or not; he kept his pleasant way, and the hours passed like mere minutes as we chatted.

"Paul," he said as always, "no matter what happens tomorrow, I want you to know how very proud I am to call you my friend."

I felt the same way. This remarkable old man and I shared a special bond now.

How could it be possible we had only met a few weeks ago? I felt as if we'd known each other forever, with fate—rather, with *Faith*—stepping in to lend a hand.

We retired at 11:00. We planned to rise at sunup, review our strategy once more, drive to the courthouse and play our final hand. As I drifted to sleep, I couldn't help smiling: A.J. Craft was in for the surprise of his life; and in a matter of just hours now, lives would be changing as our cards fell on the table.

Lives will be changing, I thought, and the image of Irene Durella came to my mind. *Maybe now's the right time to get her and the old mayor back together.*

CHAPTER
35

No way all these people will get in," I said to Joshua Gibson as we battled the traffic on the way in to court. "Courtroom only holds about 100 people."

Mayor Light, not often comfortable in such circumstances, had looked far ahead to the day's proceedings, however. With the court's permission, she had carted in 400 additional chairs, neatly placed now in rows on the great lawn outside Town Hall. Technicians had installed giant speakers and a huge T.V. monitor to provide easy viewing for the overflow crowd. I thought Mayor Light had done her homework well. "This is great," I told Joshua Gibson.

"Yes," he said, "she's thought this thing through."

"This should be some show," I said, and he nodded assent.

While we mingled with the crowd, I scanned the gathering for any sign of Irene Durella. *Not here yet,* I thought, as familiar faces greeted Gibson and me. The majority's faces wore defeated looks. Joshua Gibson struck up several conversations with old acquaintances who looked worn and depressed. They looked the way losers do after fighting hard but unsuccessfully. Their pain was still real, although numbed by time, and exhausted from effort.

Despite the meeting's apparent obvious finality, onlookers soon filled up the chairs, occupying every one inside and out, and several hundred additional residents stood behind the 400 seated outside, probably hoping and praying for delivery of a last-minute miracle.

At 11:55, the car carrying Judge Meredith Sloan pulled in front of Town Hall, ground to a halt, and stood still for a full minute before any further action. Its darkened windows added mystery to the proceedings. **Dark before the light,** I thought to myself, playing on words that compared the car's sinister look, with the name of our current Mayor, Madelaine Light.

Judge Sloan was known for starting right on time. That was her style, and we all knew it, so everyone scrambled for seats (ours inside the building) when Judge Sloan finally vacated the car and entered through the back of the building, under heavy security. **Still no sign of Irene,** I thought, as I sat down.

"All rise," bellowed the courtroom bailiff; the crowd quietly stood as one. "This court is now in session, the Honorable Meredith Sloan presiding."

Judge Sloan took her seat, pounded the gavel on the great desk, pronounced the court in order, and the huge crowd took their seats. Although it was early November, I noticed that the heat from all the bodies gathered so thickly made the whole atmosphere in the courtroom close and uncomfortable. The majority of the folks present took advantage of a handout prepared by A.J. Craft to fan themselves, vainly trying to fend off sweat. But they did occupy my eyes with lots of movement.

I didn't follow suit; I felt both disgusted and amused that the arrogant land developer had printed up these handouts, and that the crowd was making such use of his propaganda. "The Estates at Green Meadow," Craft had headlined his hype. In it, a glance told me, he'd had the audacity to offer a 10% discount on any new home built at Green Meadow "for any new resident attending today's meeting."

He just doesn't get it, I thought. But I was sure he thought he did. The fight had gone out of these people, he must be sure, and maybe by now they were ready to join instead of fight.

Craft was seated in the first row, center aisle. On either side of him sat a pair of his henchman. Incredibly, the thug on his right had been at Mayor Gibson's cabin. I pointed him out to the mayor. "That guy's in the security tape." Gibson smiled grimly and said, "He's in my sights."

At that very moment, the arsonist and Gibson shot glances at one another. Gibson smiled and winked; the man's right hand flashed Gibson a barely concealed profanity. "He looks nervous to me," Gibson asided, still staring at the man. Then Gibson chuckled, "He ought to be."

The thug elbowed Craft lightly, and Craft turned toward Gibson. Momentarily Craft's eyes flashed fear; he must not have seen us come in. But he recovered himself, flashed a smile as good as any politician's, and turned to face the judge.

"There is just one issue on today's docket," the Judge began. "I think we are all aware of why we're here today."

Judge Sloan spent the next few minutes explaining the importance of the deed, how it might possibly be permanently lost, and all the repercussions that would ensue were it not to be produced in this court. She explained clear how the Deed's loss would affect the future of the land in question; how Mayor Light would then have to decide how the land would be zoned. The judge finally explained A.J. Craft's proposal, there being none other on the table. the whole thing was simple really, I thought: Without the deed, the land would fall into Craft's hands.

Then Judge Sloan asked sharply, "Mayor Light, has the deed been located?"

A sudden silence fell on the room, and all eyes fixed on Mayor Light, who was seated a few rows behind A.J. Craft.

The mayor nodded to Judge Sloan, rose from her seat and turned to face the audience. She requested a microphone, and the bailiff handed her one. Even miked, her voice as she began to speak seemed unusually faint, though calm.

"As most of you know," the mayor began, "I've lived here my entire life. I grew up on Elm Street, in my parents house, passed down from my grandparents. One house lived in by three generations of one family. I walked to school with many of you seated here today. You attended all the football games with me, we all grew up alike, dated fellow school mates and married them."

She walked the few steps to her husband, Carl, clutched his hand for a moment, and then continued: "All these years, you've cared with me about this town, and you and I have held onto the hope that some of the great things that make us who we are here would never change."

Looking around, I noted dozens of nodding heads. Mayor Light went on. "Sure, we've seen some business development over the years. But in reality, the core of our simple little town, has remained untouched. Oh, life goes on, things change, I know all that," she said. "But I also know that we've survived without a mall, and we always have surplus money in town's account for emergencies, infrastructure and special services."

"We also have scores of family business still here. Frank Jones, your family has run that hardware store for years. And Ralph and Cindy Seeley—your insurance company is one of the oldest in the country."

Frank Jones and the Seeleys smiled back from their seats in the audience, and Mayor Light had the undivided attention of the entire courtroom.

"But when Mr. Craft came to our town several months ago with his plan, everything changed," she said. "I became so concerned about this affair, I allowed myself to become ill over the deed search. Frankly, I even thought about resigning, I heard the rumors. But I didn't want to even think about how life would be in our great town, if that beautiful land was developed during my tenure."

"I felt like an animal in a cage—that somehow the whole thing was my fault—and I felt also like I was being torn in two. The increased tax revenues from Mr. Craft's development would allow us to expand services in our schools, to build a Senior Citizen Center, and to boost our budget to a new high. But would it also encourage more new development? Yes, I realized it would; and our simple way of life, which I believe keeps many of us still here today, would soon be done and gone."

Mayor Light began pacing back and forth now, from one part of the room to the next. I could tell she sensed she was performing well, and she wasn't finished by any means. She said, "We searched high and low for that deed." She pointed toward me. "Mr. Strong here searched through years of newspapers for clues as to its location. He almost tore apart the Courthouse and the Municipal Building, too," she grinned, "but he found nothing there. I consider the sheer effort of his search alone something heroic."

To my amazement, numerous citizens burst into applause, obviously for me. I half-stood to acknowledge their gesture, and a lump formed in my throat. But quickly, the audience's attention returned to Mayor Light.

"At this point," she resumed, "I really felt we were searching for a needle in a haystack. But you know what? If someone tells me there *is* one needle in a haystack—and one I *have* to find—I'll find it. I'll look through every straw, with concentration and determination, till I find it. It's really that simple, you know. I think you'll agree—the human will is a pretty strong force when it's used at full capacity."

I could hear the audience begin to rustle in their seats now. A.J. Craft, who'd looked bored at the start of Mayor Light's words, leaned forward with sudden interest. Mayor

Light looked at Judge Sloan, who immediately signaled her to continue.

Then, in a voice hinting triumph, Mayor Light said, "I'm delighted to tell you today, ladies and gentlemen, that the will of one man, with one single purpose, has indeed turned up that one needle in the haystack."

Instantly the hushed silence of the crowd was broken by dozens of excited conversations that continued for about a minute till the judge's banging gavel concluded them. "Mayor Light," Judge Sloan said with authority, "what exactly are you getting at?"

Mayor Light said, "Your Honor, with your permission, I would like to ask this town's former mayor, Mr. Joshua Gibson, to come forward and address this gathering. He'll conclude what I began and explain further."

"Very well," said the judge. "Mayor Joshua Gibson, please come forward."

As the old mayor made his way before the Judge, the crowd erupted in a standing ovation for him—an eloquent tribute to his work as long as 50 years ago. At that moment I felt a nudge at my shoulder. I'd asked my wife to be on the lookout for me, and let me know when and if Becky Chapman arrived somewhere at the proceedings. Emily handed me a note that told me Becky, her mother and Irene Durella were sitting outside, in one of the back rows.

"Thanks hon," I said, and she exited the room and returned outdoors, where her watch continued.

In a few moments the cheers for Mayor Gibson died down, the audience re-took their seats, and the old mayor's eyes swept back and forth over the crowd. When silence was total again, he began speaking, without a mike, in a clear, penetrating voice that easily reached the back rows:

"Thank you Judge Sloan, Mayor Light—and thank you, citizens, for that gracious and warm welcome. It's nice to be back home."

Gary Kaschak

The crowd murmured appreciation for his greeting, and then an eerie silence fell over the room. I could feel the overwhelming pressure, the anticipation. This was Gibson's show now, and he was every inch up to it, in total control.

"Judge Sloan," he said mildly, "I would sincerely appreciate the patience of the court as I, shall we say, start from the beginning."

The judge nodded. "Very well, Mayor Gibson, take all the time you need."

Mayor Gibson, that eloquent 95-year-old, spoke for the next 15 minutes, like a man half his age. In fact he held the court spellbound, through bits of history about the deed, how it had been lost, and how against long odds it was at last found.

All this I knew, of course, but it had to be startling news indeed to the audience, and especially to A.J. Craft. But the truly remarkable history lesson Mayor Gibson gave us concluded with something he'd never shared even with me during all of our conversations and planning.

"When this town was first settled, a long, long time ago," he said, "our founding fathers were so struck by the natural beauty of the land, the wonderful pines and oaks, the lushness of the vegetation, and the overall purity of this particular ground, they hesitated before even knocking down a single tree."

"The wisest man of the group—and the man our "Clemensville" is named for—William Clemens, called a meeting, not only of the men, but of the region's women as well. You see, Clemens was far ahead of his time—what we call a visionary. He was so struck with the land's sheer beauty, he suggested specifically that the very land in question today be preserved—protected from any clearing whatsoever. That's how special he felt about the land."

By now the mayor was "working" the room as smoothly as a lounge singer might, and the throng was clinging to his

247

every word. He went on, with animation: "Now, in those early days of the settlers, this kind of determination to pre- serve land was completely unheard of. After all, land was what these people risked their lives for, what they wanted. So you'd think the settlers would've given Clemens a hard time, wouldn't you?"

Heads nodded all over the room, and I suspected they were nodding outside, too. Old Gibson had a storytelling style second to none. And he wasn't finished by a long shot:

"The people decided then that a vote on this question would be the proper thing to do," he said. "So that's what they did, all 224 adults present that night. Now, I know many of you fine citizens here today know some history of our town and its beginnings. But do you know, my friends, what the outcome of that vote was?"

Dozens of heads shook from side to side, several people in the crowd called, "No!"

"That's what I thought," said Gibson, and as he walked across the room, a sharp voice rang out from the front—A.J. Craft's: "Judge Sloan, I'm sure we all appreciate this history lesson from the mayor, but I don't see where it has any rel- evance to today's issue. Let's cut to the chase: do you, or do you not have the deed, Gibson?"

The audience burst into angry shouts of support for Gibson. "Finish your story!" several people yelled. Again, the loud banging of the judge's gavel settled the crowd. Looking Gibson in the eye, she said, "Mayor, Mr. Craft has a point. You're telling a wonderful story. But what relevance does it hold to the question Mr. Craft has put forth?"

"Much relevance, Your Honor," Gibson said, crisply but respectfully. "Begging your indulgence a bit longer, I'm almost through."

"Very well then. Please continue."

A.J. Craft huffed mightily before retaking his seat.

Gibson said, "That evening, the 224 adults present

unanimously voted to protect the land in question from ever being cleared. And one month later, the new town's citizens voted in Clemens as our first mayor."

The crowd showed, with loud claps and shouts, that it favored those early settlers' decision, almost as if we'd been present for that early vote ourselves.

At the judge's gavel-pounding and the mayor's raised arms, the crowd finally quieted down. Then Mayor Gibson said, "You see, this land was sacred ground to our founders, and it still should be. It shouldn't matter that a simple document is missing. What should matter is the blood and sweat shed by our founders—the wishes of those original 224 adults on that day, should be abided by."

More applause rippled through the court. Then Gibson walked toward Craft. He had a "personal" message to deliver. "Mr. Craft," he said, "you came to this town several months ago, eager to snatch this treasure of ours out from under us. But I ask you, now that you've heard this story about our people and their decision: Do you wish to stand down and let be?"

Another hush fell on the room. Craft, cocky, yet smooth, shot a grin towards the old mayor, rose to his feet, and faced the audience. "People of this great town," he began, "what happened with those settlers is in the distant past. Times have changed."

"Now, I have as soft a spot in my heart for nostalgia as any man. But I will *not* 'stand down and let be,' as Mayor Gibson puts it. You people all know this is a truly wonderful opportunity for you—one you can't afford to pass up. I'm a man it takes more than sentiment to stand down. I'm a business man. So, I ask you again, Mayor Gibson—do you, or do you not have the deed?"

Craft remained standing, all heads now turned towards the old mayor. Mayor Gibson was well aware he was the center of attention once more. He paused for a moment, then said, "Let me answer you this way, Craft. What would you say if I could show you the deed right now?"

The deep hush continued to blanket the stuffy room. Craft snorted softly but disdainfully, "Show me."

The mayor signaled for Mayor Light to come forward. She glided towards him, handed him an envelope, remained standing at his side.

"Ladies and gentlemen," Gibson announced, "I present to you Deed 10-11."

Gibson handed the envelope to a stunned Craft. He tore open the envelope, quickly scanned the contents, and announced it was a forgery.

"Anyone can forge a document," he said. "Plus, it's a photocopy. I'll need more than this fake to convince me. It's clearly bogus."

Craft was right, it was a photocopy. We had expected this reaction from Craft.

He was used to fighting tooth and nail until the bitter end, his team of lawyers prepared to lock horns with our township, probably for years, if need be. The only problem was that our town would probably run out of money fighting Craft long before he did. Craft was fully aware of this. He would fight us until we rescinded. That would be his next course of action, but we were still one step ahead.

"Mayor Gibson, may I please see the document?" asked Judge Sloan.

Gibson snatched the document from Craft and walked the document over to Judge Sloan. The Judge studied it for a while, peering through her reading glasses. Then she folded the document, slid it back into the envelope, and asked Mayor Gibson, "Do you have the original?"

"Yes," said the mayor. "It's safely hidden away."

"I'll need to see it—and *right now* would be a good time," she said firmly.

"Very well," Gibson replied. "But first, I have something

here I'd like to play for the court." He retrieved the surveillance tape from a compartment in a briefcase he had carried in and waved it above his head, for all the room to see. "I believe you'll find this to be very interesting viewing."

"I take it this tape has relevance to today's proceedings?" asked Judge Sloan.

"Without a doubt, Your Honor," said Gibson, almost reverently.

The judge ordered the court video player rolled in. Gibson handed the tape to the bailiff, and the whole room seemed breathless as he inserted it. I glanced over at Craft, he looked "puzzled" as the tape began to play.

The early footage was what I'd first watched with Gibson at the cabin, the camera showing the back of Gibson's property. Craft and his goon smiled knowingly at each other; this was nothing more than a ploy, they must be thinking.

The old mayor broke the silence. "Did you know that a fire damaged my cabin recently, Judge Sloan?"

"Really? I hadn't heard," she replied. "I'm sorry to hear it."

"Oh, there was really no damage of any significance," Gibson said, staring at Craft. "I've got a great sprinkler system and a state-of-the-art security system. And they both were very useful to me that day." In the corner of my eye I saw Craft shifting uncomfortably in his seat. "But let me fast-forward the tape," the mayor said, "it's really pretty boring—till you get to a certain crucial point."

Mayor Gibson fast-forwarded until the three figures appeared, and he let it run on to the point where the man in the middle stood on the porch and removed his ski mask. Right then Gibson paused the tape.

I noticed the guard seated with Craft growing extremely agitated. I smiled to myself. There'd be nowhere for him to hide from the truth that was about to unfold.

"Mr. Craft," Gibson said, smoothly as if the bully was the

old man's best friend, "we can stop right here if you'd like—unless, that is, you're interested in seeing for yourself the face of the person who's taking off his ski mask."

I saw the bodyguard bend down to whisper in Craft's ear. Startled, Craft shot a hateful look at Gibson. "This is all *bogus!* shouted Craft like a madman, jumping to his feet.

Judge Sloan snapped, "I'll deal *with you* in a moment, Mr. Craft. "Now, *SIT DOWN, SIR,* or I'll have you restrained!"

Craft slowly sat down, glaring from the judge to his henchman, to Gibson, and last, me. The look on his face reminded me of how he'd reacted that day at Foster's Den when I turned down his job offer.

The courtroom buzzed loudly with conversation, and I assumed the same was happening outside. Judge Sloan banged her gavel again and hollered, "Order in the Court!"

At last the audience sat down again, and Judge Sloan barked, "Let's get on with the proceedings!"

Mayor Gibson raised his hand and gestured at the judge. "Your Honor, we have the original with us. It's in the hands of one of my trusted associates, who's outside watching these proceedings on the big screen."

"And who is this person?" asked the judge.

"An eighth grade student at St. Luke's, Your Honor. Her name is Becky Chapman."

"Miss Chapman," Judge Sloan said, looking into the camera lens, "would you kindly enter the courtroom?"

Soon all eyes were searching for Becky Chapman. But the entire town didn't know her, mostly just the folks at St. Luke's were familiar with her. While the courtroom was awaiting Becky's arrival within, Emily came back in and said to me, "The entire team's sitting with Becky and Irene now. All the parents, all the players, all of us in the back rows. Becky and Irene have been talking the whole time. I think they're up to something, 'cause they're on their way down together."

Inside Becky's coat Emily had placed the manila envelope marked, "Government Document." Emily spent a few moments with Becky when she first arrived, quickly explained the plan to her, and why we wanted her to "be in" on our plan. Becky's job was to keep the document in her possession, make sure its contents were kept out of sight and bring it forward when she was called.

But both Becky and Irene began the walk from the back row, arm-in-arm, toward the front. As they both continued forward, Becky handed the envelope to Irene, gave her a big hug, and sent her off by herself. Scores of people, their faces jubilant, stood and cheered now, and formed a gauntlet directing her to the doors of the courtroom.

By the time Irene reached the front, Judge Sloan seemed to realize that banging her gavel would do little to calm the people down. She smiled broadly, as if to say, *These folks are excited, they have a great right to be, and this is my town, too. I'll let it ride.*

When the noise subsided somewhat, I saw Judge Sloan look over at Mayor Gibson and say, "I thought you said an eighth grade student would be coming in?" The old mayor just shrugged his shoulders, and Judge Sloan shrugged back and then said, "Would you please approach the bench, ma'am?" Irene did, with all eyes on her. "Do you have a document with you?" the judge demanded.

"Yes," said Irene softly. She reached into her coat, removed the manila envelope and handed it to the judge.

Mayor Gibson looked at me with outstretched hands and mouthed silently, "Who's she?" I just grinned in mock ignorance, for although I knew full well who she was, I was a bit puzzled, yet knew Becky Chapman was behind this new wrinkle in the plan.

As Judge Sloan examined the document, I saw Irene Durella gaze at the mayor. He, in turn, cocked his head and did the same. A few moments later, she walked over to him slowly, and said one word: "Josh."

As the mayor tried to place her voice, his ears seemed to perk, like a dog's would, hearing a shrill whistle. I'd never heard anyone call him "Josh" before, and figured that must have been what Irene called him 75 years ago.

The old mayor removed his glasses, rubbed his eyes and replaced his glasses on his nose. He squinted now, all attention, waiting for the woman to say something more. She repeated what she'd just said, but his time more fervently: ***"Josh!"***

The old mayor rose slowly from his seat, walked toward the elderly Irene, and regarded her with ever-wider eyes. When he'd come within less than a foot of her, he removed his glasses again and said with immense tenderness, ***"Irene?"***

She nodded, and tears welled in her eyes. "Yes, Josh...it's me."

He reached his right hand slowly, gently to her face and caressed her cheek. She accepted his caress, clutching his hand and holding it to her face. I looked around the courtroom. All eyes were on the couple. Only Judge Sloan, still poring over the document, missed out on this touching reunion after 75 long years.

Gibson took Irene's hand and, led her to the seat he'd occupied, next to mine. I rose, nodded to Irene and motioned to the mayor to take my seat. Irene sat first and Mayor Gibson followed. ***This is so romantic,*** I thought, as I watched them gaze at each other like two young lovers, just 20 years old again.

I looked up to the judge's bench. She had been examining the document for several minutes now. As I watched, she held up other town deeds, probably from the same era, comparing them with Deed 10-11. Being a political columnist had brought me in contact with these documents over the years. No doubt the judge was zeroing in on the Great Gold Seal, which each deed at the time bore. Old as the deed was, even back when it was drawn up, documents were notarized, to make them "official." I knew there was no way anyone could fake the unique old Seal of the town.

At last Judge Sloan put down the document and looked up. She struck her gavel once more, her hardest thud yet. Everyone quickly sat up straight, and now the courtroom was as quiet as a vacant church.

The judge peered directly down her half-eye glasses at A.J. Craft. He had his arms crossed, trying to look as if nothing had happened. *Arrogant snob* I thought. Then Judge Sloan spoke, straight to Craft:

"Mr. Craft, before I give my *final* ruling on the deed, we need to clear up another matter, wouldn't you say?" Craft didn't answer; I'm sure he knew the judge didn't expect him to. She went on: "The video we've just watched shows some pretty compelling evidence of criminal activity, wouldn't you say so, Mr. Craft? I for one am looking forward to watching *the rest of the tape.*"

Craft began opening his mouth as if to speak, but Judge Sloan held up a hand, signaling him to make no response. She wanted to make it absolutely clear at this point who was in charge—and that it wasn't going to be this pompous land mogul.

"Now," she said, "the 'gentleman' seated on your immediate right, the bearded one—am I to understand he's an 'employee' of yours, a 'bodyguard' for you? Mr. Craft, before you even think of shaking your head and denying any connection with that man, let me save you the trouble. I, too, Mr. Craft, happen to be a regular at Foster's Den, and it just so happens, the owner of that establishment, Conrad Foster, is one of my very good friends and supporters. I've seen you there many times, Mr. Craft, and I've seen this man as well, always near you, never straying too far away. Yours is a curious setup for a man in the land-business, I think."

"That proves nothing out of line," Craft mumbled from his seat.

"No, it doesn't **prove** anything untoward, you're right, Mr. Craft. Proof must come in a court of law. You see, Mr. Craft, in a court of law, very little can be swept under the carpet—the facts, they do come out, eventually. And the facts, so far, are certainly weighing quite heavily against you."

The judge looked over to the bailiff now, and announced in a loud voice, "Bailiff, would you please take Mr. Craft and his, uh, 'employee' into custody? Mr. Craft, I'm placing you under arrest for conspiracy in the suspicious activity witnessed in this video tape."

Bedlam broke out as the bailiff and two Sheriff's Deputies approached the two men and, after a brief scuffle, handcuffed them. As they escorted Craft by us, he sneered at me directly and said, "This isn't over, Mr. Strong, **your** turn is coming next!"

Scattered booing broke out as Craft made his way from the courtroom. He cursed at anyone in his path, vowing revenge. When Craft had departed, certainly to face the overflow crowd outside, Judge Sloan's gavel struck again. People milled around a bit, then gradually returned to our seats. She still hadn't given her ruling on the deed.

Judge Sloan appeared unflappable, waiting patiently for the courtroom to settle down. At last she was ready to make her statement:

"Mayor Light, Mayor Gibson, your words today were most inspiring. I commend you on a job well done." Turning to me, she said, "And Mr. Strong, I commend you for your diligent search for the deed. It is people like you and the two mayors here that make a community like ours a place one is proud to call 'home.'"

A loud ovation followed her words, and I could even hear the people outside cheering as well. *That was nice of her,* I thought, and she began speaking again as the cheering subsided:

"I've carefully examined this deed, and compared it to others from that era, and there is no doubt, none whatsoever in my mind that this deed, Deed 10-11, is authentic. The deed will now be carefully taken to its proper location, and will be placed in its rightful home. Case dismissed!"

Amid the now-unstoppable jubilation, I shouted into Mayor Gibson's ear, "Maybe we've seen the last of Craft!" As we clasped hands, he hollered back, "Maybe, maybe not. I wouldn't be so sure. He'll post bail right away, be out this afternoon. He may never bother us again, but you can be sure he'll surface somewhere. A snake may take refuge in a hole, but every now and again he'll need to come up for a meal."

Cheers, congratulations, back-slapping followed—an enormous outburst of pent-up emotion from our people. Just a few weeks ago we'd seemed so far from achieving this incredible victory; but we'd never given up, never given in, we'd never quit. We were like underdogs in the ultimate big game, pulling off the upset. I couldn't help imagining a repeat performance tomorrow in our championship game against St. Paul's. *Why not?* I thought. *That would really be the icing on the cake!*

We'd decided ahead of time that a victory luncheon would be in order after the day's events had transpired. Our plan had worked perfectly, so precisely, so cleanly, with not a single bump in the road today, and Mayor Gibson the star of the show.

All the while the hubbub subsided and the crowds broke up and left, I saw Irene Durella beaming at the old mayor, and soon Gibson able to turn his full attention to her. I heard him ask her quietly if she would join us for lunch. She cordially accepted his offer, and she'd be adding some very interesting conversation to the luncheon celebration, I presumed.

The luncheon, attended by Mayor Gibson, Mayor Light and her husband, Emily, Rosemary, Irene and myself, was a celebration indeed. Though we refrained from alcohol, we toasted ourselves with club soda and soft drinks for the fine performance we'd just given, and for the day's incredible outcome—especially Craft's arrest.

I couldn't resist rising from my seat to give still another toast. I stood, my glass full of club-soda in hand, and looked at Joshua and Irene, who seemed very comfortable together. Rosemary beamed, evidently enjoying the old couple's reunion. Joshua and Irene sat very close in the booth to each other; they'd been talking and laughing the whole time. I doubt if either could probably yet believe they'd found each other again—especially in this way. But it was yet another of those *coincidences,* and as far as I was concerned, *it was meant to be.*

I held my glass high and said, "I'd like to toast Mayor Gibson and Miss Durella. It's been 75 years since they've seen or even heard from each other. Here's to how *Providence* lent a hand!"

CHAPTER
36

Championship day at last arrived, just one day after A.J. Craft's historic defeat and Joshua's and Irene's reunion.

The game was set for 7:30 p.m. at Community College. The teams would be allowed on the court as early as 6:00 to practice and become familiar with the court. We planned to motor to the site on one of St. Luke's school buses that had been specially decorated and painted by the girls for the occasion. We would meet at 4:30, and leave at 4:45, followed by what we were certain would be a large convoy of vehicles trailing us.

For me, the hours leading up to our meeting in the parking lot dragged by. I was nervous, excited and eager to get going, and so, I knew, must be my team. Waiting out the hours, I reviewed strategy and prepared words to say to the girls, and finally, the moment arrived to leave for the bus.

When we arrived at the school parking lot, I saw that dozens of cars had already pulled into an open area. Music blared from tape players and car radios, and several players were putting finishing touches to the bus windows, smearing signs like "Go Eagles!" and "We're Number 1!" By 4:30, the whole team was accounted for, so we boarded the bus, took our seats, and began the 25-minute ride to the college.

And what a ride it was! As every car passed or came toward us, well-wishers honked and waved and cheered us on. The long line of cars behind us seemed endless, like some great, lighted tail that weaved with every turn in the road. We were a sight to behold.

The college parking lot was much more crowded than I'd ever seen it at this hour, even more than two hours before game time. As we drove into it, a policeman directed the bus to our drop-off point, and I spotted a long line of people at the front door, waiting to get in.

"Who are all these people?" I asked the officer, as I exited the bus.

"Oh, they want tickets," he replied. "Lots of people who got advance tickets are already in there, trying to nail down good seats. We had to open an hour earlier just to keep the lot clear."

Yeah, seating was first-come, first-serve, all general admission priced. Word had spread that an overflow crowd was expected, and these fans knew that prediction wasn't an idle one.

I waited at the foot of the bus as the girls exited, giving each one a word of encouragement, and a pat on the back. As each girl passed me on her way into the cavernous gym, I studied her with a good look in the eye. They all looked focused and ready to me. We'd soon find out if they were as ready as they looked.

Once we were all inside, I caught looks of awe on the girls' faces. They'd never been to the college before, and their jaws were dropping at the sight of the massive gym.

Mandy Morrison gasped, "Look at the size of this place, coach Paul, it's *huge!*"

Indeed it was. Our girls had been playing in ancient, rickety gyms, most of them barely retro-fitted for volleyball. Low ceilings, loose floorboards, low-hanging lights, courts without lines—that's what we'd endured in our league's low-budget gyms. We'd never played on a "perfect" court, but we sure would now—this court was volleyball *heaven.*

I looked up and told the girls, "I don't think you could hit that ceiling if you tried-and look at all the room you have for serving. This is great, huh?"

We walked all around the gym before the girls headed for the locker room; I wanted them to get a great feel for the place right away. When I gave the word, the girls ran quickly to the locker room, and returned minutes later ready for practice.

As we took the court, there was still no sign of Daryl Reed and his St. Paul's Crusaders. The fans had packed the seats, and "fight" music began to blare through the gym's giant sound system. *Why aren't' Reed and his team out here?* I thought. *He's always more than punctual.* I shrugged off his absence, and we went about our drills business. As we did, I paid close attention to my team's every move. I also glanced now and then at the excitement all around us: balloons, streamers, and signs were being hung along the court, and on the walls at the top of the stands. Interestingly, most of them were supporting our team; only a striking few boosted the Crusaders.

I watched as several teams in our league came in together, each girl wearing the jersey of her school. Opposing coaches, clergy, fans, all entered seeming to want to sit in the St. Luke's cheering section. By game time, I figured, nearly 80 percent of the 2,800 in attendance would be rooting for *us.*

At 6:30, after we'd practiced a full half hour, a hush overcame the crowd as eyes began to focus on the doorway leading to the locker rooms. Daryl Reed came out of it, his girls, the veteran champions, trailing behind him.

I understood the silence once I got a good look at the St. Paul's players: Like warriors' from some ancient time, their faces were all painted black, emblazoned with sinister-looking symbols. Each girl's uniform number was smeared in red on her right cheek; each girl's hair was pulled back and held tightly in place by a crimson and black "Crusaders" headband.

The sight was intimidating, and that was Reed's obvious plan. The crowd buzzed uncertainly as he opened up the ball bag and put his girls to work.

There'd been rumors Reed would be pulling something like this, and I'd warned our girls to be on the lookout for a weird Crusaders entry. At our final practice I'd told them, "Pay no attention to them when they enter the court. They'll be trying some diversion to intimidate you, but don't let them get inside your heads."

I glanced quickly at our girls, who were now performing a defensive drill near the net. Our team Captains, Karen and Lauren, were doing their jobs well, keeping the girls' focus on the drill, off the Crusaders.

"Watch the way that ball comes off the net!" Lauren shouted. "Use your knee-pads!" Karen barked. I was so proud of them—not one player wavered from the promise they'd made to me. Every one of them stayed focused on the drill. So many distractions surrounded them, it was a wonder they could even think straight; but I could see they were determined to finish the job they'd started four months ago.

The referee, Zach Billings, entered the gym, and I thought it was time I greeted coach Reed. I was on my way toward him when someone else caught my attention, entering right behind the ref. I neared one of the net poles before I could identify him. It was A.J. Craft, trying to shield himself from view and at the same time carry on an animated conversation with Billings.

"What's he doing here?" I growled aloud. "What could he possibly want *here?*" *Gibson was right*, I thought*, he got himself sprung on bail.*

Seconds later, Craft drew a small envelope from his shirt pocket, looked around furtively, then palmed the envelope in his right hand, and reached out, pretending to be shaking

Billings' hand. As the handshake ended, I could see that the envelope had been transferred to Billings right hand. He swiftly shifted it into his right front pants pocket. *Oh no!* I thought. *This guy Craft never quits—now he's paying off the referee!*

I looked at Billings, and he seemed nervous—unlike his usual calm, direct self, who never, ever made a bad call, the referee you wanted most to do your game. Then I saw Daryl Reed look to Billings and nod. I watched in horror as Billings nodded back. *So Reed's in on this, too,* I frowned to myself. *Think, Paul, think!*

Instinctively I started walking toward Billings. He noticed me and ducked off court, maybe figuring he was safe there for the moment. But what could I say to him, anyway? If he was in with Craft and Reed, what could I do at this point? I felt like my heart was about to fall to my feet. Game time was quickly approaching, and not only would we be fighting an uphill battle against the Crusaders, we now had to contend as well with a referee who'd apparently been paid off to make sure we had no chance to spring an upset. We were doomed, but I was determined to get at least a moment alone with Billings; we'd worked too hard to lose it all like this.

Billings appeared back on court a moment later and immediately called us coaches together for the traditional pre-game handshake, coin-toss, and review of the rules. I could tell Billings was being super careful as he went over the rules, I shook hands with Reed, and Billings tossed the coin into the air. "Heads!" yelled Reed, as the coin flipped and descended back to Billings open hand. "Heads it is," said Billings. "Serve or defend?"

"Of course we'll serve first," sneered Reed.

The game was about to begin now. Daryl Reed was returning to his bench; so was my assistant, Annie Shea, and now I had the moment I needed, alone with Billings.

He looked sheepish, but I told him, "Zack, I just wanted you to know, in all sincerity—in my opinion, you're the best referee in this league. You've been fair and honest all year, and we have great respect for you. Thank you for being that way."

I shook his hand; it was limp to my touch. He muttered, "Thanks, good luck, Coach Strong," and motioned me back to our bench.

I was far from sure my "reverse psyche" strategy would work. As I sat down on the bench, I spotted Craft in the crowd. He was glaring worriedly at Billings, who was paying no attention to him, rather, reviewing the starting lineup cards.

I gathered our girls for our pre-game prayer, a simple, "Hail-Mary." Each girl placed her good luck charm on the bench, and all that was left before the whistle blew was our team cheer.

Becky Chapman smiled at me and said, "Coach Paul, we've added some words to our cheer, specially for this game. Do you mind if we use them now?"

"Of course not, girls," I said, "let's bring it on!"

We huddled tightly together, kneeling in front of the bench, Becky began, and the other girls joined right in:

"We're all for one...we're one for all...together we stand...together we fall...but in the end...we win them all...we're all for one...we're one for all... *GO, EAGLES!"*

Even as I was relishing the power of this new cheer, the whistle blew, and moments later the starting teams took the court.

The stands were packed with people, *2,800 of them,* I thought. It looked like every player in the entire 13 team league was present, as well as every coach—and all 270 students from our school. Dozens of green and gold signs bearing messages supporting our team dominated the stands; I noticed only a few crimson and gold Crusaders signs.

But games aren't won or lost by how many signs your fans bring, or by how many people root for you. You win with hard work, skill and a little luck. ***Divine intervention would certainly help, too,*** I thought, as St. Paul's got ready to serve the first ball of the contest.

In this final contest, best three of five games would replace the usual best two out of three format played in the regular season; so the team winning three games first would be champions. Time wouldn't determine this contest; we couldn't know how long the match would take. In past tussles, St. Paul's had destroyed St. Cyril's in less than 90 minutes, but the college was allowing more than three hours before the next athletic event was scheduled to start.

St. Paul's Gloria Rappaport, one of the Crusaders' many "Amazons," was known for her deadly serve. Word was out that she had before this game served 99 straight times without missing, accumulating 86 points during her incredible streak. Her serve was not only accurate, she drove it so hard, defenses rarely even got a hand on it. With her serving, the Crusaders might easily build a 10-0 lead in no time.

But we had prepared our game plan knowing well that we'd face just such St. Paul's players. I'd focused our final practices almost entirely on defense. And we were no slouches at serving, either—that was a fact. Our team had put in over 85 percent for the season, top-rank in the league.

But I had told the team several times this past week, "Serving wins ***games,*** but defense wins ***championships.*** That's how St. Paul's wins—they have a few excellent servers, but ***they all*** play excellent defense. So will we."

Rappaport's opening serve came as hard and strong as all the others in her career. But our players let the ball, which headed deep toward the back line keep going that way. Our back-liners, Lynn Modell and Joanne Cross, both yelled "Out!"to each other as the ball sailed past their positions.

Indeed, "Out!" cried linesman Drew Mills, in perfect

position to make the call. "Serve, St. Luke's!" yelled referee Zack Billings.

Reed, Rappaport and the St. Cyril's bench argued the call, of course. They'd figured there was no way Rappaport could have missed. But Drew Mills was as good a linesman as Zach Billings was referee, so the Crusaders would just have to live with it.

"The ball was *out*, coach Reed," said Mills confidently. "Now, have a seat."

One thing I'd learned well: How an athletic contest begins is crucial to the outcome, especially for play at this level. There was no score in the game yet, but we'd passed our first test of the contest right off, with a great judgement call by our back line. Now that we'd snatched the serve quickly from the Crusaders, we had a chance to score first.

To say Karen Strong was in a zone that day would be an injustice to her heroic effort. Her serve, already the league's most accurate at 95 percent, had carried our club to several wins on the way to this game. I'd been watching her carefully, as both coach and father, and knew we'd need a huge game from her to have a chance against St. Paul's. She didn't disappoint us this night.

Karen had quickly whacked us a 5-0 advantage before coach Reed called the first timeout. Our mostly pro-St. Luke's crowd created quite a din of cheers, but the noises Reed was making and the grimace on his face came through nasty, like he was yelling at, even threatening his girls.

This was a strange position, trailing by five points, for them, and I hoped we could maintain and even increase our lead at this point. I wanted to win game number one badly, to give the girls an advantage and put St. Paul's on the spot.

But, the Crusaders side-outed the next serve, the ebb and flow of volleyball now shifting back their way. The lead went on to change hands several times that first game, and we were trailing, 13-10 when Lynn Modell stepped to the serving line.

Lynn was another of our all-stars; her powerful left-handed serve ranked second only to Karen's in accuracy. Lynn was overshadowed a mite by Karen, yet she was every bit as talented, just a year younger. The pressure was clearly on her shoulders—we needed to get at least three points to have a chance to win this game.

And Lynn did her part. Karen had begun the game with five points, and Lynn ended it with five of her own: Game one went to St. Luke's, 15-13!

What an unbelievable feeling! I had to tell the girls to cool down their jubilation; they surrounded Lynn with hugs, flashing huge smiles and screaming with delight. "Great going, girls," I shouted, "but don't forget, you've only got one win—we need two more!" That would be anything but easy, with Daryl Reed on the opposing bench. *He'd already be making adjustments for this next game*, I thought.

And so he did. The next hour belonged to the Crusaders. They bounced back hard, winning game two 15-10; then they took game three 15-6, though we made them fight for every point they got. The momentum had obviously shifted to their "Amazon" volleyball machine, and now they stood just one victory away from still another championship.

But I still had confidence in our girls, despite the results. And I needed to say something that conveyed that before we took the court for the fourth game. I shot every girl a quick look in the eye, then said calmly, "Girls, we've already scored 31 points today, and that's more than *double* what they usually yield. And when was the last time anyone took a first game from 'em? I tell you, we can beat them! But you've got to believe it," and I pointed to my head first, then to my heart, just as Mayor Gibson had done to me at the Lake, "here, *and here.*" I scanned the team once more and said firmly, "I don't doubt for a second that if you truly believe, you *can* win this thing—and you *will* win it!

Now—let's go out and *take* this game!"

As the girls took the court, I reviewed our strategy so far. We'd juggled the lineup, just like we had in previous games. Every one of tonight's games had been grueling; each contest, including the last one, which was more closely contested than the 15-6 score indicated, had taken up to 40 minutes. We'd been substituting freely, giving each girl who played adequate playing time, with the exception, of course, of Becky Chapman, who'd been cleared by her doctor to play just days before, "sparingly as needed," as he'd put it.

But I wasn't sure Becky was quite ready to play in this "big one." She'd gone to every game despite her injury, cheering us on, giving us hope. But she was still wearing a soft cast on her right hand for protection, and I hadn't seen her left-underhand serve improve, and she'd done no right-handed serving yet. I just couldn't see how it would be fair to the team to put her in a championship game at this point and hope to win it. She'd just have to remain a cheerleader on the bench.

Game four was much like game one, a point here, a point there, momentum shifting back and forth. We held leads of 3-1, 6-4, 11-9; but we also trailed, 4-3, 8-6, and 12-11. All throughout the crowd roared so we could hardly hear ourselves think.

Nobody could say we weren't creating edge-of-seat excitement for the 2,800 fans.

Karen and Megan had scored all our 11 points till this moment, but now Sharon Lee, one of our seventh-graders, was at the line. Would she seize this chance to be a new hero? To this point she'd been quiet but steady, scoring only a few points, making only a few plays on defense. Sharon took a few deep breaths, and slapped her serve.

Four serves later, she'd more than met the challenge: She'd sliced the defense like a surgeon four times, giving us our second "miracle" win, 15-12. There would be a fifth game after all, winner-take-all, for the league championship!

A raucous, standing ovation greeted us as we took the court for the final struggle. Our girls returned the ovation with little waves and smiles. They had to be tired—but so must be our opponents. We would try to use as many girls as we could this game, to keep as fresh forces as possible on that court every second.

Just then the thought hit me as I looked at Zach Billings wiping his brow with a towel. *The payoff?* There had been no controversial calls by Billings in the first four games, and now A.J. Craft was standing and glaring at Billings. *What could he do?* I thought, as Billings blew his whistle for game five to begin. *What would he do?*

This last contest soon threatened to become the longest in the league's history. Neither team built more than a three-point lead throughout the game, and how the overflow crowd kept from going totally hoarse was beyond me; they screamed and hollered at the top of their lungs at every point and every defensive stop. They were sure getting there money's worth today.

We trailed early on, 3-0, but gained back the serve and tied it, 3-3. Then we trailed or tied the Crusaders for most of the contest—but then Megan's two points gave us our first lead this final game, 13-12, and we still held serve.

Daryl Reed called his final timeout at this point, and our girls came to the bench looking like they'd already won, relishing the noise of the huge crowd, all standing and cheering wildly. I quickly snapped, "Hey, you guys, stay focused! There's nothing to celebrate yet!" They'd regained their focus by the time they took the court as Billings blew his whistle, A.J. Craft looking at him with an "I don't believe this!" look on his face. The crowd remained on their feet, craning necks to see the final action.

St. Paul's calling card all season had been defense, and they played it well now. Megan served what would have been a winner against a lesser team, but the veteran St. Paul girls reached deep down, dug the ball from inches above the floor, and stopped our offensive surge. It was an awesome defensive display, and though we still led, 13-12, we'd lost serve. If they could buzz just three points by us, it would be all over.

They did score two quick ones with strong serves, and I called our first timeout, hoping to break their concentration and momentum. I saw Reed snarl in my direction as his girls circled him. He thought it was as good as over, I figured—game point was coming up for them, and in a minute they'd have the championship.

"Girls," I began. "you all know we need a *stop, right now.* And WHEN—not if—we get the ball back, it's Lauren's turn to serve, and we all know what she can do. Now, dig down real deep and make it happen!"

I knew I didn't need to say more, and as they took the court I sensed they'd give me and our fans that one defensive play we needed to give us a chance.

And they did! Joanne Cross made the play of her young life, blocking a potential "spike" with her arms outstretched high above the net. the play returned the serve and the emotion to us; now we needed to get those three points (you have to win by two in volleyball) for victory.

Lauren proceeded to serve two points—again the lead had changed, we were ahead, 15-14 now, once again positioned to win the game. *Just one more point!* I prayed silently.

But the Crusaders once again pulled it out with yet another superb defensive stop. *They're tough,* I thought, *but we're gonna come through eventually.*

For 20 tense minutes the advantage shifted from one team to the other. The Crusaders held leads of 16-15, 18-17, and 20-19. We led 17-16, 19-18, then took another one point lead at 21-20, at which time I called for another substitution.

Janet Moore had served well today, I'd noticed, while Ellen Anderson had struggled a bit. We had to get one last point here, and I wanted Janet at the serving line.

"Moore for Anderson," I yelled at Billings.

"Illegal substitution," he barked back. "She's already been substituted for three times."

Darn! I'd forgotten how many times I'd subbed for Ellen, and the league rule was cut-and-dried: You could substitute for a player no more than three times in a game.

I'd gotten too caught up in the game as we were."O.K.," I said, "just keep Anderson in the game."

But Billings shook his head, and I knew we were in trouble. Maybe this was the big break he was looking for—to make this call at this point and "earning" his payoff from Craft. He said, "You know you can't do that, coach. You have to put another player in."

I felt panic stab me. There *were* no other players, I'd put everybody who could play in already, and he was right: In volleyball, once you've entered a particular player in a particular position in the lineup, that's it for that player.

I had only simple, but unpleasant choices. we could give up the serve. *Out of the question—Gloria Rappaport's next in line to serve for them.* My other choice? Send in Becky Chapman—to serve left-handed. I couldn't risk injury to her right hand, and besides, she'd had no practice right-handed...

What have I done? Blown it royally, that's what! I thought. I looked over at Billings; he frowned impatiently, waiting for my decision.

"Time out," I said. I had to regroup my thoughts somehow.

"Time out, St. Luke's," Billings bellowed. Then he looked me dead in the eye and said, "That's your last one, you know."

As I turned to face the girls, I felt lower than low. Our

final huddle of the season had been caused by a coach's mistake. I looked around at the girls' sweaty faces, gasping for air. They were beyond exhausted, but each one took another's hand—they were still "all for one and one for all," even looking straight at a defeat that was 100% my fault.

All right, what to do? Keep Ellen in the game and give up the serve to St. Paul's? Or substitute Becky Chapman for Ellen? What choice did I have, really? Becky alone hadn't played yet.

In a way the decision had already been made for me. So I took a deep breath and said, "Girls, we've climbed a huge mountain today, and played every minute like a *team. I've* made the mistake here, and I apologize. Now we've got to forget it—and here's what we need to do."

The girls looked intently at me, all squeezing hands. I went over to Becky and wrapped my arm around her shoulder and said confidently,"Becky's going in for Ellen. She's got serve."

I saw the girls grimace, like they were a bit startled. Maybe some of them weren't sure about Billings' ruling, or why it was I had to put Becky in. And I had no time to explain. But they showed real character, turning to smile at Becky, who was already removing her sweats.

Seconds later the girls were about to take the court, maybe for the final time. I signaled Becky over, looked her in the eyes and calmly said, "You can do this—now bring this baby home."

You never forget certain moments in your life, and I'll always cherish the ones that followed. Standing at the serving line for the first time all year, Becky looked around, into the throng of 2,800 people. Her mother, Maureen, was somewhere in the huge gathering, and I knew Becky's eyes were searching for her. I remembered Becky used to scan the audience at dance recitals, when her father, Jack, was still alive. And before each one, Becky would spy where he was seated, and they'd exchange their hand signal. Maybe now Becky needed to have her mother do the same.

"Where's Mrs. Chapman sitting?" I asked the girls on the bench.

"She's up there, coach, just below our team sign," Maggie pointed.

I scanned the crowd, and a single person, Maureen Chapman, stood up there gazing down at Becky. I looked at Becky; she'd spotted her mother and was smiling back at her. And there it was: Maureen raised her left hand and extended her index finger, pinkie and thumb. And Becky gestured back, beaming, as the whole crowd watched, most of them clearly perplexed.

One by one, each of the girls on the court flashed the signal, then so did every player on our bench. Seconds later, each parent of a team member—all had sat with Maureen—stood up around her and repeated the gesture. Moments later, half the audience was standing, too, flashing the signal at Becky, much to the remaining fans' gaping surprise.

"All right, coach, what's going on here?" referee Billings growled, "What's that signal mean?"

"It means 'I'm o.k, your o.k," I grinned back. "It means I love you."

Just then I saw something in Billings' tough face begin to melt, and I could have sworn time stood still. Could this incredible display of respect and solidarity have touched this rough man's emotions? If so, I wasn't surprised, some-how—no one in our league had ever seen anything like this.

Time began running again when Daryl Reed's enraged voice broke in. "Are we gonna play, or keep watching this freak show?"

Billings flinched slightly, then turned to Reed, nodded, and blew his whistle to get the players' attention. One by one, everyone in the stands sat down again—all but

Maureen Chapman, who remained standing.

Billings signaled for linesman Drew Mills to roll the ball to Becky for her serve, then blew his whistle, and Becky began her serving motion.

Immediately after her unorthodox, underhanded, left-handed serve left Becky's hand, its low trajectory seemed to be giving it no chance to clear the net. But as if some unseen force was lifting the ball, it not only cleared the net, it seemed headed for the Crusaders' far corner.

The Crusaders girls defending at net stood stunned—that ball *couldn't* have cleared the net. But one's instincts were keen, and she desperately dove for the ball. Her super effort paid off; her outstretched hands met the ball inches before it hit the floor. It caromed off her fingers and headed toward the back line. Back there, a second Crusader defender miraculously kept the ball in play just as it was about to tumble out of bounds. And a last defender matched the efforts of her two teammates, valiantly punching the ball back toward our side, her body lunging with every ounce of effort she could muster.

Amazingly, this third hit cleared the net, bounced somewhere on or near the out-of-bounds marker, and rolled to a stop only a few feet from where I sat.

It had all happened so fast, from my angle I couldn't tell whether the ball had dropped out of bounds, or it had barely hit the line. If the ball had landed on the line, it was in play and we'd missed it, and the serve would return to St. Paul's. If the ball had been out of bounds, we'd just won game point and the victory.

Zack Billings had to make the call; all eyes fixed on him; and for me everything shifted into a weird slow motion. My eyes slowly swept the crowd, and I found A.J. Craft. Along with 2,800 others, he was standing open-mouthed, imploring the ref to make the call, signaling "in," of course, along with the Crusader fans, players and coach Reed.

Reed stood nearly in Billings' face, waving "in" wildly; our side's fans stood by the hundreds signaling "out." A whole season had come down to one referee's call.

Zack Billings paused for a moment, looked at Reed and Craft, both madly motioning him for an "in" call, then looked at me, all in a few split-seconds.

To rule the ball were "in," he'd simply point with the index fingers of both hands towards the court. To rule the ball "out," he would raise his arms, the palms of his hands facing his body. Or he could fall back on a third, seldom-used possibility: "hands over the eyes," signifying, "I didn't see the play." If he went that way, the call would go to linesman Drew Mills, who was positioned right on the line.

Billings began to move his arms to make the call, amid the sole sounds of thousands of fans' screams, and much to my dismay, his arms began to move toward an "in" call.

But then, as Billings' arms rose past his waistline, then his chest, I knew we at least had a chance. He continued to raise them past his shoulders, and finally, he covered his eyes with both hands, saying he hadn't seen the play clearly enough to make the call.

That shifted all eyes immediately to Mills, and in that instant, things stopped moving slow-motion. Without hesitation, Mills' hands rose halfway and turned in, and one beautiful word roared from his lips.

"OUT!"

Mills signaled back to Billings, who announced the official call like a trumpet: "Point, St. Luke's, game and match!"

Instantly bedlam broke out in the crowd. Daryl Reed stamped his feet, shouting and cursing at linesman Drew Mills, and all Reed's players followed his lead. Zack Billings quickly approached me, shook my hand and winked his approval. Then I saw him head in A.J. Craft's direction.

The thousands of our fans swiftly vacated the bleachers

and surrounded Becky Chapman, our hero. Her teammates hoisted Becky aloft, cheering at the tops of their lungs. Becky rode high above them, her left hand locked in the "I love you" position.

My coaches, Annie Shea and my wife, Emily, hugged each other, then fought their way toward me. We embraced warmly; then I pointed them toward the team, promising to catch up to them all momentarily.

To my delight, I watched Zack Billings approach A.J. Craft, lift the "dirty" envelope from his pocket, tear it in two and drop it on the floor in front of Craft. "Good for you, Zack," I said silently, "good for you."

Craft muttered some words then looked threatening at Billings, but Billings wasn't listening. He was already walking away from the shouting Craft, waving him off, shaking his head, and disappearing into the locker room.

I stood alone then and watched my team carry Becky around the gym. She still held her hand aloft, and hundreds of people from the crowd, even including St. Paul's fans, held theirs up too, rejoicing with her.

I tried to take stock in those few moments of all the emotions engulfing me: exhilaration, pride, joy, relief, utter happiness, a kind of blissful peace. I never wanted to forget that I'd enjoyed all of them just that once.

And in that few seconds' span, I realized beyond the shadow of a doubt: "coincidence" doesn't exist. Sure, that thought had occurred to me many times during the last six months, but the last two days had confirmed it beyond question, as I had read one by one the signs laid out before me.

Becky and hundreds of fans turned the gym's corner towards me, and several of my players waved at me. The whole team headed toward me, and as they neared, Becky and I caught each other's eyes.

Becky Chapman was the closest thing to an angel on earth, that was for sure. She had united a team, by doing nothing more or less than staying a part of it, and not quitting. I wondered, as I enjoyed her smile, what the future had in store for this amazing young woman.

CHAPTER
37

During the following six months, Mayor Gibson seemed to have more than a little "kick" in his step. In fact, he acted much like a school-boy would around his first girl-friend. And, Irene Durella didn't behave much differently, either.

It wasn't easy for the two to see each other as often as they desired. Gibson was simply too old to drive the six-hour round-trip from Rye Lake to Chadwick Manor too often, and getting himself to the bus-station from Rye Lake sometimes seemed equally daunting. Nevertheless, arrangements managed to get made so this budding relationship could continue, and of course, I served at the center of their little get-togethers, acting as chauffeur every other weekend, until mid-December, when the weather began to become a factor inhibiting long drives.

However, we had an extra bedroom in our house that was infrequently used; and Emily and I became so enraptured by Joshua's and Irene's relationship, we offered the room to the mayor—an "open" invitation on an "as needed" basis.

"Right neighborly of you," he told me when I offered it to him. "Snow's a comin', and you just never know what the weather'll bring now. If you mean it," and he knew I did, "then I'd be glad to take you up on that offer."

Bunking in that room was his way of confirming how

deep his and Irene's relationship had become. Never did I feel his presence was an intrusion; that's how deeply *I* felt about my relationship with *him.*

The mayor took full advantage of the *arrangement,* but I never felt he took advantage of *us.* Sometimes he'd stay on a few more days than usual; but when he was ready, then off we'd go to Rye Lake. And always, our conversations were informative, provocative and enlightening.

During one of these trips, we engaged in a rather animated discussion about the factors involved in "coincidence." My life had seen one "coincidence" after the other, and I wanted to know Gibson's feelings and personal thoughts on the subject.

"Coincidences?" he grinned, feigning surprise. "You've had quite a few lately, and so have I. I reckon with all that's happened, you probably feel you're like a lightning-rod for them, don't you, Paul?"

"As a matter of fact, that's *exactly* how I feel," I said, quickly taking my eyes off the highway for a glance at him. "Is that how you feel, too?"

"Paul, it's a fair question, you know, and coincidence is a phenomenon that's always intrigued me. So let me tell you a little story from our great American history, and you decide whether it's coincidence, divine-intervention, or something else that was involved."

Storytelling was his way of sharing truth. And the old mayor was so very good at it, by far the best story-teller I knew, first, because of the content he shared; second, because his delivery was so clear it kept you riveted to his words; and third, because what he shared was "lasting," kind of like Jesus' parables in the Bible.

"I'm all ears," I said, gazing at the odometer, "and we still have 50 miles to go."

Gibson began, "Well, Paul, how familiar are you with the Declaration of Independence?"

"Pretty familiar with it," I replied. "You're not going to embarrass me with too many difficult questions, are you?"

"That depends on *you*," he laughed.

"Just get on with your story," I said with a touch of sarcasm.

"Well, then, way back in 1776, a couple of Patriots by the names of John Adams and Thomas Jefferson teamed up to write and edit our Declaration of Independence. They'd been hand-picked by the delegation in Philadelphia, Jefferson for his writing skills, and Adams for his uncanny ability to analyze and edit the written word. Adams was known for his great oratory skills as well—he was perhaps the finest speaker of his day."

"I didn't know that," I said.

"You could look it up," he shot back. Seeing I was suitably impressed, he went on:

"Now, of course we know a few things about these two men. Adams was eventually elected our second President, Jefferson, our fourth. But I ask you, Paul, would you have believed back then that both these two great men—men who were basically responsible for our Declaration of Independence, who were hand-picked to do the job—would *both* become Presidents of our great nation? Do you believe that was "coincidence," or do you believe it was "divine intervention?"

I thought for a moment, then said, "I believe it was neither, actually. I believe the reputations they made for themselves carried them to the top job, as the things they did for their country were recognized by the people as great acts. I don't really see any of that as either coincidence or divine intervention."

"Fair enough," Gibson said. "Now, would you like to hear *the rest of the story?"*

O.K., what did he have up his sleeve, now that he had just warmed me up? "Of course," I replied, "let me have it!"

Gibson geared up with a deep breath, then said, "Now, Paul, I don't need to bore you with all the events surrounding each man's long life thereafter; I think you've heard enough about those two men to know their place in history. But once I've told you a few things you may *not* know, I'll ask you *again* if you think coincidence or divine intervention came into play."

I nodded, "Fair enough," and he continued:

"Eventually, Jefferson and Adams retired to their homes after serving their country all those years. Jefferson went to his beloved Monticello, and Adams to his farm in New England. They corresponded with each other over the years—especially in the later years—until they both died... *both on the same day of the same year!"*

"I don't ever remember hearing *that* in American History class," I said.

"That's probably because you had a boring teacher, probably stuck exactly with the program, never strayed from the text."

"Why, *yes,* that's right," I said, thinking back to old Mr. Cornell's class full of yawning students.

"Thought so," the old man snorted. "Now, Paul, I ask you again, was that a coincidence, that both of these great men died on the exact same day of the same year, or was it divine intervention?"

"That's *not* a coincidence," I said quickly. "Now that's what I would call divine intervention."

"Very good," he said, rocking slightly in the seat next to me. "But Paul, that's still not completely *the rest of the story."*

"It's not?" I asked. "What more could there be to it? Did they die at the same hour, too?"

"Oh no," said Gibson. "It's much more remarkable than that."

He paused for emphasis and stayed silent till I begged

him to go on.

"Well, it was the year 1826," he said, "50 years since the signing of the Declaration, and our young country was planning a huge celebration in honor of that day. There'd be bands and fireworks and speeches, just like we have today, and an invitation went out to both men, asking them to attend the festivities, and to speak at them as well."

"Did they accept?"

"Well, it's been documented that both men **wanted** to attend, but they both were racked with physical ailments. I believe Adams was 91 and Jefferson was 83—that alone was divine intervention, 'cause those days, life expectancy was only about 40, with all the disease and war common then. Anyway, traveling to the big bash would be nearly impossible for either man, so they both declined, reluctantly."

"That's really a shame," I said, "that they'd both have to miss such a nice tribute."

"Yes, it would have been," Gibson agreed, "but now, here's *the rest of the story.*"

"While the country was planning that big celebration, Adams' and Jefferson's health continued to fail rapidly. They stayed in contact with each other as best they could, but correspondence in those times was rather slow, as you might imagine. Usually, it took weeks for a simple letter to reach its destination any distance away."

"Well, by the end of June that year, the end was drawing hopelessly near for both great men, and on the day of the great celebration, that 50th anniversary of our nation's birth, both men passed away—that's right—*on July 4th, 1826!*"

"You're kidding!" I said, dumbfounded.

"Oh no," the mayor said, hands now folded across his chest. "You can look it up."

He turned to me at that moment, his eyes a-twinkle. "Now, Paul, I'll ask you again: was that a coincidence, or did divine intervention play a part in the whole thing?"

I said nothing, only smiled. He knew my answer. No, things didn't happen by chance, they happened for reasons. I also knew that miracles like the story Gibson had just magnificently told me are **signs** to help strengthen our beliefs in the divine, as long as you can keep yourself open to **reading** them.

CHAPTER
38

By the spring of 1980, Mayor Gibson and Irene Durella had become inseparable, and the three-hour distance between them was only a minor inconvenience to him. He had more life and vitality than a man half his age should. He'd even begun to show his face around town again, and mingle in with the residents. He was a young man again, I thought.

So it came as no surprise to me when the pair decided that even though they were both 95 years old, it wasn't too late for them to be married, and so they were, at a small church near Rye Lake, and they held the reception at the cabin—on *July 29th, 1980.*

Mayor Gibson honored me by asking me to be his Best-Man, and Rosemary served as Irene's Bridesmaid. The girls from the team all helped to decorate the church and the cabin, and both the wedding and reception were very special. And all of us, young and old alike, learned some lessons that day as well.

I'd been preparing my toast to Mayor Gibson for weeks, but as I stood in front of the large crowd of well-wishers waiting to hear my words, I decided to ignore what I had written, and just wing it and speak from my heart instead:

"I never expected, at my age, to be standing in front of a group of people as Best-Man at a wedding for a man 59 years older than me," I began, and the whole room laughed. "So much has happened in such a short period of time— frankly, I'm both overwhelmed, and truly honored to be this man's, ***Best-Man.***"

The folks applauded, and I faced Gibson, seated next to me at the Head-table.

"You know," I said, "there are so many things I could say today, so many things about this man that only I know about. But let me put it this way: You never know in life, when a real hero will come along. And you never know how young or old that hero will be. You never really know, either, why ***you've*** been thrown in that hero's company. But what you will know, ladies and gentleman—***what you will know***—is that when it happens, and you begin to understand it all, you'll know how blessed you are, to be there."

I lifted my glass, faced the newlyweds, and said, "Joshua and Irene, may the remaining years you have be filled with all the blessings you both deserve; for I believe, with all my heart, that our paths were destined to cross, and that you, sir, ***are my hero.***"

There wasn't a dry eye in the house following my little speech. Gibson rose from his chair and gave me a big bear-hug. Seconds later, the band began playing, and the patrons leaped to their feet for some dancing.

"That was nice, Paul, ***real nice.***" Gibson said quietly, drawing me aside. "Let's go outside for a moment, o.k.? I have a gift for you."

"Right now?" I said. "What about the party?"

"It'll wait, and this won't take long," he said.

He took me to the back of the property, and we walked out to the wooden dock that housed his little row-boat for fishing. He bent down and gathered up a few stones in his hand.

"Lovely night, Paul," he said. "I just love this old place."

"Me too," I said. "I can't think of a better place to be. I

feel so—so *alive* when I'm here, almost like I *belong* here. I've always felt that way about the cabin and the lake, ever since that first day."

He smiled. "Yes, it does have some magical qualities about it. There's no other place on earth quite like it. It's one-of-a-kind."

He skimmed a stone across the surface of the still lake.

"Paul, Irene and I have decided that we're going to travel the world, starting with our own beautiful country. We're not sure how much longer we have on this earth, but we do want to make the most of our remaining years together, and we've agreed to travel."

"That's just great," I said.

"Well, I've never left this old place for over 50 years," he said. "Don't know how I'll feel once I go, but I can't just let the place go to blazes while I'm gone, you know."

"Sure," I agreed. "Would you like me to take care of it while you're gone? I'll be glad to..."

"That's a mighty nice offer, Paul, but it's not *exactly* what I had in mind," he said.

"Oh," I said, and waited for him to continue.

"I spoke to Rosemary several days ago—seems she's ready to move on, too, wants to go out West to Arizona. She's had some friends asking her for years to come out there. Sedona, I believe it's called. Very spiritual place, perfect for her, actually."

I was surprised. "Is she going for good?"

"Yes, I do believe she is," Gibson said. "Everyone's lives are changing now, aren't they?"

It was a rhetorical question. He held his hand open, and I took a stone from his hand and skimmed it across the lake.

"So, what do you have in mind to do with this place?" I asked.

"It's very simple, really, Paul. You've been like a son to me, and I've always known how you felt about this place.

You didn't have to tell me."

He reached into his pants pocket, removed a ring of keys and dropped them into my hands.

"What are these?" I asked.

"What do you think they are?" he snapped with a fierce grin. "They're the keys to the cabin—it's yours now."

"WHAT?" I cried.

"Yes, it's a done deal, Paul," he said. "I've had all the paperwork prepared, just needs your signature now..." Then, as if he'd just remembered out of the blue, he said, "Hey, let's go back inside, there's a party we're missing!"

I told him to go ahead of me—I needed a few moments to come to grips with the sudden sensation of being the owner—*THE OWNER!* of this great cabin and land I so loved. It was so sudden, I'd never expected this—but what had I "expected" during the last nine months? I picked up one more stone and threw it as far as I could across the lake. Then I punched the air triumphantly, and headed back in to join in the great celebration.

CHAPTER
39

By Spring 1985, a full five years after Joshua Gibson and Irene Durella became man and wife, they had settled down a bit from their travels and eventually purchased some property in Arizona, near Rosemary's. Now we made arrangements to bring the pair back to our township, for a combined celebration of their fifth wedding anniversary and both their 100th birthdays.

We had collected dozens of postcards from their travels around the world; in fact, and Emily and my daughters had created a scrapbook chock full of them. She included many photos of the two, and I noted how fit and happy they always looked.

So much had happened during those five-years. I'd stayed on as volleyball coach at St. Luke's, and we'd won the league championship in no less than five of the total six years that included our famous first championship in 1979. St. Luke's had replaced the St. Paul Crusaders as "the team to beat," and St. Paul's not only began a downward spiral following their loss to us in 1979, Coach Daryl Reed was unceremoniously dumped following St. Paul's disastrous follow-up season in 1980. Angry parents, and complaints from his former players as well, helped drive him out. I thought, *The old mayor's prediction was right again.*

A.J. Craft was tried for and convicted of arson and served

a few months' time in jail, then was placed on probation for a year. Judge Sloan made it perfectly clear to him that if in the future he made any slip-ups—even anything as petty as jaywalking—she'd find a way to throw the book at him.

Craft never again showed his face in our township, and it was common knowledge that his land deals in the region dropped off drastically in number. By 1984, following a three-year run of busted deals, he was arrested again, this time for fraud, and indicted for bilking several investors out of thousands of dollars. Last I heard he was sentenced to 15 years in state prison.

Mayor Light served out her final four-year term, winning decisively in 1980 by a landslide. In 1985, as a regular citizen, she accepted a job at Community College where she's still teaching Political Science.

The girls from the 1979's championship team did their best to keep in touch with us, sending Christmas and birthday cards, year after year. Those who stayed in the area called Karen and Megan often, and stopped in to see them frequently. I really enjoyed watching them grow from girls to young ladies over those five years.

Becky Chapman, on the other hand, became an exchange-student in her junior and senior years of high school. Then we heard that she joined a Christian ministry organization and went to Africa, to teach tribal people. Her mother, Maureen, also moved away after Becky graduated high school. She kept in touch early on, when we learned that she accepted a teaching position at a private school in Boston, teaching handicapped children, no less. *What a fitting tribute to her late husband,* I thought.

I found myself growing a bit bored with my political writing; I just didn't seem to have the drive and passion I once had to do the things involved to uncover the truth in that arena. It seemed almost as if some other force was pulling me in some other direction, but though I kept trying to "read the signs," I couldn't tell where that pull was coming from or where it was trying to pull me to.

I found the phrase, "the good news" recurring in my life and mind. I kept hearing it said to me in conversations, or catching it being said on the news, or written elsewhere. I wasn't really sure if this "coincidence" meant anything, or if I was merely making something out of nothing. Nevertheless, something inside me longed to know what, if anything, "the good news" meant for me.

Joshua's and Irene's homecoming was, as expected, a joyous occasion. We held the big party at the cabin and kept the guest list short, as per the Gibsons' request. Among those attending included Madeleine Light, Judge Sloan, and even Millie Parker. Some of the girls from the 1979 team attended, too, but most of them were away at college. Those who couldn't attend sent the Gibsons "congratulations" cards and gifts. One thing was for sure: the special girls from that team hadn't forgotten any of us.

During a lull in the party, Mayor Gibson asked me to retreat with him into the cabin. "We need to do some private talk, Paul," he said. I couldn't help but wonder how much younger-looking he seemed than his 100 years. And he still had that rascally gleam in his eyes. When we got inside, the old mayor walked over to the fireplace, like he always had, and looked up at the many old photos, still in place on the old mantle that had once been his.

"I read your column today," he said. He paused for a response, and I asked, "What did you think?"

He paused again, standing in front of the great fireplace, hands behind his back, admiring the photo we'd taken with the team following the great cleanup five years back. I knew this stance of his well, and wouldn't think of rushing him; he'd speak when he was good and ready.

"Do you remember that day at the cabin?" he finally said, pointing to the cherished photo.

"Of course," I replied. "I think about it often."

"Good," he shot back, "then maybe you'll remember something else." He finally turned to face me. "You've got to feel it here, and *here,*" he said, pointing to his heart with one hand, his head with the other. "If you no longer feel that combination of the two, it's time to make a change."

The old man was on to me. Sure, I had lost the desire to inform the public about the day's political doings; he'd seen that in the creative dullness of my column. He was right, I needed a change. "You're right—but what should I do?" I said desperately. "I can't just leave my job and start over."

He paused again. Had I disappointed him? "Paul, for five years now you've been telling me how you've learned to read the signs, like an old scout tracking some criminal in the woods. If you truly believe what you feel, *here,* and especially *here,*" pointing to his heart, "don't be afraid, be *brave.*"

He was right again, of course. I'd bragged enough about how easy it was for me to "read the signs." Now what was I going to do with that talent?

The old mayor eased into his old rocking chair and began rocking gently, his eyes closed. "Paul, you *do* know how to read the signs, and that's *the good news.*"

The good news, I thought. *There it is again!*

CHAPTER
40

hree months after Gibson's little talk with me at the cabin, I resigned my position at the paper, amidst much protest from friends and co-workers, and with a great feeling of personal trepidation as well. During those 60 days prior to my resignation, I had gathered enough advertising promises and financial support to figure I could spin off my writing talents into a monthly publication. This experience was nerve-wracking to say the least: no more guarantee of a weekly pay-check like on my cozy job at the paper. My (and my family's) survival all hung on how the general public would respond to my publication. It was as simple—and complex—as that.

I had the magazine distributed locally to start with, because I tried to fill it with everything of a positive nature I could find in and around our township. Topics ranged from little things like one neighbor doing a good deed for another, birthday celebrations, engagement stories, anniversaries; and also "harder" stuff, like the local man who lost his legs in Vietnam competing in a national Olympics for the disabled, and the local woman who never had any children of her own, but fostered more than a dozen over her long, tough life. I wanted to see if I could capture an audience who'd grown tired of the same old negative reporting they'd grown accustomed to, and instead fill their hearts and spirits full of "the good stuff." That's why naming the publication was the easiest journalistic thing I'd ever decided on—we'd call it "The Good News."

At first, we experienced great growing pains; we had to find more start-up money, advertisers, circulation—all real causes for concern. But we made it through 1985, our first year. By our second year, our circulation had doubled, and our subscriber list had tripled. In late 1990, we moved into a larger office in town. We employed 20 people, and our circulation had gone from a mom-and-pop local gig to a very popular magazine distributed statewide. Several of our feature writers had gained national prominence and won awards for their stories.

Though the magazine did run many "heroes to the rescue"- style stories and short bits on "everyday miracles," feature stories, our mainstay from the beginning, still were our bread-and-butter. Our top staff writers now traveled the globe, sometimes to remote corners of the world, reporting on individuals or groups who were making a difference through great efforts against the odds. Our crack research department never seemed to fail at pinning down some great story or other that needed uncovering.

One thing I was especially proud of: We became known for our diligence and expertise in finding these kinds of great stories. If a feature required a 4,000 mile journey to some obscure African village, we'd do it, and our readership appreciated our efforts, and continued to grow in numbers. Well, that was what I'd hoped for "The Good News."

Also in 1990, that great old mayor and my most-trusted friend, Joshua Gibson, passed away, at the ripe old age of 105, apparently in his sleep, quietly, and quickly. *With no pain,* I thought, and I was glad for that. He'd lived *105 years*, and never complained of any ailment or a physical problem, to my knowledge.

"Uncoincidentally," later that same year, Irene, who after

the mayor's death went to live with Rosemary, joined her husband in finding peace with the Lord in that same bed they'd shared during their 10-plus years together.

As a tribute to them, "The Good News" ran a feature story on their lives, their 75-year separation and their eventual, joyous reunion. I gave that assignment to an up-and-coming young writer named Kara Nichols. Kara's major writing talent had been evidenced in her resume and clippings from the small-town newspapers she'd free-lanced for before coming to us. She had a particular interest in romantic stories such as this one, and after much debate in our editorial ranks, she got the assignment, though it was her first for us.

I had to think long and hard about giving her the assignment. I thought maybe I should write the story myself; I had so much first-hand knowledge about Mayor Gibson and Irene Durella and their relationship. But at the same time, I thought back to my early writing days, and how eagerly I waited for my "big story" break. And Kara Nichols' energy cast a spell on me, one strong enough to cast my vote her way.

Kara would do the story; that was understood, I had plenty of leads and sources for her, including myself I told her. So it was an easy task for her to uncover the story; she just needed to write this tribute to my old friend with all the fervor and charm I craved for it.

The story Kara Nichols wrote turned out to be what was, at the time, our top-selling issue to date. The passion and pain of the Gibson-Durella relationship, her words captured well. People found the saga mesmerizing, especially told feature-length. Many readers called and wrote to say it had left them in tears.

Miss Nichols' story also brought the old mayor newfound stardom and admiration among the townsfolk. Soon it came out, the citizens dedicated our new *Joshua Gibson*

Memorial Park, and busy Hazel Drive was renamed *Gibson Drive*.

Kara's remarkable story won a national "Best Feature" award that year. And I was pleased to see that Kara's attitude about life matched her talent; she gave much back in time to the community, often as a guest speaker at schools, ladies' auxiliary functions, and the like. She was always ready to do anything she could to help people out, to give other young women healthy confidence in themselves—not for writing, but for anything they might choose to do. My two daughters admired her, and Kara took them both under her wing. In 1990 she was named our township's "Woman of the Year," and year after year she continued to write one inspiring story after the other.

Not long after Kara came onto our staff, I realized that her spirit reminded me a lot of Becky Chapman's, and that made it very good indeed to have her on board. (Where in the world *was* Becky these days? Time had flown and we'd lost touch years ago...).

By 1993, our publication was being distributed *nationally*. We had not only survived, we were thriving. People couldn't get enough of "The Good News." We got buy-out offers from large publishers, even offers to move us into the limelight of New York City, but we held on where we were. I never forgot that offer years earlier from A.J. Craft, and though the years were slipping by, Emily and I knew this was our town, where we lived and where we'd stay. "The Good News" would never leave, nor would we.

In the fall of 1995, as our circulation and popularity continued to grow, one staffer stumbled on a story he felt we ought to check out. After he presented in a board meeting what he'd learned, Kara Nichols was given the assignment to find out more about this so-called "Angel of the Jungle." It seemed a fitting description: An American woman whose name no one knew, teaching Christianity in some far-off

South American jungle. We'd done stories like this before, so I wasn't in any particular hurry to send Kara packing for two weeks or more. But Kara made some contacts and insisted she'd find a new angle to this old-style story, so we sent her to South America.

Kara seemed to vanish into the rain forests for a full month, and we only heard from her sporadically. When she did contact us, it was to say each time that she needed more time to "get the whole story." She assured me "This will be something *great!*—and those were to be the last words I'd hear from her till she brought the story back.

Kara returned home very thin and exhausted, yet alive with even more fervor than usual, after midnight at County Airport, a full four-weeks after she'd left us. She phoned me the moment she'd retrieved her bags. "Mr. Strong, this was one *great* assignment," she said. "Could we have a staff meeting about it first thing in the morning?"

We usually held staff meetings at 8:00 a.m., and I knew how tired she must be. "Say, didn't you just get in? Why don't you take tomorrow off and rest up—the meeting can wait..."

"No," she broke in firmly. "I've got to come in *tomorrow* morning. Maybe I'll take the afternoon off, but I've got to share the story with you all as soon as I can."

"Well, o.k.," I chuckled, "we'll have a staff meeting at 8:00, and it'll be your baby."

"Great!" she said. "See you in the morning!"

CHAPTER
41

Next morning close to 8:00, the conference room buzzed with our regular staff members (in all, seven editors were now responsible for the publication.), milling around, drinking coffee, making phone calls and small talk as usual. At 8:00 on the nose, a very thin, very tanned, Kara Nichols burst into the room.

"So, welcome home," said Stephen Malloy, one of our senior editors, greeting Kara like a daughter. Kara made her way around the room, exchanging hugs with her co-workers. *They sure do love her,* I thought, as she made her way around the room to me, *and so do I.*

"You look great!" I said.

"I feel *fabulous,*" she said back. "This was a *great* assignment."

This was the third time in our last three conversations she'd made that statement; I was certainly looking forward to her report.

The next hour she spent reviewing the wondrous deeds of the "Angel of the Jungle." Kara passed around photos of the village and its villagers that showed eloquently the impoverished conditions in which the "Angel" worked. Kara seemed in absolute awe of the woman.

"Hey, you've got plenty of photos of the villagers," our photo editor called out, "but did you take any of this 'Angel'?"

"Yes, a few," Kara replied. "She wasn't particularly eager to let herself be the center of attention. She was very humble and very private, really."

Suddenly I remembered how Maureen Chapman had described Becky 16 years ago. *Humble, and private,* I thought. *Odd coincidence, this same description.*

Kara reached deep in her bag and pulled out a few photos of the "Angel." "Here you are; that's a real angel you're looking at."

The pictures made their way around; each editor looked at them for a few seconds. One of them said, "What's her name, this 'Angel,' and where's she originally from?"

"Oh, never mind for now," Kara said evasively. "She just wants to be known as 'An-gel'—that's what all the villagers call her."

"The most amazing thing," she said, as the photos came close to passing into my hands, "was this hand signal the people used whenever they were around her."

"What hand signal?" I quickly asked.

She demonstrated with her left hand a gesture identical to the one we'd learned from Becky.

"Do you know what that symbol means?" I asked.

"Yes, they told me it means, "You're o.k., I'm o.k., and I love you," said Kara, "and they used it every time they greeted her. It was almost like they were greeting some deity."

"Please, let me see those photos," I said. I knew I sounded over-eager, but I had to know...

The photos passed quickly to me, and my eyes bore into the top one. It wasn't a close-up shot, but it was clear enough to identify the "Angel." No doubt about it—that was our Becky, standing in the middle of that far-off jungle.

"Do you know her?" one of the men asked curiously.

I looked up and looked straight at Kara Nichols. Then I looked around the room, as all eyes awaited my answer. My own eyes welled up with tears, and Kara rose from her seat and came to me and put a gentle hand on my right shoulder. "Yes," she said. "Mr. Strong *does* know this young woman."

CHAPTER
42

The popularity of Mayor Gibson's and Irene Durella's story paled compared with the response to Kara's story about Becky Chapman. "The Angel of the Jungle" was heralded around the country, and both Becky Chapman and Kara Nichols became household names.

Kara continued writing tremendous stuff, one story after the other that captivated her audiences. She let me in on a little secret following publication of her story on Becky—that she'd become Becky's pen pal. Her life was inspired by Becky Chapman's desire and efforts; indeed, Kara had become our community's new Becky Chapman.

For years after she wrote the story, Kara maintained a file on "The Angel." She kept it off limits to everyone but me. Occasionally Kara would discuss with me new information she'd received about Becky. It was now clear to Kara that Becky never stayed in one place for more than 18 months; she kept on moving; so her whereabouts were sometimes difficult to trace.

Kara even went so far as to graph Becky's moves, hoping to find some pattern in her leaps across not only countries, but continents now. Kara struck up a relationship with Maureen Chapman, trying to get as much information on Becky as she could. Maureen gave Kara a bit more than she was able to get on her own; but in the end, it all amounted to little more than a few letters and photos, plus sketchy information about Becky's deeds and progress in her Christian ministry.

During the summer of 1998, Maureen grew so lonesome for Becky, she took a leave-of-absence from her job in Boston and joined Becky in New Zealand. Amazingly, it was the first time mother and daughter actually met since Becky had left our area 14 years ago. *She's never even been home,* I thought when I heard the news.

That same summer, a few of the girls (young women, I should say!) from St. Luke's 1979 championship volleyball team started making plans for a 20-year reunion (and more) party. Mandy Morrison and Ellen Anderson, still living in town and both very active in civic affairs, got that ball rolling.

Mandy and Ellen were thinking bigger than just a single team reunion. They wanted much more than just a 20 year reunion of the 1979 championship team. They wanted to go all the way back to 1969, the school's first volleyball year, and invite every girl and woman who'd ever played volleyball for St. Luke's. That meant trying to locate over 300 women scattered across the country. It was a daunting task, but they were equal to the challenge they posed themselves.

Soon their great search took on a life of it's own. And new ideas evolved for the gathering, as they managed to contact more and more former players. Within just four months, the pair had pulled it off: Nearly 100 percent of past and present players said they expected to attend the banquet, which would (fittingly) be held in our humble old gym.

During their four-month search, Mandy and Ellen also began asking the aging Sister Fran to allow them to open a volleyball trophy area at the school, adjacent to the basketball and track wing. So many trophies and plaques had accumulated over the years, and so many team balls with signatures from past teams, but no place had been set aside to display them. Some trophies sat in the Principal's office, some occupied windows of classrooms; some graced the library. So the girls had a point: We needed a specific area designated just for volleyball.

Their persistence paid off; Sister Fran agreed to the suggestion, promising to "find" a space for volleyball.

Two weeks before the banquet, Mandy, Ellen, my two daughters, Emily and myself reviewed the names of the confirmed attendees. As designated Master of Ceremonies, I was involved up to my ears by this time, reviewing names and old photos and preparing my speech. Thirty-one tables would be set up for the big day, each table representing one team. Spouses were invited to join their wives; parents of more recent and current team members were invited, too. I figured over 600 people would cram into our little gym.

One of the few names missing from the confirmed list was Becky Chapman's, We had still received no word from her, despite Kara Nichols' efforts to reach her. But Kara warned us that messages to Becky often took weeks to reach her, and even then, they could easily be misdirected. Indeed, all who had managed to remain in some contact with Becky over the years were drawing blanks of late. None of the dozens of cards and letters, or the several phone calls, that had been sent her way had garnered any word back. So it was "wait and see" whether she would attend or not. And probably not, since she was obviously so devoted to her missionary work.

In those 20 years since she'd made "The Serve" (the phrase coined soon after Becky's game-winning play), Becky Chapman had became a larger than life, true icon of our community. She'd achieved her stardom on three accounts: A photo taken at the championship game, of Becky riding on her teammates' shoulders, her left hand held aloft, was strategically placed in the hall near the entrance to the school. Every child, visitor or teacher passed by the photo on her or his way in and out. Sister Fran had it placed in this spot as a constant, encouraging reminder to any and all, to "never give up, never give in, never quit."

Over time, Becky Chapman's legend had grown to near-epic proportions. She was a legend cherished and revered. Strange rumors had spread about Becky—some said that she was "supernaturally gifted"; others, that she was an angel who'd been placed on earth to teach us all crucial lessons about life. Her name couldn't have occupied a higher place in our township's esteem.

Of course, the 600 people expected at the reunion were coming for a variety of reasons: Simply to get together after all the years, to see old friends and teachers, to be part of the dedication of the volleyball area for trophies. But others hoped they'd finally have the chance, if she attended, to meet, talk and touch Becky Chapman. And though we were making strenuous efforts to contact her, I doubted she'd be coming. Still, I felt a bit sorrowful: her not being there would be a huge disappointment for all, on this occasion designed for memories and fun.

CHAPTER
43

You'd have sworn the 31 linen-shrouded tables spread throughout the gymnasium had been professionally decorated. Each rectangular table comfortably sat 20 people, and the green and gold linens vividly reflected the school colors. Collages of team photos served as centerpieces, and seating charts carefully positioned everyone attending. Hundreds of balloons and streamers added a boisterous festive atmosphere to the proceedings.

On the stage side of the gym two additional tables stood. The first housed the various volleyball memorabilia collected by the scores of girls, including the ten championship trophies we'd earned over the past 20 years, all neatly arranged by order of year, and hundreds of old photos taken by the yearbook staffs from the past 30 years. The table would be a magnet that drew each and every person, conjuring memories and stimulating conversations.

The second (and head) table seated 20 and was reserved for coaches, former coaches and school faculty. It was from here that I would lead my former players as Master of Ceremonies. For months now, I'd just dreamed of seeing so many of "my girls" together in such a setting. I had peculiar feelings, really. I was now 56 years old, my players ranged from 12-34. It was ironic, I thought, that on the coaching sidelines, I felt like I was still 36; yet tonight, for the first time in the last 20 years, I couldn't help but see myself as a 56-year-old.

I would lead the receiving line at the front door, much as if this were some wedding or funeral one attends—though this happening was all joy. After greeting me briefly, former players streamed quickly down the receiving line, exchanging hugs, even pausing for photos. All of us were wearing nametags, but I was often startled by particular matches of faces with names. *Well,* I thought as they made their way into the gym, *I wonder what the girls think of this old face.*

At 6:00 sharp, old Sister Fran's voice on the microphone, calling everyone to order, pierced my ears. Yes, that old high-pitch rasp still challenged the aging speakers that hung from the ceiling's four corners. A few minutes later, the great throng of nearly 600 had found their seats, and we officially began the festivities.

Father Matthew Sullivan led the throng in an opening prayer, which would be followed by dinner, final introductions and comments by me. I had rehearsed for weeks, after deciding to keep my remarks short and sweet. I intended to announce all the names of all the players, team by team, topping off the evening with a tribute to the 10 championship teams, and a special salute to the 1979 team that had started it all. After that we'd cut the ribbon and dedicate the new volleyball wing, now full of our trophies and awards.

And so the evening went. I only ate half the meal, choosing instead to mingle among my old and new players. I'd only be able to spend a few minutes at each table, but I was eager to spend the time visiting, instead of filling my gut.

These brief visits were full of nostalgia: We discussed memories of certain games, even particular plays. Former players flashed children's photos before me. *Evidence enough of how we've all aged together!* I thought.

The last table I visited before returning to the stage was marked "1979," for the team that had begun it all for me. I smiled to myself: The characters on this squad still stood out as unique in my 20 years of coaching. Maybe that's why the few moments I spent at that table took me back to the best memories of all.

I noticed that in front of each girl's dinner plate stood the individual good luck charm they used to bring to the games. Though time's ravages had caught up to the stuffed animals, all 12 girls had conspired to bring them along. Only one was missing, Becky Chapman's, of course. *But hold it!* I recalled just then. *She never seemed to have one, anyway.*

Becky's nametag sat in front of her empty plate. I felt empty, really, at her not being there, but I did my best to hide my sadness from the other girls. They had all hoped so that she'd attend, and if her absence clearly created a huge void for all in attendance, it did especially for her 1979 team-mates.

In fact, that was the general mood I felt in the gym. At every table the question came up: "Coach Paul, is Becky Chapman coming?" Amazing, it was, that even after all those years, even perfect strangers to Becky were still so eager to have a chance to meet her. Becky Chapman *was* an icon.

And still, a part of the back of my mind was just as hope-ful, and just as anxious as these questioners. But I returned to the head table and the plates were cleared, and I began my speech, it was beginning to look sure that we'd all be disap-pointed. Yet even as I called out name after name of all the girls on all the years' teams, I kept looking back at the entrance to the gym, hoping Becky would materialize some-how. But she didn't.

It took quite a while to call out the names of all the teams, and as I went along, I also called out the names of players I knew were missing. As planned, I purposely saved the cher-ished and revered 1979 team for last, as was fitting. And suddenly, I found myself down to just that one team.

I paused for a moment to gaze over at the 1979 table. *What memories,* I thought, and I looked up at the old clock above the entrance to the gym. *7:20. Right on time,* I thought; Sister Fran wanted to dedicate the volleyball wing around 7:45, so the maintenance crew could start to clean up at around 8:00.

After a few more remarks I called out the name of each player at the 1979 table, and each girl stood up to receive gentle applause. My two daughters, Karen and Megan, blew me a kiss as I proudly called their names. It took only a few moments to go through the first 12 names. I had saved Becky's name for last.

For years, past and current players had enjoyed hearing the story of Becky Chapman, and now I prepared to tell it— the short version, of course—to all 600 attending. I wanted to highlight what made her so special. I'd spent weeks preparing notes for this part of the evening, but as I stood at that microphone with all those faces looking my way, I decided to keep the note cards in my pocket. I wouldn't need them.

"I know most of you realize whose the final name will be tonight," I began. "Many of you have asked me—and often—to tell about her, to share some of my thoughts on *the* legendary player in our school's sports history. So, let me tell you a little bit about Becky Chapman."

The room fell utterly quiet. I glanced at the clock once more. *7:27—better wrap it up quickly,* I thought, *or face the wrath of big Sister.*

I took a deep breath and said, "Becky Chapman played just one sequence in her *entire* volleyball career here at St. Luke's. She made contact with the ball *one time,* and she never had to move from her position—and yet she made the one play that will forever identify volleyball with St. Luke's."

I paused and heard the silence broken by some movement in the hallway. *Ah, just the maintenance crew, jostling about with their equipment.* For a moment I thought: *How fitting it would be if instead that noise were Becky.* I looked again at the clock; it said *7:28. Well, it's fitting anyway that I'll finish my story at 7:29.*

I was saying just a few more words about Becky, when I heard more noise in the hallway. I looked to the back of the gym just as the clock hit that magic *7:29.*

A woman, maybe in her 30's, blond hair, thin, stood in the doorway. She was moderately dressed, looking quite tan and fit. I squinted, trying to see her better, and as I did I drew the attention of all 600 heads in the gym to the entrance. She just stood there for a moment, her eyes fixed calmly on me. Then she smiled, *just as she always did,* I thought, and spoke six words I'll never forget:

"Coach Paul, I'm sorry I'm late."

The women at the 1979 table didn't hesitate a moment. Like they were 13-year-olds again, they rushed to the young woman's side, in a welter of embraces and tears.

I didn't need to say another word. Everyone knew who had just walked through the door.

CHAPTER
44

Becky Chapman's sudden and unexpected arrival at the banquet sent the whole place into a frenzy. Soon she was completely surrounded by a huge circle of women and girls, who all closed in to get a good look at her. It was as if she were a newly discovered, marvelous species of animal, and these were the first people in line to see her on display.

But Becky handled the commotion and the attention with all the poise and friendliness I had been accustomed to see in her. She was all smiles, beaming that wide, ear-to-ear grin, those flashing white teeth, those dazzling blue eyes. *She still has it all,* I thought, as her old teammates finally led her to her place at their table, and the place began to settle down.

I hadn't yet moved from my position on that podium. *I'll bet she's done all this for the girls,* I thought. And I finally said into the microphone, "May I have your attention, please!"

Even now it took a bit longer for things to quiet down so I could speak; Becky remained the center of attention for awhile. I let it go on for a few moments, let everyone have their fun. I looked at Sister Fran, seated a few seats away. She nodded her approval, indicating she was no longer concerned with the time-table she'd set. Nor could her eyes hide her glee.

When I felt the time was right, I went back to the microphone, held my hands high, said, "Let's settle down, please, everyone—would you all return to your seats?"

A few seconds later, the gym fell quiet enough for me to continue. I looked once again at that table full of "girls"; but as hard as I tried, I couldn't hold back a few tears. Most of them were now in their mid-30s, yet somehow, as I moved from eye to teary eye, they were 13 years old again, and I was 36 once more.

At last I said, "It seems we've had the pleasure of an old friend deciding to drop in on us. I'd like you all to welcome... Miss Becky Chapman!"

Now, I'd seen standing ovations in my lifetime, at Broadway shows, retirements and other events. This one's spontaneity topped them all, though. Instantaneously, 600 people rose from their chairs, cheering and clapping with all their might. I stepped back from the podium and let it happen. Becky looked at me just then, her head cocked to the side, as if she were asking, "Why all this fuss over *me?*"

Then, as the cheering began to wane, Sister Fran signaled me over to her side.

"Coach Paul," she said, "maybe now would be *just* the right time to dedicate the volleyball wing."

"I agree, Sister," I said, "it's perfect timing, all right."

I announced we were going to dedicate the new wing, and the noise of 600 chairs sliding back again rang throughout the gym. I walked down from the stage toward the 1979 table, hoping to steal at least one hug from Becky.

But that wasn't possible; she was swallowed up by her old teammates, who surrounded and escorted her along with many others towards our destination. I strode out front and led the way, along with Sister Fran, down the corridors of the old hallway and up to the second floor near the library. The great procession followed with high anticipation and excitement; 600 voices rang and echoed all down the old hallways. I was as eager as anyone; even I hadn't been allowed to see the wing until now, where I'd see it for the first time along with all the others.

When we reached the turn in the hallway that led to the new volleyball wing, I spied a giant green and gold banner, filling the area from ceiling to floor, concealing what lay behind it. Across the banner in huge letters was written the motto that began with that first championship 1979 team; "All for one, and one for all." *Great touch,* I thought, and we all stopped in our tracks, blocked by the giant sign.

"Folks," Sister Fran said as loud as she could, "I'd like now to hand coach Paul these scissors, which he will use to cut the ribbon on this sign and officially open our volleyball trophy wing."

Sister handed me the scissors, I made one quick, sweeping cut down the middle, then pushed my way through the breakaway sign and, led the way inside, followed by my 1979 girls, then the rest of the years' many players.

What a sight! The long corridor had been beautifully transformed to hold glass-enclosed trophy-racks, filled with all the trophies, medals, and team photos and balls we'd accumulated over 30 years. We walked slowly down the hallway, stopping to view each showcase for a moment, yet also very conscious that lots of people trailed behind us. I figured it was up to me to maintain a steady pace forward, so though I did stop and take in some old memories, it would be only at a later date that I'd return to really get a good look at this incredible, wonderful sight.

The 1979 display was located near the end of the hallway. Although I was every bit excited about viewing the whole thing, I was mostly looking forward to this one.

We came to another stop this moment, and Sister Fran asked loudly for the members of the 1979 team to come forward. It only took a moment, as they were just behind us in line.

"Girls, we've left a spot open in the glass for your old "lucky charms," Sister said. "Would you be kind enough to place them inside?"

Apparently this had been planned without my knowledge, and I thought, *What another great touch,* as the 13 women walked past me towards the shrine. Katrina Glover led the way, placing her little brown bear inside; my daughters came next, and as the rest of them followed one by one, the glass-enclosed display took on a new look.

Becky Chapman hung toward the back of the line. *Ah, she'll be last again,* I thought. *Now I'll find out what Becky Chapman's charm was,* as she made her way to the display case and waited for the rest of her teammates to place their charms inside.

When it came Becky's turn the rest of the team huddled together around her. She reached into a small bag and pulled out something wrapped in cloth. She carefully opened the cloth, revealing a plaster cast, yellowed with age. *It's the cast from her broken hand!* I thought, and I remembered then that one of the girls had long ago told me, "Becky always has her charm with her."

Becky gingerly placed the cast in the display case, between the team photo and the ball with which she'd served her winning point. Weathered as it was by several decades, it was still in fairly good shape. And I thought, *That's the most important memento of them all*

Epilogue

I spent the rest of that great weekend at Rye Lake, where my wife and I hosted the entire 1979 team in a joyous party. All the young women bonded again, just as they had 20 years earlier. And Becky Chapman was again, as always back then, the center of attention. She told us all about her life in the jungles. She shared her grief over the despair so many of the world's people experienced, and what she and her co-workers were trying to do to help. Sad indeed were the conditions she described; yet we were deeply inspired to know that someone of the character of Becky Chapman was out there, making a difference. *As I always knew she would,* I thought.

And something else incredible happened at this party that night. As all the young women shared their stories about he past 20 years, and their great memories from 1979, they began to notice that they had some peculiar things in com-mon—the vocations each had chosen in life, all choices they had made independently.

The Shea twins, Colleen and Maggie, owned a Christian book-store, which they called "Two-Shea's." Sharon Lee was Director for a center for foster-children. Joanne Cross was a Pediatrician, Janet Moore a Special-Education teacher. Lynn Modell ran the local Special-Olympics, Mandy Morrison assisted low-income families. Katrina

Glover, the girl who'd had the ball fly off her fingers in our heart-breaking loss to St. Cyril's 20 years earlier, was a motivational speaker now, and Lauren Carter had just been appointed the new Director at Chadwick Manor.

Ellen Anderson, our great artist, had honed her craft to paint inspiring landscapes and, paintings of surreal places. She also depicted heaven, and angels. My own daughters, Karen and Megan, had similar careers; Karen had become a literary agent, specializing in "inspirational fiction," and helping talented writers find there way to publication in the literary market place. Megan wrote short-stories of fiction for children, inspiring stories of hope, the "feel-good" type, and was very busy with both writing, and book-signings.

I didn't take me long to realize as the stories and the life experiences unfolded that night, that these girls' choices of lives of service to humankind were no coincidence at all. I believed that our Becky Chapman, broken hand and all, had brought us the first sign along the way. After that, everything else just fell into place, like a great plan from *The* great source, God Most High.

As the women talked animatedly in the great room of the cabin, my mind took me back in time to my own experience in 1979. My life, too, had been so deeply affected by that year's events, by the people I'd met and, the things that had happened. I thought of Joshua Gibson and Irene Durella, of A.J. Craft and Daryl Reed, of Millie Parker and Rosemary Gibson. I thought of my players, my own daughters and my wife, of Maureen Chapman and, Becky Chapman.

I thought about Mayor Light and our great search for the deed, about the courtroom battle and, the championship game. I thought of the great cabin and Rye Lake, the fire there, the day the team cleaned up after the fire. I thought of the many ways each of these events had shaped my life—as had those that followed: "The Good News," all the later signs I'd followed, the time I'd spent at Chadwick Manor.

As the girls continued chatting I walked over to the huge fireplace. I looked at each old photo on that vast mantle. They all meant so much to me: The photo taken the day of the great "cleanup," a picture of the girls carrying Becky Chapman off the court after our win over St. Paul's, her hand aloft giving "The Sign." To the far left, the old, nearly sepia photo of Joshua Gibson and Irene Durella, taken long ago, in 1904.

I turned to gaze at the old grandfather's clock. It was still stuck on 7:29, and as I pondered that number's significance, I broke down and wept.

I thought then, as I retreated into my study to get back my composure, of hands and the things they had touched for good. I thought of how a young girl's broken hand and, an old clock's broken hands had brought so much together. I thought of the Spirit's invisible guiding hands that had so directed my life. And I thought, watching the girls from my vantage point near my study's open door, of how hands that break—whether physical, man-made, or spiritual—can also be—the hands that heal.